Only an Earl Will Do

To Marry a Rogue, Book 1

TAMARA Gill

COPYRIGHT

ONLY AN EARL WILL DO

TO MARRY A ROGUE, BOOK 1

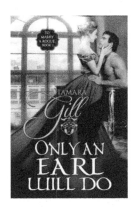

The reigning queen of London society, Lady Elizabeth Worthing-
ham, has her future set out for her. Marry well, and marry without
love. An easy promise to make and one she owed her family after
her near ruinous past that threatened them all. And the rakish
scoundrel Henry Andrews, Earl of Muir who's inability to act a
gentleman when she needed one most would one day pay for his
treachery.

Returning to England after three years abroad, Henry is determined to make the only woman who captured his heart his wife. But the icy reception he receives from Elizabeth is colder than his home in the Scottish highlands. As past hurts surface and deception runs as thick as blood, so too does a love that will overcome all obstacles, unless a nameless foe, determined with his own path, gets his way and their love never sees the light of day...

PROLOGUE

England 1805 – Surrey

"You're ruined."

Elizabeth stood motionless as her mother, the Duchess of Penworth, paced before the lit hearth, her golden silk gown billowing out behind her, the deep frown between her eyes daring anyone to follow her. "No. Let me rephrase that. The family is ruined. All my girls, their futures, have been kicked to the curb like some poor street urchins."

Elizabeth, the eldest of all the girls, swiped a lone tear from her cheek and fought not to cast up her accounts. "But surely Henry has written of his return." She turned to her father. "Papa, what did his missive say?" The severe frown lines between her father's brows were deeper than she'd ever seen them before, and dread pooled in her belly. What had she done? What had Henry said?

"I shall not read it to you, Elizabeth, for I fear it'll only upset you more, and being in the delicate condition you are we must keep you well. But never again will I allow the Earl

1

of Muir to step one foot into my home. To think," her father said, kicking at a log beside the fire, "that I supported him to seek out his uncle in America. I'm utterly ashamed of myself."

"No," Elizabeth said, catching her father's gaze. "You have nothing to be ashamed of. I do. I'm the one who lay with a man who wasn't my husband. I'm the one who now carries his child." The tears she'd fought so hard to hold at bay started to run in earnest. "Henry and I were friends, well, I thought we were friends. I assumed he'd do the right thing by our family, by me. Why is it that he'll not return?"

Her mother, quietly staring out the window, turned at her question. "Because his uncle has said no nephew of his would marry a strumpet who gave away the prize before the contracts were signed, and Henry apparently was in agreement with this statement."

Her father sighed. "There is an old rivalry between Henry's uncle and me. We were never friends, even though I noted Henry's father high in my esteem, as close as a brother, in fact. Yet his sibling was temperamental, a jealous cur."

"Why were you not friends with Henry's uncle, Papa?" He did not reply. "Please tell me. I deserve to know."

"Because he wished to marry your mama, and I won her hand instead. He was blind with rage, and it seems even after twenty years he wishes to seek revenge upon me by ruining you."

Elizabeth flopped onto a settee, shocked by such news. "Did Henry know of this between you and his uncle? Did you ever tell him?"

"No. I thought it long forgotten."

Elizabeth swallowed as the room started to swirl. "So, Henry has found his wealthy uncle and has been poisoned by his lies. The man has made me out to be a light-skirts of little character." She took a calming breath. "Tell me, does the letter really declare this to be Henry's opinion as well?"

The duke came and sat beside her. "It is of both their opinions, yes." He took her hand and squeezed it. "You need to marry, Elizabeth, and quickly. There is no other choice."

She stood, reeling away from her father and such an idea. To marry a stranger was worse than no marriage at all and falling from grace. "I cannot do that. I haven't even had a season. I know no one."

"A good friend of mine, Viscount Newland, recently passed. His son, Marcus, who is a little simple of mind after a fall from a horse as a child, is in need of a wife. But because of his ailment, no one will have him. They are desperate to keep the estate within the family and are looking to marry him off. It would be a good match for you both. I know it is not what you wanted, but it will save you and your sisters from ruin."

Elizabeth stood looking down at her father, her mouth agape with shock and not a little amount of disgrace. "You want me to marry a simpleton?"

"His speech is a little delayed only, otherwise he's a kind young man. I grant you he's not as handsome as Henry, but… well, we must do what's best in these situations."

Her mother sighed. "Lord Riddledale has called and asked for your hand once more. You could always accept his suit."

"Please, I would rather cut off my own hand than marry his lordship." Just the thought was enough to make her skin crawl.

"Well then, you will marry Lord Newland. I'm sorry, but it must and will be done," her mother said, her tone hard.

Elizabeth walked to the window that looked toward the lake where she'd given herself to Henry. His sweet whispered words of love, of wanting her to wait for him, that as soon as he procured enough funds to support his Scottish estate they would marry, flittered through her mind. What a liar he'd turned out to be. All he wanted was her innocence and nothing else.

Anger thrummed through her and she grit her teeth. How dare Henry trick her in such a way? Made her fall in love with him, promised to be faithful and marry her when he returned. He never wished to marry her. Had he wanted to right now he would be on his way back to England.

She turned, staring at her parents who looked resigned to a fate none of them imagined possible or ever wanted. "I will marry Viscount Newland. Write them and organize the nuptials to take place within the month or sooner if possible. The child I carry needs a father and the viscount needs a wife."

"Then it is done." Her father stood, walking over to her and taking her hand. "Did Henry promise you anything, Elizabeth? The letter is so out of character for him, I've wondered since receiving it that it isn't really of his opinion but his uncle's only."

"He wanted me to wait for him, to give him time to save his family's estate. He did not wish to marry a woman for her money; he wanted to be a self-made man, I suppose."

"Lies, Elizabeth. All lies," her mother stated, her voice cold. "Henry has used you, I fear, and I highly doubt he'll ever come back to England or Scotland, for that matter."

Elizabeth swallowed the lump in her throat, not wanting to believe the man she'd given her heart to would treat her in such a way. She'd thought Henry was different, was a gentleman who loved her. At the look of pity her father bestowed on her, she pushed him aside and ran from the room.

She needed air, fresh, cooling, calming air. Opening the front door, the chilling icy wind hit her face, and clarity assailed. She'd go for a ride. Her mount Argo always made her feel better.

It took the stable hand only minutes to saddle her mount, and she was soon trotting away from the house, the only sound that of the snow crunching beneath her horse's hooves. The chill pierced through her gown, and she regretted not changing into a suitable habit, but riding astride in whatever they had on at the time was a normal practice for the children of the Duke of Penworth. Too much freedom as a child, all of them allowed to do whatever they pleased, and now that freedom had led her straight into the worst type of trouble.

She pushed her horse into a slow canter, her mind a kaleidoscope of turmoil. Henry, once her father's ward, a person she'd thought to call a friend, had betrayed her when she needed him most. Guilt and shame swamped her just as snow started to fall, and covered everything in a crystal white hue.

She would never forgive Henry for this. Yes, they'd made a mistake, a terrible lack of decorum on her behalf that she'd never had time to think through. But should the worst happen, a child, she had consoled herself that Henry would do right by her, return home and marry her.

How could she have been so wrong?

She clutched her stomach, still no signs that a little child grew inside, and as much as she was ruined, could possibly ruin her family, she didn't regret her condition, and nor would she birth this child out of wedlock. Lord Newland would marry her since his situation was not looked upon favorably by the ton; it was a match that would suit them both.

Guilt pricked her soul that she would pass off Henry's child as Lord Newland's, but what choice did she have? Henry would not marry her, declare the child his. Elizabeth had little choice. There was nothing else to be done about it.

A deer shot out of the bracken, and Argo shied, jumping

sharply to the side. Elizabeth screamed as her seat slipped. The action unbalanced her and she fell, hitting the ground hard.

Luckily, the soft snow buffered her fall, and she sat up, feeling the same as she had when upon her horse. She rubbed her stomach, tears pooling in her eyes with the thought that had she fallen harder, all her problems would be over. What a terrible person she was to think such a thing, and how she hated Henry that his refusal of her had brought such horrendous thoughts to mind.

Argo nuzzled her side as she stood; reaching for the stirrup, she hoisted herself back onto her mount. Wiping the tears from her eyes, Elizabeth promised no more would be shed over a boy, for that was surely what Henry still was, an immature youth who gave no thought to others.

She would marry Viscount Newland, try and make him happy as much as possible when two strangers came together in such a union, and be damned anyone who mentioned the name Henry Andrews, Lord Muir to her again.

America 1805 – New York Harbor

Henry raised his face to the wind and rain as the packet ship sailed up the Hudson River. The damp winter air matched the cold he felt inside, numbing the pain that hadn't left his core since farewelling the shores of England. And now he was here. America. The smoky city just waking to a new day looked close enough to reach out and touch, and yet his true love, Elizabeth, was farther away than she'd ever been before.

He rubbed his chest and huddled into his greatcoat. The

five weeks across the ocean had dragged, endless days with his mind occupied with only one thought: his Elizabeth lass.

He shut his eyes, bringing the vision of her to his mind, her honest, laughing gaze, the beautiful smile that had always managed to make his breath catch. He frowned, missing her as much as the highland night sky would miss the stars.

"So, Henry, lad, what's your plan on these great lands?" Henry took in the captain on the British Government packet; his graying whiskers across his jaw and crinkled skin about his eyes told of a man who'd lived at sea his entire life, and enjoyed every moment of it. He grinned. "Make me fortune. Mend a broken family tie if I can."

The captain lit a cheroot and puffed, the smoke soon lost in the misty air. "Ah, grand plans then. Any ideas on how you'll be making your fortune? I could use some tips myself."

"My uncle lives here. Owns a shipping company apparently, although I've yet to meet the man or see for myself if this is true. I'm hoping since he's done so well for himself he can steer me along the road to me own fortune."

The captain nodded, staring toward the bow. "It seems you have it all covered."

Henry started when the captain yelled orders for half-mast. He hoped the old man was right with his statement. The less time he stayed here the better it would be. He pushed away the thought that Elizabeth was due to come out in the forthcoming months, to be paraded around the ton like a delicious morsel of sweet meats. To be the center of attention, a duke's daughter ripe for the picking. He ground his teeth.

"I wish you good luck, Henry."

"Thank ye." The captain moved away, and he turned back to look at the city so unlike London or his highland home. Foreign and wrong on so many levels. The muddy waters were the only similarity to London, he mused, smiling a little.

Henry walked to the bow, leaning over the wooden rail. He sighed, trying to expel the sullen mood that had swamped him the closer they came to America. What he was doing here was a good thing, an honorable thing, something that if he didn't do, Elizabeth would be lost to him forever.

He couldn't have hated his grandfather more at that moment for having lost their fortune at the turn of a card all those years ago. It was a miracle his father had been able to keep Avonmore afloat and himself out of debtor's prison.

The crewmen preparing the packet ship for docking sounded around him, and he started toward the small room he'd been afforded for the duration of the trip. It was better than nothing; even if he'd not been able to stand up fully within the space, at least it was private and comfortable.

Determination to succeed, to ensure his and Elizabeth's future was secure, to return home as soon as he may, sparked within him. He would not fail; for once, the Earl of Muir would not gamble the estate's future away, but fight for its survival, earn it respectably just as his ancestors had.

And he would return home, marry his English lass, and spoil her for the remainder of their days. In Scotland.

CHAPTER 1

Two years later – London

In the arms of Lord Dean, the Earl of Thetford, Elizabeth danced a minuet, enjoying his easy style and competent ability. She looked up at his charming gray hooded eyes, straight nose, and strong jaw. A gentleman as alluring as the music was entrancing. Her new green silk gown slid sensually about her body as they moved around the room and between other couples.

The air smelled of blossoms picked from the hothouse and an alarming amount of different perfumes. She chuckled as he murmured sweet words in her ear that were amusing if nothing else. She allowed his banter to a certain point. He was a sweet man.

Sweet on her.

"The season's already halfway gone, Lady Newland. Are you going back to Dunsleigh or your own home in Wiltshire?"

Elizabeth checked her footing. "Dunsleigh, I think. It's where my family wishes me to go. It's been a while since I visited with them there." She looked away from his disappointed face and watched the other couples dance. Dunsleigh was where her heart was and not her married home and certainly not London. As for the man in her arms, he was nice enough, but neither he nor any other fop who considered himself enamored of her could persuade her to stay or marry again.

"Ah, a shame. Perhaps if you would allow it, I could visit when I'm next in Surrey."

She smiled. "Of course, you are always welcome, my lord. I'm sure my brother would be delighted with a visit. As you know, he's been down at Dunsleigh for quite some time learning all there is about the estate."

"How is your father? I had meant to inquire of his wellbeing."

"The duke is well." She smiled. "Much better, thank you. The doctor's stated he has to slow down, that is all. Josh is stepping up to fill the void, as he should. Father would like to see you, too."

"I have been meaning to call…"

Elizabeth looked up at him as the dance drew to a close and hoped his final quip didn't mean what she thought it did. She hated having to deny one's proposal, but she would should he ask, just as she would any other.

He left her with her younger sister, Victoria and took himself off toward the card room. Victoria raised her brow and smiled as she caught her attention. "Another one fawning at your feet, I see."

Elizabeth fiddled with her hair. "He believes he is 'the one.' He's even hinted at speaking to Papa for my hand. I'll not marry again. Lord Newland was quite enough."

Victoria frowned. "Surely Lord Newland wasn't that bad. He seemed smitten with you."

She nodded, knowing that under the circumstances she'd

married, Lord Newland was a very lucky blessing for her. "I used him, and I know he used me just as much, but it still does not make such matches right. He brought up a boy who was not his own, loved him even. I cannot forgive myself for that."

Victoria clasped her hand, compassion in her gaze. Compassion she did not deserve. "I know it must be hard, but should we know the true fathers of half the ton's children, I think it would be an eye-opening experience. Lord Newland was a happy man. You did that, no one else. Do not torture yourself so. You do not deserve it." Her sister gestured across the room and Elizabeth cringed at who she noted. "So you're not going to marry Lord Riddledale, then? His lordship will never recover from such a blow."

Elizabeth hid a repulsed shudder over Lord Riddledale, who stood pompous and proud across the floor, the ever-present scowl on his face no surprise. No doubt her stepping out with another gentleman other than himself had put him out of countenance. She turned back to her sister. "I cannot summon any remorse for annoying Riddledale. As for Lord Dean, I'll be sorry to hurt him, but no, I will not marry him no matter how much his heart breaks over my decision."

"Could your feelings change in time, do you believe?" Victoria asked.

"No."

"No?"

Elizabeth shook her head. "No."

"Why?"

She swallowed the familiar lump which formed in her throat every time she thought of him, the man she refused to name, even in her own thoughts. "I'm not the loving kind. I don't believe it's healthy to rely on such feeble unstable emotions when someone is entering the marriage state. Men and their need to be adored, looked up to in awe, can go hang. Lord Newland's name protects me now. I have no need to marry again."

Victoria threw her a dubious look. "I believe there is nothing purer and good than love, especially if you are fortunate enough to have it in a marriage." Her sister sighed, the sound tinged with sadness. "You promised Papa you would try."

"I am well aware of what I promised Papa, but he did not stipulate marriage is what I should try. I'm friendly and affable. That is enough." Elizabeth clamped her jaw shut. Lashing out further about marriage would not be helpful here, no matter how her temper spiked every time she thought of the Scottish rogue who'd ruined her and left her to face such undoing alone.

Where was Henry when it was time for him to step up and claim responsibility for their actions? New York, that was where, thousands of miles away and with little care he'd left her pregnant while she had to face disgrace, heartache, and a future forever changed because of one careless act.

Tears pricked her eyes at the thought of the life she could have lived, not the one she endured. Her husband had been kind and gentle, but he had not loved her as a husband should love a wife.

"Elizabeth?" Victoria said, nudging her a little. "What are you thinking? I've been talking to you without a word of response."

She shook herself from the depressing thoughts and looked out to the throng of guests, some still arriving and being welcomed by their evening's host. "Nothing of importance. You were saying?"

"Just that our host, Lord McCalter looks mighty pleased with the latest guests who've arrived. The gentlemen are very dashing, I must say."

Elizabeth looked back to the ballroom doors and

frowned. She kept her eyes peeled to the group, but the gentlemen turned, placing their backs to the room and obscuring her view.

"It must be because his lordship is Scottish," Victoria said with a decided nod.

Elizabeth's heart sped up and her skin prickled at the mention of Scotland. She sought out the small party again, inwardly cursing herself as a silly fool for doing so. So what if a Scottish man had arrived? So what indeed.

"Why do you believe his lordship is Scottish?" Elizabeth asked at length, curiosity getting the better of her.

"I noticed one of the men had a piece of tartan in his coat pocket. I doubt an Englishman would wear such an article." Victoria stated in all seriousness.

Soon after, Elizabeth and her wayward thoughts were twirled out to dance a quadrille with Lord Stanhope. Then next, a country dance with Lord Riddledale, which annoyed her greatly, as he took the opportunity to berate her over her conduct, which was perfectly proper. She strove not to set his lordship back in his pompous box as he held her stiffly in his arms. Each time she was near the man, her skin wanted to crawl off and run away from the gentleman. Ghastly didn't even come close to how she felt about him.

"There was something in particular I wished to discuss with you, and since I have pointed out my dislike of your conduct this evening, now is the time to talk."

Elizabeth fought not to roll her eyes. Really, the man knew no bounds when it came to decorum. "What is it you wished to discuss?"

He smiled, his crooked, smoke stained teeth making her cringe.

"I have considered our history, the friendship your family has had with my own over the years, and I think you'd make me a suitable wife." He pinned her gaze with his cold eyes. "I wish you to marry me."

It was a statement, not quite a request, and her temper frayed. "You mean to ask if I will marry you."

He glared, the muscle in his jaw clenching in annoyance. "Of course. What do you think I just asked?"

"You stated, not asked." She looked over his shoulder, noting some of the guests' attentions were still fixated toward the door. Pulling out what little manners she had left when it came to Lord Riddledale, she threw him a pitying smile. "I'm honored, tru—"

"At least think about my offer" he said, interrupting her. She conceded, not wanting to make a scene should he take offense. "Very well. I'll think on your proposal."

He preened like a dandy looking at himself before a mirror as he swept her to a stop, bending to place a light kiss on her glove. He lingered over her hand like a kitten over a bowl of milk. She counted to ten as he took his leave; better that than to slap him with her fan.

"Oh, the insufferable coxcomb. I don't know why our parents keep up an association with that man. And why he would think I would wish to marry him, when I've given him no hint of particular regard, is beyond imagining." Elizabeth glared at his lordship's retreating back.

Victoria sighed. "He hasn't asked you yet," her sister stated, diplomatically.

"He just did. Would you like to congratulate me?" Elizabeth laughed at her sister's mortified visage.

"He never."

"He did, during the dance. I've agreed to think on his offer, but you know I cannot accept him. There's something about him that I do not like, an inner sense that I've always had around him. He makes me feel uneasy."

"I agree wholeheartedly." Victoria stilled beside her,

placing her hand on her arm. "Never mind Lord Riddledale, my dear, you have much bigger and definitely more worrisome problems to deal with."

"What do you mean?" Elizabeth turned to look at Victoria and noted the alarm across her features.

"It looks as if the Scottish guests are headed our way."

"Really?" Elizabeth looked toward the doors, and the secure little world she had built up around herself tumbled down. A chill pooled in her chest, rivaling the cold his presence created around her heart. Then anger fired her blood, replacing the chill with molten lava.

How dare he...

It took all of Elizabeth's breeding to not flay him alive and leave him alone and defenseless in this viperish society.

Her hand fisted at her side. It would at least be a fitting end for him, the same in which he'd left her when he'd not returned after the missive they'd sent him, begging him to do so. And by the looks of his superfine coat—cut to perfection around his shoulders, the highly starched cravat and tight-fitting breeches—he'd found his riches in America, and good for him in doing so, but now he could leave.

Elizabeth glared at the earl and his friends as they made steady progress through the throng, women's gazes devouring the tall, well-proportioned man in their midst. In the two years since she'd seen Henry he'd changed. He was no longer the gangly youth of four and twenty, but a man. A man whose eyes no longer held innocence, but rather learning and life. A life without the burden of sired children out of wedlock. A life where one walked away from such problems without remorse.

With heartbreaking missives where the word "strumpet" was used.

She braced herself for the coming introductions, her attention wholly focused on the couple who accompanied him, the people appearing more autocratic than herself when she decided to play the lofty duke's daughter. And over the last two years, Elizabeth had learned to master such a guise well. Thanks to Henry.

Untouchable was unbreakable.

The Elizabeth of old was no more. He would not get a smiling, happy welcome from her if that was what he expected. The day his letter arrived was the day they no longer were friends. And by his stony features, his hardened jaw that looked like it was cut from rock, Lord Henry Andrews wasn't pleased to see her again, either.

Well that was just perfect.

Elizabeth focused her attention on the accompanying man and woman, refusing to look any longer at Henry, although she knew by the pricking of her skin that he was watching her.

The gentleman with him was tall, though perhaps an inch shorter than Henry, his frame more athletic compared to Henry's larger shoulders and muscled thighs. The woman was around Elizabeth's own height, ethereal-looking with her golden blond locks pulled up into tight curls atop her crown. Her eyes were a cold, piercing blue. Elizabeth swallowed as the party came to stand before her and Victoria. She smiled her welcome to Lord McCalter, the mask of detachment firmly set on her features.

She would not acknowledge Henry until she absolutely had to, and even then she would not for long. He deserved no such acknowledgment now or ever.

"Lady Victoria, Lady Newland, may I say how happy I am to reunite you with an old friend, Lord Henry Andrews, Earl of Muir and of course, his cousins from America, Mr. Richard and Miss Amelia Andrews of New York."

Elizabeth looked back to Victoria and noted her sister's tight smile as Lord McCalter made the introductions.

"Good evening, Lord Muir, Mr. Andrews, Miss Andrews." Although her sister's addresses were welcoming, the strained edge to them wasn't hard to discern.

Elizabeth cursed her inability to stand true to her word and looked at Henry. She flicked a cursory glance his way and noted his perfectly formed cravat, his jaw still angular with a slight shadow of a beard. How uncouth not to shave before a ball. Her attention snapped to his lips, ones she'd once enjoyed kissing, nibbling when toying with each other, which now were pressed into a hard, thin line.

With his glowering at her, her stomach knotted. She ignored the fluttering in her belly, cursing it to Hades. Never would she allow feelings to blossom with any man again, and especially not this man. Ever.

"Good evening." Henry's deep baritone thrummed through her, rich and fulfilling. Damn him and his voice. He even sounded wiser, primal almost, and she shivered.

"We had not thought to see you again, Lord Muir, but we're always very pleased to make any acquaintance of yours," Victoria said, her smile directed at Mr. Andrews, who blushed under her sister's polite words.

Elizabeth nodded. "Yes, of course." Her own reply dripped with sarcasm, not that she cared. Henry certainly hadn't cared when she needed him, so there was no way she would start to now. "How was your journey over to England? I hear the crossing can be quite treacherous at times."

Mr. Andrews smiled, and the aristocratic mask eased. "It can be, Lady Newland, but our father runs an import export company out of New York and has vessels of the highest standard at our disposal. Our journey over was never a concern. His biggest worry was if his daughter would return to America come the New Year."

Elizabeth met Victoria's gaze and refused to react to the man's implication. What was he trying to say? Was there an understanding between Miss Andrews and someone… Miss Andrews looked up at Henry, her coquettish gaze saying without words what gentleman she had in mind. Elizabeth narrowed her eyes.

"Do you wish to make England your home, Miss Andrews?" Victoria asked.

"No, not at all," Miss Andrews replied. "But I wouldn't be against Scotland or Ireland. I find the people in the north more to my taste."

Elizabeth started at the barely masked insult against those who lived south of the Scottish border. Again Miss Andrews fixed her attention on Henry, and the lady's liking of everything north of the border became clear. Elizabeth cleared her throat, taking her sister's arm. "Well, Miss Andrews, perhaps you could join the society in Edinburgh or Dublin, since those are more to your taste. We would not wish to keep you here if it makes you unhappy."

Henry stepped forward and bowed when Miss Andrews didn't reply but merely glared at Elizabeth's remark. She smiled.

"Lady Newland, would ye care to accompany me for the next dance? I believe it's to be a cotillion."

Elizabeth ignored the longing that the request brought forth in her. She steeled her resolve to remain strong, detached, withheld. "That is kind of you, my lord, but I do not wish to dance. My feet are feeling poorly after my earlier efforts."

"Come, Lady Newland, surely there is one more dance in ye," Lord McCalter said jovially.

"Perhaps another time," Victoria stated, clearly sensing her growing unease. "Elizabeth did say when she finished the last set that she wouldn't dance again this eve. But the season still has many more dances in it. I'm sure Lord Muir can wait to take advantage at another ball."

Henry smiled, but the gesture never reached his eyes. "Of course. I would never wish to cause unease for Lady Newland."

Elizabeth bit back a nasty retort and directed her attention to the dancers swirling about on the dance floor. Henry's years in America had turned him into a hypocrite.

"How is Dunsleigh? And ye father? We've only been back in the country a week or so, and I've not heard how ye family goes on."

Like you care.

The bitter thought should shame her; to think so cruelly wasn't something that was in her nature, and yet the man before her was the very reason she'd married a total stranger. Had used him poorly.

"We're all very well. Although Father hasn't accompanied us to town; he remains in the country," Victoria said.

"Are ye staying at Newland house or the Duke's London residence?" Henry's eyes burned with a hatred Elizabeth wondered at. That he was annoyed with her was odd, since it was by his own doing that she'd married someone other than himself. Had he returned when they'd written him, they would be married right at this moment.

"I'm staying at my brother's home." Elizabeth's reply was clipped, and Mr. Andrews shifted with unease. The tension among the party was almost palpable, and uncomfortable to say the least.

Henry laughed, the tone mocking. He took a sip of his wine, draining the contents. "How diverting. Ye English husband doesn't mind that ye stay with your family when in town. I thought he would wish ye beside him at all times."

Victoria met her gaze, her eyes wide with disbelief.

"I do not believe my husband would wish me to be beside him at this very moment, Lord Muir, since he's buried in the family plot in Wiltshire."

Henry started at her words, his eyes widening in shock. "Ye're a widow?"

Elizabeth glared at the Scottish oaf. "Lord Newland passed away over a year ago."

"I'm sorry for your loss, Lady Newland." Mr. Andrews threw her a consoling look. "We apologize for bringing up what must still be so painful for you."

"Thank you." She looked back at Henry, who watched her, or more like contemplated her every move like a fox watches a rabbit. "Lord Muir, do you have something to say?" she asked, annoyed he would study her so.

He cleared his throat. "Sincere condolences, my lady." Henry took another glass of wine from a passing footman. "I'm relieved to hear ye father is doing well. I shall travel down to Dunsleigh and call on him before returning to Scotland."

"That won't be necessary, Lord Muir. I'm sure you're busy here with your visiting family from abroad."

"I admit we're very busy, but I will always have time for His Grace. He was my guardian, after all."

Elizabeth made a noncommittal sound, looking toward the supper room doors that were being opened by liveried footmen. "Well I'm sure you'll do as you please." Victoria's hold on her arm tightened, a silent warning to behave. The first strings of a cotillion sounded, and the tittering about the room increased.

"I will dance with you, Henry. This dance is such a favorite of mine, and you do it so well. I'm sure, given the amount of times we've stepped out together, I will prove adequate for this society's standard," Miss Andrews said, her voice as sweet as ratafia.

Elizabeth watched as Henry smiled down at Miss Andrews, and a rage as strong as she had ever known consumed her. This woman believed she was acceptable for

Henry, and no doubt wished to become more to him than just his cousin. She watched as the woman boldly set her hand on his arm, her expression riveted on the earl.

Miss Andrews was in love...with Henry. Elizabeth hated her on the spot.

Henry chuckled, the sound deep and throaty, and one Elizabeth had heard only sparingly in his youth. She studied his profile and realized she no longer knew him. His voice, body, mannerisms were all different. Had she ever really known him? She doubted she did right at that moment.

He took Miss Andrews's hand and bowed over it. "Shall we, my dear?"

Elizabeth looked away from the retreating pair and refused to let past emotions over Henry hurt her a second time. No, she no longer knew him and really never did, if she were honest. Never had she been so wrong about someone's character as she had been with Henry.

Needing to get away, she pulled Victoria toward the supper room doors, determined to stuff herself with food to fill the aching hole she felt in the pit of her stomach. Of course she'd known one day Henry would walk back into her society, possibly married and with children. But to see him again, to be so close to him and yet so distant, was something she would have to get used to. Perhaps he would tire of town and leave for Scotland soon and all would go back to the way it was before.

Normal. Mundane. *Lonely...*

Elizabeth heard a familiar laugh and turned to see Henry and Miss Andrews, their enjoyment of the dance and of each other clear to see.

She growled under her breath. Damn him.

CHAPTER 2

*H*enry finished the dance with Amelia and managed to dislodge his cousins from his side during supper. He leaned against the ballroom wall, watching the play of the ton before him, all of the guests oblivious to the turmoil coursing through his body.

After walking past a group of meddling matrons he decided, at the look of fear they threw his way, that perhaps he ought to stop glaring at everyone present. He took another glass of brandy from a passing footman, confident the beverage would amend him to a more affable manner.

Or perhaps not.

The reason for his sour mood stood talking in deep discussion with the pompous Lord Riddledale. The older gentleman, at least fifteen years her senior, seemed to be too close, leering at her like a man who'd never seen a woman's form before. And with Riddledale, that was surely a possibility. Henry gritted his teeth, forcing another sip of the burning liquid down his throat.

"Is this the chit you've been pining over the last two years?"

Henry huffed out a breath, but didn't deny the charge his cousin Richard laid against him. "What was there to pine over? She married another not long after I left. Lady Newland was a child of my guardian. Nothing more, I assure ye."

His cousin raised his brow, considering his words that Henry had to admit sounded false. "She makes a beautiful widow." He paused. "In fact, all the sisters I've been introduced to this evening are striking beyond measure. Lady Newland has three sisters, I'm told, and one brother."

Henry nodded, unable to disagree with his cousin on both counts. Elizabeth had always been handsome. The memory of them as children, of the delightful girl who had no qualms attempting anything he or his friends could manage. A girl who hadn't minded the mud and scrapes of venturing outdoors. He'd loved her even then, although in a different kind of way from the love his affections had morphed into as an adult.

"Beautiful they may be, but believe me when I say they're as fickle as snakes if in need or want of something." As if his thoughts conjured her, Elizabeth looked across the room, and their gazes locked. His hands fisted at his sides, and for the life of him he could not look away. How could she have married Newland after promising him only weeks before that she would wait for his return? Yes, his time away equated to two years, but Elizabeth had known his time in America could be lengthy. She'd promised that no matter how many seasons her parents afforded her, she was his.

So why did Elizabeth do it?

"Most women are, I find, although that's what makes the chase all the more enjoyable. Wouldn't you agree?" Richard nudged him, smiling. "So now that you're not looking to the striking Lady Newland as a wife, on whom have you set your sights? Father would be pleased to see you settled and happy.

You were so focused on gaining a fortune that we thought your heart ceased to beat for the opposite sex in New York."

Henry shuddered at the thought of marrying anyone at all. Of course he wasn't foolish enough not to know he must marry one day, but it wasn't a priority. Now was the time to enjoy himself. Acquire a mistress perhaps and drown himself between her legs whenever he wanted. "The sole reason I came to America was to gain my fortune and secure my estate. Now that I've done that, I can take my time in surveying the diamonds of the ton. And paramount to that, no father can call me an heiress hunter."

Richard nodded, his cousin's gaze fixed on Elizabeth still. Henry frowned, not liking the appreciative glint in his relative's eyes. "I must say Lady Newland wasn't cordial to you. In fact, her very finely veiled dislike of your presence was quite obvious."

"Yes, but the sentiment was mutual, so my feelings remain intact." Henry looked about the room, anywhere but where Elizabeth stood, laughing, drinking, her beautiful eyes that once looked upon him with favor now turned toward other gentlemen, all of them more than happy to take whatever she would bestow upon them.

She was a rich widow, which meant the proprieties in this society no longer applied to her, within reason, of course. If she were not obvious in her regard or affairs, the ton would not care what she got up to behind closed doors. Elizabeth could take a lover, and no one would chastise her for it.

The image of them beside the lake, of her flushed cheeks and thoroughly kissed mouth, tormented him. Of knowing another man may hear her whispered gasps of pleasure, of taking from her what he'd always thought of as his, near buckled his knees.

"Who is that gentleman with her now? He seems quite cross."

Henry's lip curled at the sight of the pompous bastard. "Lord Riddledale, Marquis Ridges."

Richard laughed. "Your tone tells me all I need to know. You're not old friends then?"

"No, not at all. And why the fool thinks Elizabeth would have him is beyond me. He's old enough to be her father."

"You mean Lady Newland."

Henry cursed, taking another sip of brandy. "Yes, of course. Lady Newland."

"It's sad about her husband. He died well before his time, poor chap."

Well before his time. How would anyone wish to die when the delectable Lady Newland was your bed partner? He knew how Elizabeth was in the throes of passion, giving, needy, absolutely delightful in every way.

Henry pulled at his cravat, the damn thing awfully tight all of a sudden. Why was he tormenting himself in this way? She was nothing to him. Nothing but an immature chit who used him, lied to him, and yet...he could not shake the feeling of her legs about his hips, her breasts free from her gown, the dampness of his kiss on her pebbled peaks glistening in the afternoon sun.

Henry cleared his throat, needing to pull his thoughts away from memories that only made him want what he could not, would not, have again.

"Yes, terrible tragedy, I'm sure. Although I dinna know the particulars of his death. In fact, I had no idea at all he had died."

"Why did the family not write you? You were their ward."

That Henry couldn't answer. In fact, after the letter of Elizabeth's forthcoming marriage, he'd not heard from the family at all. They cut him off with no word as to why, even after he'd written numerous times to see if all was well. Communication ceased, and it had puzzled him greatly.

He took another sip of brandy and realized with embarrassment his cup was empty. "Who knows how these great aristocratic families work. Ye guess as to why they never wrote me is as good as mine."

Richard nodded in agreement. "Will you seek her out and ask why you were never told of Lord Newland's death or why the family ceased all communication with you?"

"That, cousin, ye can be assured I will." And he would take great pleasure in telling Elizabeth what he thought of her treachery and lies.

Richard clapped him on the shoulder. "Good man. Now, our dearest Amelia is looking bored. I had best save the chits of London from the vocal capabilities of an American when she becomes annoyed." Richard went to leave, but stopped, turning to face him. "Good luck with it all, man. If there's anything I can help you with, let me know."

"Thank ye, I shall." Henry watched him go before seeking out the one woman who'd haunted his every thought since the day he left. He looked back to where he'd last seen her only to see the space empty.

He caught a glimpse of blond curls disappearing through a door into an adjoining passage.

Henry marched after her, making the passage only scant moments after Elizabeth. He scanned the corridor, noting a conservatory at one end, the door slightly ajar. Was she rendezvousing with another gentleman? Fury tore through him, and heedless to the clip of his boot heels on the polished tile floor, he marched toward the perfumed room.

She stood before the fountain, her profile clear to see in the moonlight that pierced the glass roof. He shut the door, and she turned at the sound of the click.

"What do you want, Henry?" Her bored tone hurt more than he liked to admit.

"I wish to talk. Now."

*E*lizabeth fought to control her voice lest she give way to emotions that no longer served her any good. There was no future with Henry, not after his abandonment of her. She had escaped to the conservatory for some time to gather herself, to stop her eyes from constantly seeking out the man before her. And now here he was, looking more handsome than she ever remembered him.

"What? No kind salutations on seeing me again? Ye greeting of me in the ball earlier was unpardonable for a duke's daughter."

"Or a viscount's wife."

Pain flickered in his gaze before his eyes narrowed with another emotion she herself was feeling right at this moment. Anger.

"We're not friends, Lord Muir. I do not have to be nice to you."

"And why is that, madam? Pray tell me, what did I ever do to ye to make ye throw our friendship away?"

She laughed. What was he? Foxed? "I have my reasons, you know I do."

"I would like to know of them."

Elizabeth moved away toward the stone bench, not liking how the closer he came, the more she wished to throw herself at him like the lovesick fool she had been in her youth. "Why don't you tell me why we're no longer friends, Henry? I'm sure you have some inkling."

His lip cured into a snarl. "You married Lord Newland without a care to the promises we'd made to each other. How could ye, lass? Did ye lose ye heart in some way as to treat me with such little respect?"

"How could I? How could I not! You would not come back and marry me."

Henry stepped back, running a hand through his hair, leaving it on end.

Elizabeth fought the urge to pull it back to order, to run her hands through it and touch it one more time. But she would not; never would she touch him again.

"Ye knew I would not marry ye as poor as I was. I refused to let society class me as a Scottish fortune hunter after a rich English lass. I wanted to marry ye, give you the life you were accustomed to, without the help of your dowry. What is wrong with that? Why did ye not wait for me?"

"We wrote you, Henry. Asked for your return. You did not."

He shook his head, frowning. "I never received such a letter."

Elizabeth held up her hand, needing a moment to think. None of this made sense. Was Henry lying or telling the truth? And if he was in fact being honest, that meant he did not know of their child.

Oh dear God. "But you replied saying you would not be returning to England any time soon."

"I never wrote such a thing." He shook his head, confusion replacing the anger in his tone. "I don't understand what ye're talking about."

She bit her lip, her mind whirling with thoughts. If he did not know of Samuel, their son, was that such a bad thing? Her son was to inherit Newland Estate and the abundance of wealth that came with the viscountcy. If Henry knew Samuel had been birthed under the guise of another man's name, he'd murder her.

"I," she paused, thinking for the first time that perhaps Henry had never abandoned her. Had never in fact treated her with such utter disrespect that she would never forgive him. That the man before her had never willfully broken her heart… "I don't know what to say but, in any case, it's done now. I fell in love with another, and I married him. You left for America to gain your wealth, and you've succeeded if your superfine coat is anything to go by. There is nothing left to say now that could change our past."

"Someone has meddled, and I want to know why. I never wrote such a letter, and I certainly never received a letter from ye family requesting that I return."

She bit her lip, confusion warring with the long-held anger she kept within her. The urge to run far away from Henry made her restless. "I do not know, and I'm not interested in opening old"—she was going to say wounds, but she would never allow him to know how much it hurt that he hadn't come home—"opening up what no longer matters. It's done now, just as we're done."

He came up to her, leaning over and cowering her smaller stature. Elizabeth lifted her chin, refusing to step back. "We're done?" he mocked, his gaze flicking to her lips. Her mind fought with her heart to give way, to close the scant space between them and see just if what she said were true.

"Yes." She cleared her throat, hating that her voice would betray her at such a time and sound breathless. Needy even. Damn him.

They stood within the conservatory, the air crackling with denied need and perfumed hothouse plants.

A little disappointment pricked her when he stepped back, his eyes darkening to the color of coal. "Ye're absolutely right. Good night, Lady Newland. I hope the remainder of the ball is to ye satisfaction."

Elizabeth's mouth opened in shock as she watched Henry bow and depart. A severing pain, similar to the one she felt the day her father had read his missive, tore through her. How dare he again be the one to leave? But with the thought came guilt. Had he written the letter, or was it Henry's way of getting out of a bad situation to deny all knowledge of it?

Neither seemed to sit well with her, especially since—up to Henry's leaving—he'd been of sound character and mind, not fickle or in need of lying to those who supported him.

So if she were to give Henry the benefit of such doubt, who had written the letter and why? Elizabeth walked back to the ball, wanting nothing but to return home, away from all the intrigue and scandal that the ton thrived on. In no way did she wish for her scandalous past to be known or gossiped about. And in no way did she want Henry to find out his son held another title and name that was not his rightful father's.

CHAPTER 3

*H*enry slammed the front door of his home, startling the sleeping footman in the entrance hall, the young man falling off his chair and landing with a thump on the tiled floor.

He strode into his sparsely furnished library and slumped into a leather-clad chair, thumping his feet atop the small table before him.

Richard, asleep on the settee, one arm lazily thrown over his eyes, woke and looked at him. "You spoke to her, I gather?"

Henry gritted his teeth. "Yes, I bloody well spoke to her, and I'm no clearer on anything than I was when I first returned to England."

His cousin chuckled and sat up. "What did she say? Don't forget you've been gone two years or more. Things change. Women change."

Henry looked into the hearth and watched the wood turn into black coal. "Aye, I know, but I thought she would at least tell me why she chose to forget the understanding between us and marry Newland." She had given herself to him, honored him with her body, but she no longer trusted him, nor liked him very much, if he was any judge of her emotions.

"Look elsewhere before you drive yourself mad, man. You said yourself before leaving New York you no longer had feelings for the chit, so why get all high in the instep about things now?"

Because he'd lied, that's why. "Hmmm," he replied, noncommittally. Having returned to England and being in the same room as Elizabeth had proved what a complete ass he'd been. Tonight in the conservatory he'd wanted to yank that defiant miss against him and kiss her bloody senseless. Prove to her that they were far from over or "done," as she'd stated.

"I know you won't like me saying this, but as your friend I fear I must. Father would like you to offer for Amelia. Now I know," Richard said, silencing him with his hand, "you do not see her in such a romantic light, but perhaps after finishing things with Lady Newland you could look elsewhere, start afresh, and move on, as it were, with someone else."

It was what Henry ought to do, but an unrelenting, restless fury wouldn't abate. Something told him someone had kept them apart, had written to both of them to ensure such a separation occurred.

"Do ye know of any letters arriving for me from the Duke of Penworth that I did not receive? Lady Newland spoke of a missive that I did not know of."

Richard looked up, frowning. "I do not, I'm sorry. Any mail that came into the residence was given to Father to look over before allocating it to whomever it was for. I'm sure had anything arrived he would not have kept it from you."

Henry clenched his jaw, not so certain that that was true,

but willing to let it go. For now. "Drink?" He lifted the decanter of brandy.

"If you're pouring." Richard sat up. "But as your friend and closest relative, please take some time and think on what I said earlier. The love you felt for Lady Newland, if it was love at all, could've been nothing but youthful folly."

Henry gnashed his teeth. What he felt for Elizabeth was anything but youthful folly. Had he been like so many of his friends, flush with blunt, not a care in the world for finances, he would've married her as young as she was. "Amelia does not care for me in that way, Richard. No matter how much ye father may wish it." He sat across from Richard, after handing him his drink, staring at the dark fire grate.

"You're wrong. Amelia cares for you a great deal. Hell, we all do. But don't you think it's time you forgot about whatever happened between you and Lady Newland? A clean start and all that. And how often do you have your family from New York staying? I have not been to Whites yet; however will I face society back home if I do not look out the famous bowed window?"

Henry laughed, his cousin always managing to pull him from a sullen mood. "I shall take ye to Gentleman Jackson's as well. A bit of sparring is what we need."

"Indeed, but make sure you leave the face unharmed, if you don't mind, good chap. I have ladies to court."

"More like seduce." Henry took a sip of his brandy, the golden liquid relaxing him finally. "A night at Covent Garden may suit ye. What say ye?"

"Oh, garden and night sound most intriguing. When do we go?"

Henry closed his eyes, groaning when the fiery glare of Elizabeth flashed before his eyes. "Not soon enough."

*E*lizabeth sat at the edge of the Serpentine in Hyde Park and penciled in the last of the duck feathers she was sketching. She smudged the edges to give the image a little depth, then sat back and scrutinized her accomplishment. She would never be as good as her younger sister Victoria at drawing, but the effort wasn't too terrible, she supposed.

"What do you think, Tony? Could my sketch win an art prize?"

Tony, her groom, walked over from the tree he'd been leaning against and stared down at her drawing. "Very good, my lady, if I do say so myself."

Elizabeth chuckled. "I think you're being too kind, but I'll keep it in any case. Samuel loves ducks."

Her groom cleared his throat, and she looked up to see Lord Riddledale purposefully striding toward her. She inwardly groaned, her desire to roll her eyes only stopped by the years of proper manners drilled into her. Not wanting to have to deal with his lordship, she looked back to her sketch, hoping he'd not seen her. The shadow of his top hat landed across her paper and she knew her wish wasn't to be. "Lord Riddledale, how nice to see you again. I hope you're enjoying your stroll." She didn't look at him, just continued to study the birds that flitted about on the grass.

He shook his head—or his shadow did, anyway. "Not at all, Lady Newland. I find the air most troublesome this morning, full of coal, if I'm any expert on the matter."

Ever the expert on everything. She fought back a chuckle. "Oh dear, what a pickle you seem to be in then, for what can one do without air. I hope it hasn't offended you enough that you've stopped breathing altogether." She could only hope.

"Do be serious, my lady. Of course one must breathe." She

made a noncommittal sound. "As you can see, I'm drawing and enjoying the lovely weather."

"How opportune it was to see you here, as there's something in particular I wish to continue to discuss."

She looked up inquiringly, hoping he wasn't going to chat about his marriage proposal again. "What is it, my lord?"

"I wanted to know if you've given my declaration of marriage any thought."

What an indomitable fellow. Elizabeth cursed her inability to let him down nicely. One would think after a year of marriage she would've learned the art of telling people what she thought and wanted. "You wish for an answer now? Here at the park?"

"Yes. And then I'll know how to proceed."

She frowned at the hardened edge to his voice. There wasn't anything he could do if she said no. Riddledale stood before her, arms clenched behind his back and his lips pursed as if he'd eaten something distasteful.

"I'm sorry, Lord Riddledale, but I cannot marry you. Friendship is all I can offer, and I hope that is enough."

His lips twisted into a sadistic snarl, and he sat down next to her, crossing one leg over the other. It looked less than comfortable.

"I thought you may say as much, and I do not mean to hurt you, so please remember this with what I have next to say."

Elizabeth swallowed, not liking the turn of the conversation. "You cannot possibly love someone who's given you no reason to seek her affection. We've been neighbors at Dunsleigh for many years, yes, but never in all that time have I sought your love."

"Be that as it may, I've thought you the perfect candidate for my wife for some time. You're young enough to bear my children, have in fact had a child, so there is no fault with you there. Your family is titled and well sought after within the ton, and you're kind of nature. And I think a young son such as you have needs a guiding hand when it comes to estate matters etc. I shall run Newland Estate until Lord Samuel comes of age."

Coldness swept down her spine at the mention of Riddledale having anything to do with her dear boy. "Does your decision to fix me as your wife have anything to do with real feelings, my lord? Or is it only my monetary value that holds sway with you?"

A light blush stole over his features, making his skin blotchy and red. "Of course not," he huffed, his chin—that was a little too far set back in his face—jutting out with annoyance. "I cannot believe you would suggest such a thing."

"I'm sorry if I offended you, but as the mother of an heir to Newland Viscountcy and a woman of independent means, you must see that I would never agree to an understanding unless I was fully engaged in heart and mind with the gentleman. I'm sorry, but I'm not, in this case."

"You will be my wife, Elizabeth, or everything you hold dear will be ripped from under you."

She looked at him sharply, narrowing her eyes. "Do not threaten me, Lord Riddledale. You forget yourself." She stood, and he followed.

"No, you forget, Lady Newland. In fact, you seem to have forgotten a lot." He laughed as if she'd said something amusing.

"And pray what did I forget that you seem so determined to remind me of?"

A laugh sounded across the lawns, and Elizabeth cringed at Henry's uncanny ability to catch her at such a moment. Could this day become any worse?

"I will speak with you at another time." Lord Riddledale

bowed and left. His retreat in the opposite direction of where Henry walked was hasty, to say the least.

Elizabeth took a calming breath and turned to face her next guests. She noted Miss Andrews hung off Henry's arm like an annoying growth one could not cut off. The sight of them together irritated her more than it ought. She dismissed them and started to pick up her sketching supplies, fumbling with her paper in her haste.

What did she care if Henry had turned his attentions toward someone else? He was nothing to her. Nothing but a mistake of colossal size that had thrown her into a future she'd never thought to live.

"Good mornin', Lady Newland." Henry smiled, but the gesture didn't reach his eyes. If anything he looked as annoyed as she was at their meeting. Again. "I hope we weren't interrupting your tête-à-tête with Lord Riddledale."

Elizabeth pulled on her gloves, casting them a furtive gaze. "Good morning." She passed her supplies to her groom who carried them over to the carriage. "And no, you didn't interrupt anything of importance with his lordship." Elizabeth looked to where the gentleman concerned continued to stroll along the Serpentine banks, wondering what he'd been about to say. She frowned, not liking the feel of Riddledale's words. "I'm afraid you've caught me packing up to return home."

Henry raised his brow, his gaze mocking. If only she knew what was going through his mind right at this moment. If it was anything like her own it was a kaleidoscope of thoughts, and not any of them good or helpful. She was a walking muddle these days.

"Would ye care to join us? We are heading toward Rotten Row. Miss Andrews would like to see the horses that are going for a run."

"No, thank you. I really have dallied longer than I ought."

Elizabeth started toward her groom, relieved when he opened the carriage door preparing for their departure.

The touch of Henry's hand on her arm pulled her to a stop. She faced him, her skin burning where he touched. How could he, after all their time apart, what he'd done to her, what she'd done to him, create such a reaction within her?

She cast a glance over his shoulder and noted his cousins had walked on to give them privacy.

"Why are ye being like this? Ye're the one who married someone else, lass." His whispered words were only for her to hear, and she yanked her arm out of his hold. Henry stepped back, his jaw hardening in anger. "I don't understand, Elizabeth."

"I'm not being anything to you."

"Ye're avoiding me, cutting me dead at every chance ye get."

She continued toward the carriage, ignoring his question. "I have nothing to say to you, Henry." Elizabeth grabbed her groom's hand and stepped into the vehicle. Henry shut the door, but didn't say another word, just watched her.

Elizabeth looked away from the confusion and hurt she read in his eyes and settled her skirts about her legs.

"Who was the letter from that ye supposedly received from me?"

"I told you last night."

He shook his head, a dark lock falling over one eye and making him look more roguish than ever before. For the life of her she couldn't look away. How many times had she pushed that lock away from his face, spiked her fingers through his hair, and pulled him down for a stolen kiss?

"No, you didn't."

His reply pulled her from her musings, and she hoped the

heat she felt on her cheeks was only in her imagination. "It was signed by both you and your uncle."

"I will find out who wrote that note, but there is also something else I wish to know. Ye never told me why ye needed me to return. What was the reason?"

She bit her lip frantically trying to come up with an excuse. "I ah...I confessed to my parents my feelings toward you had grown beyond friendship after you left, and Father, liking you as much as he did, wrote for your return."

"Ye talk as if your family no longer wishes my association. Should I have sent that letter and denied ye marriage, I could understand being treated like I had the pox. But I did not." He paused. "I deserve an explanation, Elizabeth."

She couldn't look at him, for surely he'd see the lie clouding her gaze like the dirty little secret that it was. All of Samuel's future hung in the balance, his inheritance, his security. The way she played the next deal of cards between Henry and herself was of high import.

The last thing she wanted was to lie to him, but no matter who sent the letters, who received them and who did not, they were sent, and the damage was done. "Your denial hurt me, and therefore my family rallied around me, supported me. Mama and Papa knew, you see, of us lying together at the lake that day. I'm sure given the circumstances such reactions on their behalf are warranted."

"I hope ye will tell them that I did not write the letter, and I will find out who did, ye can be assured of that, but I will not apologize for having ye, Elizabeth. Never that."

Heat bloomed on her face and the reverence behind his words told the truth he spoke. She cleared her throat. "It's all in the past, Lord Muir. My feelings toward you were youthful and fickle. I fell in love with Newland, and I married him. No harm done and no need to look into the missing letter."

"I disagree." His clipped words were unrelenting and primal.

If he found out about the missing letter he would find out the real reason her father wrote him. She'd be ruined. Samuel would be cast out as a bastard. Her head swam, and she clasped the carriage seat to steady herself.

"Are ye well, Elizabeth? Ye've grown quite pale." Henry clasped her arm, supporting her, and she wished he had not. His nearness had always affected her, made her long for things no well-bred lady should think.

She smiled, nodding. "I'm very well. Perhaps I have sat in the sun a little too long today. I really must return home. Alice will be wondering where I am."

"I shall keep ye informed on my progress. Give your sisters my regards."

She nodded. "I shall. Good-bye." Elizabeth sighed in relief as the carriage rocked forward and finally out of Henry's scrutiny. Nerves rolled about her belly like a storm, and a forthcoming sense of disaster settled on her shoulders. This was terrible, worse than she could ever imagine the situation would become.

It was only a matter of time before Henry found out about their child. If the letter stayed forgotten, or better yet, destroyed by whomever decided to meddle, the parentage of Samuel could never be proven. The thought of someone else in the ton knowing the truth was little comfort and more troubling than everything else put together.

---

*L*ater that evening, Elizabeth stood surrounded by the many gentleman admirers who thought they could triumph over her indomitable attitude toward marriage.

They could not. But for a few hours it was fun to forget her worries and enjoy their flirting and humorous bantering all the same. Her sister Alice glided through the throng, looking amused and confident, two traits she'd always wished for within herself. Alice always saw the funnier side of life and what larks one could get up to. She was glad her sister arrived from the country to attend some balls and parties; she'd missed her when at Newland Estate more than any other of her four siblings.

Alice clasped her arm, wrapping it about her own. "Come walk with me. I want to have a little chat."

Elizabeth bade the gentlemen good night. "What do you want to talk to me about? You seem quite determined."

"I've heard Lord Muir is back in town. Is this true? Has he returned from America a rich man, and seeking a wife?"

Elizabeth sighed, wondering when her sister would take a breath. "Yes. It's true. Well…" She paused, clasping two glasses of champagne from a passing footman and handing one to Alice, who certainly needed a drink. "The first is indeed correct. He's back and wealthy, but as for him looking for a bride I could not say."

"Did you confront him about his denial of you all those years ago? What did he say?"

She pushed the glass up to Alice's lips. "Drink and take a breath." Alice smiled but did as she was told.

"I have, and he denies ever knowing of the letter we sent him. Furthermore, he has no idea of the reply that we received." Elizabeth steered her sister over to a vacant settee that was slightly concealed behind a potted fern.

"That is absurd. Someone must have read and replied to the letters." Alice paused, sitting and staring ahead at the throng of guests. "His uncle? But then we're left wondering as to why."

"Yes, that's the question. If it was Henry's uncle who

wrote the letter and it was certainly signed by that man, why would he do such a thing? Other than the rivalry he had with Papa all those years ago, but surely he would not act in such an underhanded way."

"What rivalry?" Alice turned to look at her, and Elizabeth told her of the story of how Henry's uncle wished to marry their own mama prior to her marrying their father. "So he sees Mama's marriage to a duke as a slight against an earl's second son." Alice slumped back in her chair and Elizabeth did the same. "I can see why he would hate our family, if that is the case, especially if he loved Mama and was broken-hearted by her marriage to someone else."

Elizabeth finished her drink, nodding. "If he hadn't ruined my future, I could almost feel sorry for the man." To be denied marriage to the one you loved was something Elizabeth had in common with Henry's uncle. Infuriating ass notwithstanding.

"And so if Henry is innocent of the crime we laid against him, what are your feelings on the matter? You used to be so close."

They were once best friends, long before anything romantic had occurred between them. "Nothing has changed, Alice. Don't you see? If anything, the situation I'm now in is worse."

"Why?" Alice took her hand, and Elizabeth noted hers was shaking.

"He doesn't know of Samuel, Alice. Henry has no idea that he even exists." Tears smarted from behind her lids, and she blinked. "If he finds out who wrote the letter, he'll find out why we wrote it in the first place. It could ruin my son."

"Do you not think he deserves to know?"

Elizabeth looked at her sister, wondering if she knew this woman sitting beside her at all. "I cannot tell him. That you must see, and, anyway, Samuel is at Newland Estate for the season; Henry will be back to Scotland soon and never need know of our child."

"But if he somehow reads or is informed about the letter and its content, wouldn't it be better to have come from you first? If you spoke to him, surely he would see the dilemma and not create any trouble for you or Samuel."

If only that were true, but something told Elizabeth should Henry find out about their son he'd want to claim him for his own. Henry had never cared for what society said, or their rules and regulations when it came to what was correct form or acceptable behavior. "He'll be angry, and rightfully so. But Samuel is to inherit Newland Estate. Marcus loved the boy and wanted nothing but the best for him. It seems wrong somehow to tell Henry about something that cannot be undone."

Alice sighed. "Very well. We'll not say a word about the boy, but you know that it will only take a word from someone else mentioning your son, and he'll know."

"But he'll only know that I birthed a child, not that it is his. Surely he would not suspect anything from such news. And without the letter, nothing can be proven as to Samuel's parentage." Elizabeth took a calming breath. "All I can hope is that whoever orchestrated this severing of us is not Henry's uncle and is no longer interested in our lives."

"Elizabeth, do be serious. Of course it is his uncle, and Henry will only have to write him to find out the truth. You should prepare yourself for what I fear will be an unstoppable culmination of terrible events."

Dread pooled in her stomach at the thought and she stood, wanting nothing other than to leave...to hide, to run away.

Her sister stilled beside her and Elizabeth looked to see what had caught her attention. "Oh dear, I see Moore and Miss Hart have arrived."

Elizabeth nodded, noting Moore's attention was fixed not on his wife but their sister Isolde across the ballroom floor. "She's Miss Hart no more, Alice. Should you not call her your grace?"

"She'll always be Miss Hart to me, which I will admit is the nicest name I can think to call her. There are many others I'd like to use."

Elizabeth couldn't agree more. "He cannot take his eyes off of Isolde. I believe he still loves her, you know."

Alice nodded, gazing at Isolde with pity. "I know, and Miss Hart loves nothing but to flaunt her marriage status before Isolde's face at any opportunity that arises. That woman is unrecognizable to the girl we grew up with and loved."

Elizabeth was glad her sister used past tense to describe their feelings toward the duchess. They certainly no longer loved the woman. "Let's not talk anymore of anything troubling. It'll ruin the ball for us both if we keep being so dreary."

Another footman passed them by, and Alice returned their empty glasses before taking two new filled ones. "I'm going to leave you, my dear. I see Lord Arndel has arrived." Elizabeth took a sip. "And what do you have to say to our 'elusive viscount'?"

An impish grin formed on her sister's lips. "Many things that I'll divulge in good time, but for tonight I want to let him know I'm here should he wish to further our acquaintance."

"You are acquainted. He's our second closest neighbor at Dunsleigh, you silly girl. And don't be too forward or you'll have our mother, whom, by the way, is watching from across the room, over here making us dance with the likes of Lord Riddledale."

Alice chuckled. "We are acquainted, yes, but I wish to be more so. I will see you later."

Elizabeth smiled after her sister as she all but floated across the room toward the gentleman. Lord Arndel, somehow sensing her sister's approach, physically stiffened when Alice came to stand beside him. Elizabeth wondered what Alice was playing at. For it seemed to her that his lordship wasn't at all favorable to a match with the highly placed Lady Alice Worthingham.

"May I have the next dance, Lady Newland?"

Elizabeth strove to quell her racing heart at the sound of the deep baritone behind her. She took a calming breath and turned to face her nemesis, her ruination, her past. She looked up and met Henry's eyes, and lost herself for a moment in their deep blue depths. Lost herself in the past that had no right to meddle in her future.

"Elizabeth, would ye dance with me?"

The note of need she heard in his voice had her nodding and taking his hand. Damn it, she really ought to learn when to refuse.

She disregarded the warmth that flowed into her limbs as his strong, gloved hand enfolded hers. Ignored the defined muscles beneath his superfine coat that left a fluttering deep in her womb. She had fought hard to forget such feelings. She would not allow him to awaken them now. Not when it was too late.

By the time the dance began, her nerves were beyond repair. Her determination to never allow him to affect her again was a poor showing indeed. She reminded herself she hated him. Hated him to the very pits of Hades. Oh yes, she really hated him. Yet, it was hard to hate someone when he could possibly be innocent of the crime you'd placed against his character...

"Ye've changed from the girl I once knew," he stated matter-of-factly.

Elizabeth kept her eyes focused over Henry's shoulder and fought not to meet his gaze. She wanted to look at him, wanted to see all the contours of his face this close to hers, if only to remind herself of what she'd once dreamed. "I have changed. And for the better, I believe."

"In some respects, yes, I'd agree with ye."

Her eyes narrowed. "In all ways. And anyway," she continued, "who are you to judge me? A poor earl from Scotland? Or is it an impoverished earl? Or is it now a rich earl trying to win a wife?"

Henry stiffened in her arms, and he yanked her hard against him, leaving her breathless. "Look at me, Elizabeth." A moment passed and then, furious at her lack of self-control, she turned and looked at him.

Elizabeth read a multitude of questions in his eyes, along with the hurt she'd intentionally inflicted. She raised her brow, annoyed more at herself that she'd brought up the mention of Henry looking for a wife. Of course he was looking for a wife, and so what if he was? He could do whatever he wanted.

"I'm not sure how it is done in Scotland, but in England, my lord, unless I have given you leave, you will address me as Lady Newland."

A muscle worked in Henry's jaw. He swirled them about the floor, their steps gliding and smooth, the opposite of how their conversation was progressing.

"You will not give me leave to address ye as I once did, even in a relative private dance like this one? You are high and mighty now."

Elizabeth shrugged at the disdain in his voice. "You will address me as Lady Newland or I'll not speak to you."

A muscle ticked in his jaw before he averted his attention

over her shoulder. "I am no longer ye friend? Is that what ye're saying?"

They twirled to a stop; Elizabeth stepped back as soon as she was able and curtsied. Hating the fact that his words severed her soul in two. "Lord Muir, only hurt can come from us being acquaintances. I think it best we leave the past where it belongs—in the past—and start our futures as we are now. Apart."

------

*H*enry pulled Elizabeth to the side of the room, away from the dancers setting up for a quadrille. "I'm not in agreement. I've written my uncle and will know the truth of the letters soon enough, but I do not see why we must be strangers. Enemies, even."

"He may deny it. He may never have received them and knows nothing of them at all."

"You talk as if you'd rather me not know why ye wrote me. Are you hiding something?" A light rose flush spread over Elizabeth's cheeks just as it always had when she was fibbing.

"I hide nothing. I told you," she whispered." I thought myself in love with you and wished for you to return. Nothing more, I assure you."

Henry took a calming breath, wanting to pull the determined, angry minx into his arms and kiss her senseless. Remind her of how well they did together. The two years he'd worked in America, diligently saved and invested until his estate was safe and he had enough funds to marry the minx before him, made her denial of him maddening.

"You married Newland so fast I'm sure had I received ye letter in the first place I wouldn't have made it back in time."

Her eyes went wide before they narrowed to piercing slits

that, should they be able to throw fire, Henry would be aflame. "You're an ass."

Her use of a profanity made him start before he laughed. "Ass? Is that the best ye can do?"

"Here at the ball it is?"

"Come, lass. Why won't you tell me what ye really think?" He stepped closer, the smell of roses wafting up to tempt his senses. He watched her watch him, and he noted the instant her thoughts went from platonic to, well, not platonic. Right at this moment he wanted to kiss her, pull her close and feel the delicious curves that haunted his dreams. Remind Elizabeth just what she really thought of him...of them.

She stared up at him, her mouth open with a gasp, and he ran a finger down her cheek, following the curve of her chin. "Do you know what I think?" he whispered against her ear.

"What?" she said at length, the shiver of her touch running through his arm.

"I would lay good blunt down to say that right at this moment you would like me to drag ye behind the ferns at your back, take ye in my arms, and remind you that ye think me anything but a donkey."

She grinned, his heart hammering in his chest at the gesture. He'd missed making her laugh, making her happy. "Oh, Henry," she chuckled, running her finger up his arm, her touch burning him through his coat. "I never took you for a simpleton, though. Perhaps I should call you a fool instead of an ass."

He shook his head as he watched her saunter off into the crowd, her gown of blue silk swishing about her long legs. How was it that she could madden him and intoxicate him at the same time? Smiling, he set off for more of the good brandy and some gambling, having had enough of the fairer sex this night. Or one particular fair sex, at least.

*E*lizabeth entered the library at her parent's London home and into a whirl of controversy. Her mother, who'd accompanied Alice from the country, tittered over a posy of bluebells.

"Elizabeth, come see," Alice said, gesturing. "You have received a gift. An anonymous one."

She frowned at the bunch of violet flowers that sat atop a ribboned corsage. "It's very pretty, I'm sure. Was there a card, Mama?"

The duchess pulled the bellpull and rang for a servant. Within moments, Thomas, the head butler, walked in. "Your grace?"

"Thomas, did you recognize who it was that left the gift for Lady Newland? There was no card attached."

"I'm sorry, your grace, but no. A street urchin delivered it. Practically threw the box at the footman and skittered off," the butler said, his face a mask of distaste.

Elizabeth smiled her thanks and turned to her mother. "Well then, we shall have to wait and see if someone owns up to such a gift. I'm sure whoever it was will come forward. It isn't proper not to do so. The poor boy who delivered it probably lost the card and was scared he'd be scolded. That is all."

"Maybe not. Perhaps Elizabeth has a secret admirer. One who wishes to be sneaky with his courting," Alice said, her eyes alight with teasing.

Elizabeth shushed her sister before picking up the box and examining it. She supposed Lord Riddledale could've sent it in his haste to sway her no to a yes. Or even Lord Dean could be finally coming forward with his regard, but more likely it was from Henry, baiting her like he teased her the other night. A donkey was too sweet an animal use to proclaim him. Maybe boar, as in pig, would suit better.

"You look a little troubled, my dear. Is something the matter?" Her mother pulled her into the parlor. Alice followed, close on their heels, and shut the door behind them.

Elizabeth sat on the settee, folding her hands in her lap to stop them from fussing. "I'm thinking over who may have sent the posy, that's all." And Henry. Always Henry.

"The esteemed Lord Riddledale could've sent them. Oh, what a lucky girl you are." Alice chuckled.

"Alice! That is rude and I'll not countenance it. His lordship is a much sought-after gentleman. Either of you girls would be lucky to marry such a man."

"I heartily disagree," Alice mumbled under her breath. "I heard you." Their mother threw Alice a pointed stare.

"I don't understand you girls. All of you are out and yet none of you is married. I despair of ever being a grandmother to more than one child."

"Oh, Mama, you will be a grandmother many times over, I promise. Why, just the other day Victoria and I were talking of the act itself, and that since our marriages will be nothing other than love matches, you'll have a horde of grandchildren soon enough." Alice grinned, mirth rampant in her gaze.

Their mother sat silent, her eyes wide with shock before she rallied her argument. "Take heed, my dears, you do not want to cut off your noses to spite your face."

"What do you mean?" Elizabeth frowned, having never heard of such a saying.

"I would suggest you do not slight men who could make you happy and give you a good life just because they do not meet your ideals. It reeks of vanity, and you could end up with no one at all."

"They're not ideals, Mama, only that we wish to marry for

love. Surely there is nothing wrong with that," Alice said, playing with her hair.

Elizabeth glared at her vexing sister who didn't know when to be quiet. "For all your ideals on love, Alice, I for one will never marry again. I have my son and a comfortable life, thanks to Newland. I'm quite content."

The duchess replied. "Even so, it would please me if you wore the posy tonight, Elizabeth. We must find out who your admirer is."

"Mother, I cannot." Elizabeth sat up, the thought of doing such a thing making her stomach curdle. "The gentleman will think I welcome his suit. I will not do it, especially without knowing who it was from."

"Yes, you will. The gentleman may think what he likes, but your father will determine if he is suitable as a husband, so you needn't worry on that score. I'm sure by wearing the posy the gentleman will come forward."

"I'm sure Lord Riddledale sent it," Alice declared, nodding.

"Father knows I'll never marry again, so wearing the flowers is a moot point."

"You will wear it, Elizabeth, if only to please your dear mama. Do not fret, my dear. It is nothing scandalous."

Elizabeth walked from the room, leaving the dreadful posy in the parlor where it belonged. Even as a widow it seemed she was not in control of her life, that the play of others and their wishes sat forefront to her own feelings on the matter.

She stormed up the stairs, not caring if she portrayed a child in pigtails who'd not been given her every wish. The thought of going back to Newland Estate ran through her mind, and she paused mid step. Little Samuel would at least be glad to see her, and she'd love nothing more than to see him again, too.

But if Henry found out where she'd gone and why, he could start to wonder why she'd never mentioned a child to him. Perhaps he'd even want to meet Samuel. Elizabeth sighed, continuing up to her room. No. She would wear the damn posy and be done with it. And if the gentleman was so brave to proclaim himself as the one who'd sent it, she'd let him know exactly what she thought of the gift and of it having no card. That's if she didn't box him about the head with the posy first.

CHAPTER 4

*E*lizabeth fought not to roll her eyes as Lord Riddledale bent over her fingers, his attention fixed upon the posy at her wrist. And by the excited gleam she read in his gaze, she had her answer as to who'd sent the gift.

"What beautiful flowers, Lady Newland. Pray tell, who gave them to you?"

Elizabeth pulled her hand out of his clasp and felt the need to go wash, to rid herself of his touch. "That's the oddest thing, my lord, I do not know. It arrived yesterday with no card." She looked away from his salacious smirk and out toward the floor. She spied Henry dancing a cotillion with a girl she didn't recognize, their similar height making the dance seem effortless.

"What a shame." Lord Riddledale preened like a peacock, patting his hair and giving a decided sniff when he finished. "For it seems you have an admirer who wishes to remain anonymous."

Henry lead the debutante from the floor, and an ache formed in her chest. Elizabeth looked back at her not so secret admirer, and fought not to hit him over the head with her fan. Pompous fool. Did he really think she was so daft? She leaned closer to him to ensure privacy.

"Are you not jealous, my lord? To have another man sending me gifts must vex you after you asked me to be your bride."

He, too, leaned closer, his voice but a whisper. "I think we both know who your admirer is, my dear. And since my proposal seems hasty to you, I thought a little courting was in order. You may show your gratitude now."

Elizabeth took a calming breath, taking a sip of wine. "Mama was very cross there was no card." She stifled a giggle behind her fan as his lordship paled at her words, a sheen of sweat breaking out on his brow.

"The duchess will forgive me when we're married."

"I have not said yes, my lord. Nor do I feel inclined to." Elizabeth couldn't think of anything worse than to marry this man. There had always been something she hadn't liked about the gentleman, and now she knew what that was. He was self-centered, with no care toward others.

Alice started toward them and, thankfully, Lord Riddledale noted their little tête-à-tête would be disrupted and stopped talking. Thank God.

He bowed to her sister before turning his attention back to her. "The posy suits you, my dear, but now I must beg your leave. I'm expected at another function. As you know, I'm a most sought-after gentleman."

She fought not to roll her eyes. "Good evening, my lord. I would not keep you for anything," Elizabeth said, her tone sarcastic even to her own ears.

He picked up her hand, placing a small kiss against her glove. Elizabeth glared. "Do not overstep your bounds, Lord Riddledale."

He laughed, strutting away like the peacock he was.

She glared after him, hating him more than she thought

possible. After all, he'd only asked her to marry him, but there was something about the man...

"I thought he'd never leave." Alice sighed, coming to stand beside her.

Elizabeth turned her attention to the dancing couples. "He is determined I'll be his wife." She paused, looking down at her wrist. "I cannot believe Mother made me wear this posy."

Alice fanned her face and greeted Lord Arndel as he walked past. Elizabeth smiled at the gentleman, unsure as to what to do with Alice's forward manners. Lord Arndel nodded but did not speak nor slow enough to converse.

"Alice, your manners will become the town's fuel for gossip if you keep up such antics."

"Oh fiddlesticks. Look about, there is no one watching us." Alice paused. "And I like annoying him. It's entertaining." Lord Arndel looked back to see if Alice was watching him and ran into a young woman. His coloring turned bright red as he profusely apologized to the girl and hurried on. "Perhaps he isn't as uninterested as he seems," Elizabeth said.

"I ought to marry him and shock him even more." Alice's determined gaze was locked on the gentleman, and Elizabeth could almost feel sorry for the man. Her sister could be quite a minx when provoked.

"You admire him that much?"

"Why not? He is titled, not too young or old, has a face that pleases me, and I need a husband. He'll do as well as any other. Shame he's so reclusive, though. He may be a little boring."

Elizabeth took in Lord Arndel's handsome features, strong shoulders, and height. There could be worse people to be around than him. He glanced back at them and the heated, determined gaze he bestowed on her sister gave Elizabeth pause. "Or he might just surprise you, Alice, and be anything but boring. He may even be exciting."

Her sister laughed. "Oh, one can only hope."

A week later saw the arrival of another anonymous gift, again delivered by the raggedy-looking boy of the streets. Elizabeth looked down at the single white lily sitting on a bed of crimson paper within a long white box. She chewed her lip. If her mother thought she would wear that tonight or carry it around, she was cork-brained. Lord Riddledale's pride was beyond measure when she'd worn the posy, nevertheless this.

Elizabeth started upstairs—there was no way she'd allow her mother to see this flower if she could help it. The front door swung open and in walked her brother, Josh, and his friend Lord Dean. Elizabeth paused, knowing she should do the right thing and greet them. Her mama exited the library, and she bit back a curse, glaring down at the lily.

"Greetings, family. I have arrived."

Elizabeth turned, rolling her eyes at her younger brother's antics. She held the parcel behind her back and hoped no one would notice. "I don't know how we managed without you, Josh, dear," she said, grinning at her sibling.

He kissed her cheek. "You have not, but never fear, for I'm here, and all will be well."

She laughed, shaking her head.

"Elizabeth, what is that you are holding behind your back?" Her mama stretched out her hand as if to take the parcel from her.

"A flower."

Josh peeked over her shoulder, passing the footman his

coat as he did so. "A gift to our Elizabeth, is it? Who's the unlucky gentleman?"

Elizabeth turned and whacked him with the box. Her mother gasped and took it away, glaring at them both.

"What are you doing in town anyway? Come to acquire your own future duchess? Father will be pleased if you do." Her brother paled, and she smirked, enjoying his discomfort over her questioning. "No need for me to find a wife, I'm not the duke yet."

"Look, there's a card today." The duchess smiled. "See, what did I tell you, my dear. Wearing the posy the other evening has brought the gentleman forward. Now let us see what he says."

Her brother lifted his chin, his lips curved in a smug smile. "Just came up for some town influence. You being a female, I wouldn't expect you to understand a man's needs."

Elizabeth scoffed. "You need more than town influence. In fact, I think a good—"

"Elizabeth! That is enough." Her mother turned her attention back to the card in her hand.

Elizabeth gave her back to her vexing brother, ignoring the subtle chuckle from both gentlemen. "Perhaps we could go into the study, Mama. I'm sure Josh and Lord Dean do not wish to learn about flowers and cards."

Lord Dean stepped forward and bowed. "On the contrary, Lady Newland, this is all very exciting."

Josh laughed. "Oh, of course we want to know who is courting you. Do not worry about Dean here." He punched his friend in the arm. "We've known him for years. He won't go telling anyone your little secret." Josh winked.

Elizabeth bit back an unladylike term she'd like to fling at Josh's head but instead ignored him. Her mother paled, and she clasped her arm. "What is it, Mama? The card is not offensive, I hope."

"No, my dear, nothing like that. It is just…I believe it to be a verse. Although it is a little strange. I do not believe he is very good at poetry."

Elizabeth's cheeks heated as both her brother and Lord Dean laughed. Her mother continued. "It reads:

With eyes as green as emeralds. So are mine with envy.
Every flower of the season will be yours.
As you will be mine for eternity.

"Oh my word," Elizabeth groaned. What on earth was Lord Riddledale up to? Other than to ruin her or make her die of embarrassment.

Her mother flipped the card over and looked up. "There is still no name. Did no one come forward at the ball last week when you wore the posy?"

"No one." Elizabeth lied as she caught Lord Dean's thoughtful expression. "May I be excused?"

"Of course," her grace said.

Elizabeth headed upstairs, leaving the lily with her mama. She ignored her brother's continued teasing as she turned down the hall toward her room. Lord Riddledale and his ridiculous gifts would have to be dealt with and sooner rather than later. Tonight, in fact, if she was unfortunate enough to see him again.

———

*M*uch to Elizabeth's dislike, her mother requested she wear the lily, and so, like a child once more, not the widowed lady that she was, Elizabeth stood before the Standley family ballroom, the lily safely clasped in her hand.

She narrowed her gaze when she noted her mama deep in

conversation with the gentleman himself, Lord Riddledale, her face animated in conversation.

Although Elizabeth hadn't told her parents she suspected Lord Riddledale, she wondered watching them both if her mama hadn't come to the conclusion herself. For some absurd reason that Elizabeth had never known nor understood, her parents' approved of him. In a way, she'd been lucky to marry Newland, if only to keep Riddledale from courting her.

For all of her rushed wedding to Lord Newland, he'd been a kind, caring husband who, although slow of mind, was a gentleman through and through, unlike Riddledale, who only ever thought of himself. Period.

"I see her grace has gained her way once again." Elizabeth turned to look at Lord Dean, his lips quirked into a warm smile.

"Yes. Unfortunately."

His lordship glanced at her mother, a contemplative look in his eyes. "For what it's worth, it makes you look even prettier with the blossom than without."

Elizabeth smiled. "Thank you. You're very kind." They stood in silence a moment, lost in their own thoughts, before his lordship cleared his throat, rocking on his heels a little.

"Would you do the honor of calling me Anthony when we're alone, Lady Newland? I feel we are good friends, are we not?"

Elizabeth lost herself for a moment in Lord Dean's deep blue orbs that swirled with a storm of emotions she could never return. Even if she had decided never to marry again, she would not look to Lord Dean for a husband. He was like a brother to her, a friend. And most importantly, the butterflies that she longed to feel take flight in her belly never came forth when she looked at him; only one man had caused such a stir within her, and he could go to the devil… maybe…

Movement behind Lord Dean's shoulder caught her attention and her gaze flew wide, noting Henry's hard glare on his lordship's back. "I would like that, Anthony. Thank you, and in return you may call me Elizabeth."

He bowed and kissed her glove. Elizabeth noted, much to her dismay, that she felt nothing at the touch, just as she expected.

"Shall we dance, Elizabeth?"

"Lady Newland has already promised the next set to me, Lord Dean," Henry said, coming up to them and holding out his arm. Henry's deep voice, full of menace and steel, brooked no argument.

The men eyed each other, and a simmering of dislike settled between them like a shroud. She took note of Henry's determination and took pity on Lord Dean. A brawl would never do in polite society. "So I had, Lord Dean, but I have the next set free, if that is suitable?"

Always the gentleman, he bowed. "I'll await you here until you're free."

She nodded. "Thank you. I look forward to it." Elizabeth placed her hand upon Henry's arm and walked out onto the floor, now filling with patrons for the country dance. She tried to ignore the hardened muscle beneath her hand and the man beside her, who all but simmered with suppressed anger. He led her to the end of the line of dancers and pulled her close to his side.

"Lord Dean? Your head turns in that direction, Elizabeth?" He hissed against her ear.

Elizabeth looked at Henry and let his cloaked anger spark her own. "What if it does? It's no concern of yours."

"The hell it isn't," he stated, the words louder than they ought to be. Others noted their heated exchange and furtively watched. He lowered his voice. "How can ye play the man after what we shared?"

Elizabeth scoffed and went to step into the line. "What we shared was nothing but a mistake that I will be paying penance for the rest of my life. I'm no concern of yours, Lord Muir, so it's best you keep out of my business."

---

*H*enry fought to control his temper as the twists and turns of the dance separated them. He watched Elizabeth with growing anxiety. Why did she hate him so? Why did she deplore their past? Not for one moment did he regret what they'd shared that day down by her family's lake. The sweet kiss that had turned into so much more, more than he'd ever imagined at the time.

With every day they were apart, memories of Elizabeth, her wit, her temper, and sweet features drew him toward home. He'd thought of little else, and certainly no one had turned his head in New York.

The dance brought them together, and he pulled her closer than he ought. "I had to leave to secure Muirdeen Castle. I returned to England as soon as I could. Why this animosity toward me when I have told ye I've done nothing wrong?" He frowned at the air of detachment that settled on her features. How could she feel nothing for him? He pushed down the panic clawing at his gut and waited for her reply.

"I accept the fact that my letter and your correspondence may have gone astray or been meddled with, but you never wrote me once after that. Not once. And here you stroll back into society a wealthy lord and expect me to fall at your feet. Well, I won't." Her tone was unlike any he'd ever heard from her before, swathed with distaste and contempt.

"I have changed, Henry. I'm not the girl you once knew, and I don't want to be her again. I'm sorry, but there is nothing between us and never will be."

Henry spotted the terrace doors over Elizabeth's shoulder and towed her outside, ignoring the guests who stole surprised looks their way. Elizabeth attempted to dislodge his grip without success.

"Why can ye not understand?" he asked as he pulled her toward the end of the darkened terrace. "I couldn't marry you as poor as I was. I admit that was possibly a mistake, but I needed a fortune. I couldn't marry ye a poor earl looking for a rich wife. I refused to be termed a fortune hunter." He paused, needing her to understand at least some of why he left and stayed away.

Henry tipped up her chin and made her look at him. The need to kiss her defiant mouth overrode all decorum, and he leaned close. "Tell me ye do not feel this overwhelming attraction, this need when we're together."

"I do not." She looked away, biting her sensual lips. He growled. "Elizabeth, you lie."

"You abandoned me, Henry. Left me to defend myself against risks we both took." Elizabeth pushed him away, and he stumbled. "I wasn't worth your trouble two years ago, so why the change now?"

"I dinna abandon ye. Someone has played us both fools and I will find out who it was and when I do, they'll wish they were dead." He followed her up the terrace, away from the other strolling couples and farther into the shadows. "Furthermore, I find it odd that none of my letters reached you. I wrote often until I realized it was a pointless exercise when I received nothing in return."

"All contact from you the moment you set foot on that packet ship ceased." She crossed her arm over her chest. "I cannot forgive you for that."

Henry ran a hand through his hair and fought for calm. "And now ye're just being obstinate. You've held onto this anger for me for so long that ye can no longer see reason."

Hurt flickered in her eyes and he ignored it. Damn it, he wanted her and no one else. Wanted to kiss all her hurts away and make them better.

"I'm not obstinate."

"You, Elizabeth, are the stubbornnest Worthingham I know." He raised his brow. "I would've returned had I received ye letter. Of course I would've. I loved ye."

Her surprised gaze met his, and he took her hand, cursing the silk glove that stopped him from feeling her flesh.

"You never said you did before you left."

A self-deprecating laugh escaped. "No, I did not. I was too much a fool. I thought ye would wait for me, as ye promised, I might remind." He played with the buttons at her wrist, undoing two so he could touch her. He felt the shiver that ran through her body at his touch. Damn it, the need for her almost buckled his legs.

"I ruined ye, Elizabeth. I would not have touched ye had I not loved ye with all of me heart. You were a duke's daughter, and your father is an excellent shot, I might remind ye. I certainly dinna want to die before my life had even begun."

As soon as he said the words, Elizabeth stepped back, shutting him out and putting too much space between them. He frowned, wondering what it was that he'd said that offended her. "Elizabeth, please." Henry swore as her brother stepped out onto the terrace. Henry moved back, not liking the hard gaze in Elizabeth's brother's eyes.

"Go inside, Elizabeth. I wish to speak to Lord Muir for a moment. I'll meet you for supper shortly."

Elizabeth cast her brother a glance and then left. Henry let her go, his mind whirling to make sense of it all. He leaned against the terraced balustrade, crossed his arms, and watched as the Marquis of Worth stalked toward him. He braced himself for the coming confrontation.

"Worth," Henry said as the future Duke of Penworth

stopped only a few feet away. He was only slightly shorter than himself but was of similar build. Henry narrowed his eyes and wondered if the conversation would entail words or fisticuffs.

"Lord Muir, I'm surprised to find you outside with my sister."

Henry shrugged. "I wished to speak to her. Since the terrace sits beyond the ballroom doors, I hardly think it scandalous to talk to her here. And let's not forget she's a widow, not a debutante."

The marquis laughed, the sound far from humorous. The gentleman turned toward the lawns, focusing on some spot in the garden. "Ah, but you see I think it highly improper you should be here at all. After all, your treatment of Elizabeth is hardly worthy of friendship with our family."

Henry didn't wish to argue with the man, but what did he mean when they spoke of such poor treatment? When he'd left for America he'd parted as friends with the whole family, Elizabeth included. "I had to work to keep my estate in Scotland. I would think even you would do such a thing should Dunsleigh ever be threatened by debt."

The marquis scoffed. "I would never allow my estates to stoop to such a level in the first place. Nor will I allow my sister to marry a man who is not fit to wipe her silk slippers."

"You were always too high in the instep, Worth." Henry's temper slipped a little at the insult.

"It would be wise of you to keep your distance from my family, especially Elizabeth. She has moved on since her youth's folly that nearly ruined her. She does not look for an association with an impoverished earl."

Henry stilled at the word "ruined." He knew Elizabeth had told her parents of her growing affections toward him, but did her siblings know of their liaison? And why would Elizabeth have said anything to her siblings at all? It was none of their business. A thought niggled at his mind, but he couldn't capture it. "I am no longer impoverished." He paused, running a hand over his jaw, feeling the light stubble of regrowth already. "And what do ye know of Elizabeth and me?"

The marquis looked almost feral. "All of it," he stated.

A cold chill swept down Henry's spine. Why would Elizabeth tell anyone of what they did? Unless something he didn't want to contemplate had happened. "In the hopes this conversation does not decline to the point where I knock ye off ye polished boots, you'd better explain the meaning behind ye words."

Worth laughed. "Slipping further into your natural brogue, Muir. Not at all well to do in this society. Perhaps you should leave for Scotland and return to England only when you can speak correctly."

Henry's eyes narrowed, his hand clenching into a fist. "And perhaps ye ought pull yourself out of your own ass so ye can see daylight and remove the pasty shade of white your skin resembles."

"Typical Scot, always looking for a fight."

Henry's temper snapped and before he could think better of it, his fist had connected with the marquis's nose. No sooner had he made contact did Worth tackle him to the ground. Punches rained, and they rolled across the terrace. Henry grunted as Worth landed a solid blow in the pit of his stomach. He retaliated with a solid uppercut to the man's pompous jaw.

On it went until the faint sound of raised voices intruded into their brawl. Hands clamped about his shoulders, his cousin Richard pulling him off Worth. Henry stilled and looked up at the gathered crowd who stood in watch at their less-than-gentlemanly behavior.

Ladies swathed in silk stood with hands covering their

mouths. Gentlemen with amused grins looked on with interest. With a groan, Henry stood and dusted off his breeches, noting Worth doing the same. He looked up and saw Elizabeth, her face uncommonly pale in the moonlight, her eyes bright with unshed tears.

Worth came to stand before him, wiping his bloodied nose with his sleeve. "Take heed of my warning, Muir. Or you'll find yourself back in Scotland without any society contacts and no wife in the foreseeable future."

"Go to hell," Henry said, watching as Elizabeth was led away by Lord Dean. Where would he go from here? Henry had thought he was doing the right thing when he'd left for America. Had he been wrong? Should he have married Elizabeth before he left and be damned his poverty-stricken status? Her dowry, grand as it was, would've only gone so far. Within five years such funds would have dried up. His estate in Scotland was large and took a lot of coin. Why did Elizabeth not understand this?

Henry swore, pushing his way through the throng, and strode down the steps. He'd had enough of watching her be courted for one night. He needed to get a grip on his temper before he lost all decorum and argued with her before the ton. It was bad enough he'd fought with her brother. No doubt with such a show of base manners, the event would spread around the drawing rooms of the ton before noon tomorrow.

He needed solitude, needed to decide what direction he would take next. Henry rounded the front steps of the home and called for his carriage, cringing at his less-than-polite tone to the footman. He needed a whisky. Drowning oneself in spirits seemed the thing right at this moment.

CHAPTER 5

"What do you think you were doing fighting with Henry like that?"

"So it's *Henry* now?" Josh wiped his nose to stem the constant stream of blood. "You would call that debaucher of innocence by his given name?" he asked. "Look at my nose. It's broken, I'm sure. It will probably be crooked now thanks to your Scottish ass."

Elizabeth looked out the carriage window and sighed. She still could not fathom what she'd witnessed. Her brother and Henry fighting it out like ruffians at the Standley ball. Their time would've best been spent at Gentleman Jackson's, an entertainment that was most sought out by the highest of the ton, but not at a ball! And now her brother and the man she'd once adored had fought like common criminals. She masked a shudder over what her parents would say once they heard of this. "Does it matter what I call him? You cannot go about town picking fights with other men of the peerage."

"Why not?" Josh asked, looking petulant. "He started it."

Elizabeth shook her head, not believing that for a second.

"And you didn't insult him? Why then did he respond in such a violent manner? He was never a violent man."

Josh met her eyes. "Well, of course I insulted him, but he deserved it after what he did to you."

Elizabeth started at his words. "You did not mention Samuel, did you? Please tell me you did not."

Josh shook his head. "No, but what does that matter? He knows of the child and still has not apologized to the family for his slight to you...to all of us."

She sighed, wondering how it was that she could get herself into so much strife with very little effort. "I spoke to him about the letter and why he never returned. He stated he has no knowledge of such missive, and he denies ever writing one to us in return in relation to our plight. He knows nothing of Samuel."

Josh met her gaze, his face a mask of shock as the streetlamps cast shadows within the carriage. "And you believe such a lie? Do not let him play you a fool again, Elizabeth."

"Of course I will not, but don't you see how odd this is? Should Henry know of Samuel he would demand to see him. To be part of his life and perhaps even refuse my son the chance to inherit Newland Estate. But he has not, which makes me believe he's telling the truth, and that he does not know." She sighed. "And do you not see what strife Henry not knowing of the letter has come to? He could ruin me." Her voice broke on a sob and she sucked in a breath of air, needing to calm down. Tears would not help the situation, only clear, level-headed thinking.

"Bloody hell, Elizabeth."

Her brother's words summed up her situation quite perfectly. "I know. I don't know what to do."

"Who does he suspect of this interference?"

"His uncle, and he has written to him. If his uncle is the

one to have taken the notes and tells Henry of why I requested him to return in the first place, he'll kill me."

Her brother raised his brow. "I don't believe it to be of that severity, but still, it's bad enough. But let's not get ahead of ourselves. His uncle has yet to reply, and he may not even remember as to what we wrote."

Elizabeth snorted, a most unladylike sound, but in this situation she no longer cared about etiquette. She'd certainly not cared about rules and propriety three years ago. "Do you really believe his uncle would not remember Henry had left a duke's daughter pregnant? Do be serious, Josh, or I will punch you in the nose myself."

He held up his hands in mock defeat. "Easy, love. All I'm saying is that it is a possibility. All is not lost yet."

"There is no future between Lord Muir and myself, so I think under the current situation that it would be best for Henry and Samuel if they did not know of each other. Samuel is happy at Newland Estate and Henry will soon be happy and married in Scotland."

"What did you say to Muir as to why you wrote him? I assume he asked."

"I told him I thought myself in love with him and that only he would do as my husband. And Father, doting on us as he did, requested he return and agree to an alliance."

Her brother looked at her, and she didn't like the silence her answer garnered. "What? Tell me what you're thinking."

"You won't like it."

"I don't care. Tell me." She clasped her fan tight in her palm, her brother's answer worth more than she thought.

"He deserves to know the truth. Hell, I would want to know in his situation. If, for whatever reason, his uncle does not disclose that information, that is, if the uncle had anything to do with it in the first place, he ought to know he is a father."

Elizabeth slumped back in the squabs. That thought, the very one that haunted her every waking moment, said aloud, was even worse than thinking it. Damn it. She hated it when her brother spoke sense. "But can't you see that I can't tell the truth? If Marcus's family finds out about my betrayal to them and Henry, for that matter, Samuel will be the one to pay. And Marcus doted on the boy; they were the cutest pair. I cannot ruin the memory of that in my mind to tame the guilt I have."

"It's not all your fault, Elizabeth. Someone played a game with our family, and if Lord Muir is unable to gain confirmation that it was his uncle, I should like to know who it was myself."

She rubbed her temple, a slight thumping starting behind her eyes. "Very well, let us wait and see what Henry's uncle replies, and then I'll know what's to be done. And I will also think on it, regarding telling Henry the truth no matter what comes of his reply from his family. But please, as my dear brother, do not go getting into any more brawls on my behalf."

"The hell I won't. You're my sister. I'm the future head of this family, and I will look out for all of you." He paused as the coach rounded a corner into the heart of Mayfair. "But I promise to behave the next time we meet." He sighed. "What a blasted mess."

"Yes, your nose is quite awful looking at present."

Josh growled but did not reply. Elizabeth gazed out to the terraced houses of Mayfair. The homes were a blur as her mind fought to comprehend what her brother and Henry had done, of what she should do, and what would happen in a matter of weeks.

Blasted mess indeed…

*S*ome days later Elizabeth received another flower arrangement from her anonymous admirer, delivered in the same manner and again without a card. This time, Elizabeth took it down to the kitchen and handed it to Mrs. Arthur, who said it would make a lovely table decoration for the staff. Elizabeth headed toward the library and without knocking, entered.

"Oh, forgive me, I didn't know anyone was in here," Elizabeth said, turning to leave.

"No, wait, Elizabeth, come in." Her brother answered in a voice as sweet as honey.

Elizabeth wondered what her brother was up to using such a tone, but closed the door as asked and smiled at Lord Dean who sat in the chair opposite her brother. She came and sat beside him, folding her hands in her lap. "Was there something you wanted, Josh?"

"Nothing in particular. I just wanted to know what the parcel was in the front foyer."

Elizabeth grimaced. "Another flower arrangement, accompanied yet again without a card."

"Do you have any idea who is behind these offerings?" Lord Dean asked, his attention fixed on her more than she liked.

"I do, and there is something I wish to discuss with you, Josh, but…" She frowned, not really wanting to speak openly in front of Lord Dean.

"But what, Elizabeth?" Josh sat forward, as eager as ever to meddle in her life.

"I will come back later when you're not busy."

Lord Dean stood, pulling his gloves from his pocket. "Stay, Lady Newland. I had best be on my way. I promised my sister I would accompany her to the theater tonight."

Elizabeth smiled at his lordship's kindness and bade him

good-bye, relieved to be alone with her brother with what she was about to disclose. Nerves skittered about in her stomach as to how Josh would react to more news.

As soon as the door clicked shut, Elizabeth took a fortifying breath. "Two weeks ago I received an offer of marriage from Lord Riddledale, which you'll be pleased to know I refused. And furthermore, he is the gentleman sending me the gifts."

Her brother laughed, throwing himself back in his chair. "Something tells me he's not accepted your answer as final. Am I right?" he asked, laughing some more.

"He has not. Do you think you could use your influence to keep him away from me? He's really starting to be bothersome at balls, and you know I do not wish to marry again, and certainly not to Riddledale in any case."

"I will speak to him for you, of course. Consider his pestering of you dealt with."

She smiled, leaning back in her chair. "Thank you. I was hoping you would say that."

"Have you heard from Lord Muir as to the missing letter?"

"No, nothing yet, but I can't help but feel it will be soon." Her brother stood and came around the desk, taking her hand. "No matter what Muir ends up knowing, or what he thinks, or how he acts, know that your family will stand behind you, and nothing will happen to injure Samuel. I'll not allow that."

Elizabeth stood, pulling her brother into an embrace. "You're the best little brother a sister could have. Thank you."

He hugged her back. "You're welcome."

*E*lizabeth entered the Featherstone's ball, and her eyes widened at the vision before her. Hundreds of candles sprinkled light throughout the grand-proportioned room. Gold leaf framed every painting and fire surround. Hothouse blooms filled the air with wonder, making the outdoors seem like it lived within.

The terrace doors stood open, and from where Elizabeth stood she could see people milling about outside, enjoying the balmy night air. With the orchestra starting up a quadrille, she stepped into the throng of guests and looked about for people she knew.

"Ah, my dear Lady Newland. How lovely you look this evening."

All but this person. She cringed, pasting a smile on her lips and turning toward his lordship. "Lord Riddledale." Elizabeth brought forward all of her good manners that were instilled in her over the years as she fought not to give him the cut direct. "It is lovely to see you, my lord. Are you enjoying yourself this evening?"

"I am now that you have arrived," he whispered conspiratorially, moving closer than he ought.

His smile made her skin want to crawl away and hide. She looked about, hoping no one else heard his inappropriate words.

"Perhaps you would accompany me to the terrace? I would like to be alone with you if I may." His lordship held out his arm.

"I'm sorry, my lord, but I really ought to pay my respects to our host then find my brother. He is expecting to meet me here."

Elizabeth stilled when his lordship placed her hand onto his arm and pulled her along with him. "Well, allow me to converse with you as I take you to your brother."

73

Elizabeth swallowed her unease. "If you wish, my lord." They walked, edging the dancers on the floor. Elizabeth spotted Henry among the guests already taking advantage of the talented musicians, and her stomach knotted when she noticed him dancing with Miss Andrews. A moment later Josh came into view, and some of her unease left her before Lord Riddledale pulled her to a stop some distance from him.

"Lord Muir is certainly enjoying society and all the niceties wealth entails."

Elizabeth frowned at the menace, which laced his every word. And now she understood why Lord Riddledale hated him so much. She looked toward the throng of dancers and watched with a steel-encased heart as Henry twirled a more-than-willing American about the floor. "I believe Lord Muir is enjoying the season, as are his guests and everyone else here, I hope."

He made a noncommittal grunt, his mouth turning up with distaste. "His years spent in England before his trip to America have taught him how to act a gentleman, I suppose. No Scot could be termed as such if not for this great country and our manners." He pulled her closer than he ought, and the smell of sweat made her stomach churn. "To think he assaulted you while living under your father's roof is beyond reproach. I ought to call him out."

Elizabeth stilled, her racing heart pounding too hard against her ribs. "You're mistaken, my lord. Lord Muir never assaulted me."

He raised his brow, his eyes void of any emotion. The dead look on his face made dread claw up her spine. "I know he did. I saw you. Both of you the day you gave yourself to him by the lake." He shook his head, distaste clouding his eyes. "How could you do such a thing, Lady Newland?"

Elizabeth looked about, sure everyone was watching

them, but they were not. The ton, frivolous and fickle, continued to thrive about them as her world crumbled around her feet. "You watched us? You should've made your presence known, sir."

He wiggled his brows, and she fought not to be sick. "And miss the show? I may be a gentleman, Elizabeth, but I'm still a man. And you were worth watching."

She yanked her arm free, her hand flexing, wanting to slap his face. Her brother's concerned look gave her pause, and she smiled to hide her unease. "How dare you?"

"Oh, I dare, madam. And not only do I dare, you will be my wife because of what I saw. Do you understand?"

"I will never marry you. Ever."

He laughed, and it was tinged with madness. "You have no choice. You lay in a bed of grass and now, my fair lady, you will lie in my bed for the rest of your days. Make peace with it. I do not want to create a scene here or in the future with you, but I will have you."

"Good evening to you." Elizabeth walked off, ignoring as best she could the mocking laughter that followed her every step. Tears smarted behind her eyelids and she cursed the day she gave herself to Henry. How could she have thrown her innocence so carelessly away without any thought to what her actions could create? A bloody mess in the future, that's what.

She smiled at Josh as she came to stand beside him. He nodded in welcome and then continued on with his conversation about the excellent cattle going up for auction at Tattersalls.

The multitude of guests flowed about them as she thought of ways in which to leave early, the ball no longer holding any importance to her. Everywhere she looked it seemed people were staring at her, dismissing her as a wanton woman who gave the most valuable prize away before marriage. She swallowed her rising nausea knowing she had indeed done just that.

Dear God, how could she be in the situation she now found herself? Panic threatened to consume her, and she seized a glass of wine from a passing footman. Taking a few sips in quick succession did nothing to calm the nerves that rioted her body.

She refused all offers to dance, in no mood for conversation or idle talk of the latest scandal or new family in town. All she wished for was the comforting solace of her bedroom, to leave and never come back to this viperish world that would eat her and her son alive should they know the truth.

It was one of the reasons she loathed high society so much in her youth. The smearing and lies, all done so others could advance within their social sphere. The devious deals made when it came to marriage, fathers giving over daughters for a title, and daughters giving away love for money.

She bit her lip, furious at herself for becoming one of them. A member of the ton who had bowed down to society's standards and married a man she did not love while she was carrying the child of another. She was going to hell. Of that she had no doubt.

Excusing herself, she walked out into the gardens, and then proceeded toward a hedge where a stone bench sat secluded in the foliage. Fragrances of trimmed lawns and flowers met her senses. A slight wind moved the leaves, swaying the branches to-and-fro and making her gown cling to her legs.

Spying the bench illuminated in the moonlight, she made her way over to it and sat, sighing her relief that she was finally free from the claustrophobic ballroom. She raised her face to the sky and took a much-needed, calming breath.

"Elizabeth?"

She jumped up and only managed to stifle a yelp. Henry stood in the shadow of an old oak, the outline of his body as familiar to her as her own, not to mention his voice that she was wont to forget. "How did you come to be here? Were you following me?" she asked.

He stepped out of the shadows and walked toward her. His dark hair and eyes gave him an air of danger while possessing none. He was not a man Elizabeth could ever fear. Not in that way, at least.

"I saw ye distress when speaking to Lord Riddledale and followed you when ye snuck away. I didn't mean to frighten you."

Elizabeth sat back down. "You didn't frighten me."

"What is wrong then, lass?" Henry joined her at the bench and moved to take her hand, but then seemed to think better of it and folded them in his lap. He sighed, the sound tinged with sadness, and something inside her eased. Right at this moment she wouldn't mind a friend, someone to tell her it was all right, that what she'd done, she'd done out of fear and love.

He took in the gardens, his presence reminding her of their past. Of how they could sit for hours in silence, saying nothing at all, and neither one feel the need to fill the quiet with meaningless chatter.

"It was nothing, truly. Do not concern yourself with me."

"I will always be concerned when it comes to ye." He turned toward her, the moonlight casting half his face in shadow, but not enough that Elizabeth couldn't see the sincerity in his gaze.

A flutter took flight in her stomach. Looking at him now made her yearn for the past to be so very different. Of them, together, married...happy. "You should leave before you're seen with me." She didn't want him here, this close, consuming her every thought when she had so many others bombarding her mind. Just his company made it hard for her to think straight. His mere presence was intoxicating.

He lifted her chin and pulled her around to meet his gaze. A quiver of awareness shivered down her body and pooled in her core. This was wrong, and yet, never had she felt so right as she did this very moment with Henry.

His gaze searched hers before he said, "Why do ye continue to push me away? Can ye not find it in your heart to forgive our past mistakes, as I have forgiven you for marrying Newland? Believe me when I say I truly thought leaving for America was the right path for us. I had a title, yes, but nothing else. I wanted more for you, Elizabeth."

"I've hated you for so long, Henry. I'm not sure if I can forgive you."

Henry seized her face, his eyes beseeching her to alter her thoughts. "Damn it, lass. Say ye forgive me so we might be friends at least. I'll not push you for more, even though I want a lot more from ye than mere friendship, but it's a start, and we must start somewhere."

She frowned, torn as to how she should answer. To say they were to be friends felt like a betrayal to him. Even forgiving him for not coming back and marrying her, she'd still not told him the absolute truth. Her brother's words floated through her mind that she ought to tell him of Samuel. No, no, she could not do that. Not unless it was absolutely necessary and, at this point, it was not.

"You wish to be friends?"

"I do." He grinned, and her heart thumped hard in her chest.

She smiled a little. "I would like to be your friend, Henry."

He pushed a lock of hair behind her ear, meeting her gaze. Heat coursed between them, hot and wild, and the breath in her lungs expelled. For the life of her she couldn't look away even though she knew she should. If they were to be friends, this fierce attraction that had always been between them needed to stop.

Elizabeth stood and started toward the house. "We should return."

In two strides Henry was before her. His cologne wafted from his heated skin and she shut her eyes, hoping to control the reaction she had to him. It didn't work, for his image was etched on her mind, forever engraved and never to be removed. Of a large, muscular Scot, long dark locks and fierce blue eyes that had melted her heart the moment she'd laid eyes on him. Of his wide shoulders and delectable legs that were very nice beneath a kilt.

"I never took you for someone who ran. Are ye afraid of me, lass?"

"More than you know…" The words left her lips, and the moment they did she wanted to rip them back. Worse was that Henry heard her utterance and reveled in them if the anticipation and determination in his gaze was anything to go by.

He stepped toward her, coming closer than he ought. A delicious shiver of expectation rippled through her. It had been so long since she'd kissed a man, and not just any man, but Henry.

She shouldn't want to lose her head with him, but a wicked part of her longed for it. Months after he'd left, Elizabeth had longed to be held within his arms, to have him make everything perfect once more. But if they were to be friends from this night on, they would have to keep a platonic distance from each other. It could prove challenging if he looked at her as he now was, with dark hooded eyes that spoke of sin and pleasure.

Even with so little effort he pulled at her heartstrings. "Elizabeth, lass…" His gaze beseeched her, making her resolve falter. "I missed ye so much. So very much."

The sound of crunching gravel and laughter on the terrace pulled her from the fog of desire, and she stepped back, giving them both much needed space. "Friends, Henry, and nothing more."

———

*H*enry took a calming breath and righted his cravat— anything but to reach for her. "Then friends we shall be." How could anyone refuse such a bonny lass as Elizabeth?

She smiled, and Henry wanted nothing but to yank the minx into his arms and kiss her senseless no matter what they'd agreed—or better yet, into sense where she would agree to marry him and move to Scotland.

"I hope from this night we can move forward and carry on without any emotions involved."

Not bloody likely. He raised his brow but didn't reply, merely held out his arm to her. "Shall we return?"

"Yes." Her hand shook a little when she clasped his arm and he smiled, knowing that she wasn't as unaffected as she portrayed. Friends they now may be, but not for long.

Not if Henry had anything to do with it.

He would win his bonny lass back yet.

CHAPTER 6

The following morning, Elizabeth sat in the library of their townhouse, her mind going over what Lord Riddledale had said the night before, not to mention her almost kiss with Henry...

She sighed, remembering his mouth, hungry against hers, that even now made her stomach clench in desire. An emotion she'd not felt since the day he'd left England. And damn Lord Riddledale for impinging on her life. How dare the brute threaten to disclose her disgrace with Henry by the lake in order to make her marry him. He was the very devil. She rubbed her brow, knowing she would have to tell Josh of her latest dealings with the ass.

Speaking of the gentleman himself, he walked into the breakfast room and went straight to the eggs and ham, piling his plate with kippers and anything else he could see.

"Hungry this morning?" she asked, taking a sip of tea. He nodded, mumbling a reply as he ate a piece of bacon.

"I am," he said at last, grinning. "The season this year is taxing on one's health. I need sustenance."

Elizabeth eyed his mountainous piled plate. "Late in last night, were you?"

He grinned, throwing another large serving of eggs into his mouth. "Maybe."

"Well, since you're in a good mood I need to tell you something."

Her brother eyed her, and his chewing slowed. "Why do I get the feeling my jovial mood is going to be severely diminished by the time we're finished speaking."

"Probably because it is." She pushed her plate away, wiping her mouth with her napkin. "Lord Riddledale has proposed once more, but this time he's threatened me."

Her brother's fork cluttered to the table. "What?"

For a man who'd probably spent a good deal of the night carousing London's East End, he'd sobered quickly at her words.

Elizabeth nodded. "Oh yes, he offered with the added threat of ruining me."

"The bastard did not." Josh threw his napkin on the table, his mouth set in a severe line she only ever saw when he was livid, which wasn't very often. "What were his exact words?"

"Well," she said, meeting his gaze. "He stated that he had seen Henry and me the day we were beside the lake." Elizabeth let her words trail off, knowing how much the memory of that day was something that sparked her brother's ire as quick as a clap. "Lord Riddledale threatened to go public with that slanderous titbit unless I became his wife."

"I'll kill him." Josh ran a hand through his hair, making his combed, perfectly set hair stand on end. "How dare he." She shrugged. "He's desperate to make me marry him, I suppose, for whatever reason, and one I cannot fathom. I've never given him any inclination as to feelings that went any deeper than friendship. And I certainly do not like him even as that any longer."

"Did he mention Samuel?"

Elizabeth's eyes flew wide and she met her brother's hard gaze. "No. Why would he?" she paused, thinking over the situation. "You think he suspects Samuel is not Newland's son?"

Josh frowned. "It's a possibility we should expect. If the blaggard has no qualm bringing up your ruin in an attempt to make you marry him, I'm sure he'd have no uneasiness at bringing up your son, or even suggesting that Samuel was sired by another to seal the deal."

Elizabeth stood, pacing beside the dining room table. The thought that Riddledale knew of Samuel's correct father was not something she'd even thought to consider. The repercussions of such a truth coming out would ruin her whole family. And should Riddledale know of such a thing, she would indeed have to marry him. A shudder of revulsion slid down her spine, and she clasped the table for support. "Oh dear God. What if he knows and just hasn't played his final card in this game?"

Josh stood and came over to her, turning her so he could see her face. "We will deal with such problems if they do in fact arise. And you are not to draw attention to yourself by worrying about things that may not happen. We know Riddledale is watching you, wanting you, so do not give him any reason to suspect you of anything more than he has already accused you of."

She nodded, taking a calming breath. "Very well. I'll continue on as before and hope he only knows of what Henry and I did that day and nothing else."

"I'm sure should he have known anything more he would've mentioned it, Elizabeth. Now come," he said, helping her to sit again. "Finish your breakfast, and tell me what your plans are for the day and this evening."

Elizabeth sat spooning porridge into her mouth and not

tasting a morsel of it. She listened as her brother prattled on about his plans and she nodded and agreed when required, but her attention was not on the conversation at hand.

Her mind whirred with the thought that Riddledale could go public with her ruin should she refuse him. That if he did know of Samuel's heritage, and she continued to deny his suit, there was a possibility that Henry could find out about his child and not from her.

The thought of telling Henry of her predicament flittered through her mind, but no sooner had she thought it than she squashed it like a bug. He would hate her, loathe her for her handling of the situation, even if others had played them and the situation occurred because of someone's spite.

Her eyes smarted, and she sniffed. She'd made such a mess of things. Whatever was she going to do? Right at this moment the only sane course seemed to flee the country and move to Europe. They had family in Rome. It could work… Elizabeth took a sip of tea, wishing it was laced with brandy. A lot of it.

---

*L*ater that night, dressed in a deep emerald gown, Elizabeth passed her evening cloak to a waiting maid and followed her family into Lord McCalter's receiving room for a dinner party followed by music and card games.

Alice took her arm, and her sister chatted about her latest run-in with Lord Arndel and how she'd made him dance, something the gentleman apparently loathed to do. Elizabeth's reply halted on her lips when her attention snapped to Henry. He nodded slightly in welcome, and she knew he was thinking of their time together in the gardens the other night. Her own thoughts had gone straight to that location when spying him, the idea of being near him again, talking as they once had forefront in her mind.

She licked her parched lips, taking a glass of champagne her sister handed to her before they made their way across the room to stand with a group of other ladies with whom they were acquainted.

Lord Dean greeted them and declared he was to take her into dinner. Elizabeth listened with half interest as he spoke of the weather and the latest town gossip of a young debutante who'd run away to Gretna Green. Much to her annoyance, her attention kept snapping back to the other gentleman present, whose gaze burned her soul each time she was engaged elsewhere. This would never do if their relationship were to remain platonic.

She was being absurd. A sigh escaped. She was such a fool, and it helped no one to lie to oneself.

Elizabeth downed her glass of champagne faster than she ought and turned her attention to Lord Dean, focusing on his moving mouth and the words coming out of it. Surely if she watched him speak she'd know what he said.

It didn't seem to be the case.

Much to her dismay, Lord Riddledale chose that exact time to stride into the room, his sister, Lady Emily, on his arm. Elizabeth held back an unladylike curse, knowing she wouldn't be able to ignore him with his sibling in tow.

Conversation swam around her, and she took a moment to admire the latest fashions the women wore, their silk gowns and extravagant hair adornments glistening in the candlelight. Henry stood beside his American cousins, Miss Andrews's pursuit of him continuing, it seemed, with the lady concerned hanging off his arm and word like a ninnyhammer.

Her eyes raked over Henry's attire, his tight skin breeches, long black coat, and gold and silver threaded waistcoat that suited his dark features, making him look like a pirate ready to plunder or, more fitting, a Scottish high-lander ready to raid English settlements.

Lord Dean held out his arm to walk her into dinner, and she placed her hand upon his sleeve. They walked into the dining room in silence, and she smiled at Miss Andrews when she noted she was to be her dinner companion, although it hurt her face to do so. Lord Dean held out her chair and then went to sit across from her, her brother Josh seated beside her.

Her brother conversed with the woman beside him, but the silence from Miss Andrews was deafening as the first course of soup and marrow pudding was placed before them. Elizabeth spooned a delicious mouthful of soup and listened with little interest while Miss Andrews complimented the chef and their host's beautiful table arrangement to anyone who would listen.

Elizabeth took in the extravagant fruit platter running the length of the table and conceded it was beautiful, but not to the point where gushing admiration was required. A simple compliment after service would've sufficed.

"Lady Newland, I wonder if I may ask how you came to know Lord Muir? We haven't had much chance to get to know each other, and I gather you knew him from his youth."

Elizabeth patted her mouth with her napkin. "Lord Muir came to live with us a few years before leaving for America. He was under the guardianship of my father, the Duke of Penworth, after his own had sadly passed away."

Miss Andrews puckered her mouth in thought, bringing to attention her overuse of rouge on her lips. "Henry is a true gentleman. I'm surprised he needed guidance from your father."

Elizabeth coughed, choking a little on her soup. What was

she implying? That her father, a duke no less, wasn't fit to guide an earl?

Miss Andrews's attention snapped to Henry sitting across from them. Unaware he was the current on-dit, Henry continued with his animated conversation with her sister Victoria. He threw back his head in laughter, a deep throaty sound that shot a pang of envy straight through Elizabeth's heart. She looked away, not wanting to be reminded of all that she'd lost.

"Henry is an attractive man, is he not?" Miss Andrews smiled, her eyes dreamy, no doubt with imaginings of the two of them married.

Elizabeth shut her mouth with a snap. Henry? Miss Andrews was now calling him by his Christian name? "I have no opinion on the matter, Miss Andrews," she replied.

Miss Andrews snorted. "I find that highly unlikely."

"You don't believe me?" Elizabeth leveled her gaze with the obnoxious woman whom she was starting to despise.

Miss Andrews chuckled. "Perhaps it is your breeding that blinds you to the harder sex and their looks, but believe me, Lady Newland, Henry is one of the handsomest men I've ever known. And never have I known a gentleman to toil as hard as he did when working for my father. His drive to succeed had him retire to bed early most nights. I do not know what his deep need for success was due to, but he never deviated from his goal. No matter how hard I tried to divert his lordship's ways." The woman giggled. Giggled! "And I did try very hard."

Elizabeth ignored the woman's telling words and remembered to breathe. She looked down to her plate as the aroma of lobster tail, the next course, met her senses. At least she knew one of the reasons why Henry had been determined to succeed. And it wasn't due to the little minx sitting beside her.

"Is society here in London much different from what you are used to?" Elizabeth asked, hoping Miss Andrews would expand on her association with Henry. The thought of them socializing together, having intimate conversations, made anger simmer beneath her skin.

"Only in the sense there are not as many titled families in New York as there are here. We do not need such trivial matters to show off our wealth."

Elizabeth took another sip of wine, unable to ignore the insult. "Well of course you don't, you simply speak of it aloud." Miss Andrew's eyes narrowed, and Elizabeth could feel the hate radiating from her.

"I formed a close association with Henry when we were home in New York. And between you and me, Lady Newland, I wait in hope that he'll ask for my hand."

Elizabeth nodded, the urge to scratch the woman's eyes out almost impossible to deny. "You have reason to believe he has formed an attachment to you?" She cleared her throat, hating the fact her voice sounded distraught and that there was a lump in her throat the size of an orange. Henry had almost kissed her only a few nights ago—surely he would not act with such rashness without honorable intentions.

Miss Andrews's smiled gleefully. "Of course! As a widow I don't think I'll shock your sensitivities by telling you Lord Muir kisses very well," she whispered. "I must declare that his bottom lip, just the slightest bit plumper than the top, is delightful to nibble on. If I was not so in love with him, I'd most assuredly be in lust."

Elizabeth adjusted her seat and fought not to bring up all that she'd eaten.

Henry had kissed Miss Andrews? Had kissed another woman? Pain mixed with anger sliced through her, and she ground her teeth. "I'm sure his lordship's declaration of love and an offer of marriage is not far away, Miss Andrews."

Elizabeth spooned the moist white lobster meat into her mouth; the seafood tasted like the dirt between cobbled streets.

"Perhaps," Miss Andrews replied with a devilish glint to her eyes. "Maybe it will even be tonight."

Elizabeth couldn't reply even if she wanted to. She'd heard enough of the woman's relations with Henry to last a lifetime. The lobster was taken away and was replaced with an assortment of game birds garnished with vegetables.

The picture of Henry taking Miss Andrews in his arms in a passionate embrace flittered through her mind, and her eyes smarted. She focused on her food and nothing else, less others notice her upset. She was being absurd, a silly woman, looking further into stolen moments with a man who, if Miss Andrews was correct, handed them out often and without care.

Elizabeth fleetingly gazed at Miss Andrews and didn't miss the triumph written plainly across her features. She took a good sip of wine. What Henry did with Miss Andrews, or had done, did not matter. They may have thought themselves in love years ago, but miscommunication and her marriage had put paid to that. Henry was free to see and like whomever he wanted.

Elizabeth motioned the footman to refill her glass of wine, taking another sip. Perhaps if she were foxed the ache in her chest would dissipate. Maybe.

The conversation around the table increased in joviality as the courses came and went. Finally, and with much relief to Elizabeth, Lady McCalter stood and excused the ladies, the men deciding to partake in their after-dinner port in solitude. Elizabeth followed close on her ladyship's heels, only too eager to get away from Miss Andrews.

In the front parlor where the musical loo was to take place, Elizabeth sat at the pianoforte and looked through the music sheets. She didn't want to play a difficult piece; something light was in order that would allow her to think and not have to concentrate too much on what she was doing.

Elizabeth was still undecided when the door swung open and the gentleman strolled in to join them. She inwardly groaned when Lord Riddledale strolled over to her.

"What are you going to delight us with tonight, Lady Newland?"

He sat himself beside her and, frowning, she shuffled over less he sit on her lap. "I've not picked a piece yet, my lord, but her ladyship has quite the variety of music. I'm sure I'll find something soon."

"Of course, my dear." His lordship cleared his throat. "I've been thinking about us, and how wonderful it'll be when we're married. I can hardly stem my urge to have you to myself...on our wedding night."

Elizabeth fought not to box the idiot over the head. How dare he speak to her in such a way. A man who claimed to be a family friend for as long as she could remember could not be so callous, surely. "You forget, sir, I have not accepted your proposal, and no matter the ruin, nor am I likely to."

Her hand fisted on the piano keys as the lightest touch ran up the outside of her leg.

Lord Riddledale chuckled, licking his thin lips. "A woman of your experience must yearn for a man. I cannot tell you how honored I am that it is I who'll ravish your sweet flesh after so long."

Elizabeth's mind seized in panic as his labored breaths rasped against her cheek. "It would be wise not to stroke me in such an inappropriate way lest you want to be a gentleman with only nine digits instead of ten."

"Do not play coy, my lady. It does not suit you." He laughed, throwing his head back and making himself look like a right pompous git. "And as for your name, not even a daughter of a duke or the Newland ancestry could save your reputation if I were to reveal your dirty little secrets. I am not scared of you, Elizabeth."

Elizabeth reached down and bent back the digit running against her thigh until his lordship wrenched free of her grasp with a yelp. "How very fortunate you believe what you say, but such threats will be your downfall. I've told my brother of your request and why you made it. He's not impressed and let's not forget, it's your word against mine, your word against a Worthingham." Elizabeth placed a piece of Bach music onto the piano shelf, ignoring him completely.

He didn't leave, merely took a sip of his wine. "I think in time you'll change your views on that." He paused, running a finger around the crystal stem. "I have the letter, after all, and with your dearest father's seal to prove its authenticity. The ton will believe me, not you."

Elizabeth felt the blood drain from her face, and her gaze flew to his. "What letter?" she asked, her voice stripped of its indifference.

"The one your father sent to Henry. I had to intercept it, you see, for I knew Lord Muir would travel back immediately to save your reputation. The Scottish heathen was in love with you, even if he didn't know it at the time."

"You stopped the letter to Henry?" Elizabeth fought to control her heart, beating fast in her chest. "But he answered. He refused to come back. Did you play a part in that scheme as well?"

He tsk-tsked her like a silly child, and she couldn't have hated him more at that moment. "I sent the reply, not that you can prove it, as I had it delivered to America to be posted from there. A little blunt into the right hands can secure a seal easily enough." He shrugged.

"How did you know the letter would be sent at all? We told no one of my condition." Elizabeth didn't want to think it, but servants, even supposed loyal ones were wont to gossip if enough money was waved before them. Damn them.

"Blunt will open the mouths of the tightest lips." He sighed, frowning. "It is hard to find servants who are honorable and faithful, don't you agree?"

She watched him blankly, unable to process what he was saying. That her family's servants had broken their trust was nothing to how a gentleman claiming to be friends with her father, a neighbor even, could act in such an atrocious way. "How could you do that to me?"

"I wanted you for myself. I always have." He growled. "I was most displeased when your father had you up and marry Newland, but of course I knew why. I'm left wondering if you've told your highlander that his child is alive and well and with another man's title bestowed upon his head."

The room spun before her eyes. Oh dear God. What was she going to do? Panic crept about her, wanting to enfold and suffocate her. Spying her forgotten glass of champagne atop the piano, she made to pick it up but instead knocked it into Lord Riddledale's lap.

"Apologies, my lord. How unfortunate for you." Her words were without care, and she watched with little interest as Lady McCalter fluttered over with napkins and ready apologies.

"A little wine will not change your future, Lady Newland," he whispered, standing. "No matter how much you wish it."

Elizabeth watched as he took his leave. Elizabeth sat and played Minuet in G to the best of her ability, her mind a whir over everything Riddledale had disclosed and what it meant for her son should she not marry him.

Her attention snapped to Henry, and she missed a note. He watched her, his intense gaze flicking between her and the now departing Lord Riddledale. Other ladies came to stand beside the pianoforte, and Elizabeth gave up the instrument, only too happy to let them have their turn. She walked over to a nearby window, the grounds outside as dark and gloomy as her mind.

She would have to marry Riddledale…unless she spoke the truth.

The jarring sound of Miss Andrews singing pulled her from her thoughts, but only for a moment. Henry was innocent, and so too was his uncle. That, at least, was a small comfort, but most definitely the only one.

---

*H*enry watched Elizabeth and Lord Riddledale's conversation at the piano and unease crept across his shoulders. Her pallor, and sometimes the blatant hate that sparkled in her green depths, told him more than any words could that the conversation was in no way pleasant. His body tightened, and a fury took hold when he saw his lordship caressing her leg.

Highhanded rake!

Henry sipped his brandy and welcomed the burn to his gut. He would rip the bastard's hand permanently from his body if he didn't stop. He took a step toward them, only to see Elizabeth deal with the fiend's finger herself.

His eyes narrowed as Elizabeth struggled to hide her emotions from the gathered guests. If Henry didn't know better, he would assume the man was threatening her in some way. But over what would Lord Riddledale threaten Elizabeth? She was a well-respected widow, a woman above reproach.

Henry took a large sip of brandy and slapped the glass down on a nearby table. He started across the room. Miss Andrews stepped into his path, and he mentally swore.

"There you are, Henry," she cooed, clasping his arm and pulling him to where her brother stood speaking to Lord McCalter. "You look all sixes and sevens. Is everything well, my lord?"

Henry smiled and tried to banish his annoyance at her interference. "Of course." He muttered a few replies to the inconsequential conversation while keeping vigil on Elizabeth. She played her piece of intended music, but there was no passion, no emotion behind the music, she was distant...distracted.

They needed to talk, at length and without interruption. Not tonight, but tomorrow. Ever since his return something wasn't quite right, and it was time he found out just what that "something" indeed was.

---

*H*enry walked toward the Duke of Penworth's residence the following day, determined to find out the truth of what was going on between Elizabeth and him, if anything.

This morning his manservant had delivered him the missive from his uncle, who had no recollection of such a letter ever being received, and he'd been adamant, if not a little hurt, that Henry had accused him of such foolery.

He rapped the knocker hard on the Worthinghams' front door. If his uncle had not played a part in keeping him from marrying Elizabeth, then someone else had, and Henry couldn't help but wonder if that "someone" was Elizabeth's brother. They'd never really been close as boys, and were certainly less than friendly now.

A butler he'd known for some years opened the door and greeted him with an arctic nod.

Henry stepped past the man. "I'm here to see the Duke

and Lady Newland." He pulled off his gloves and set them upon a hall stand before handing the butler his coat.

"His grace is not in residence, and I'm not certain when Lady Newland will return. If you wouldn't mind coming back, my lord—"

"I'll wait in the library." Henry entered the room, one he knew as well as any of his own, and took a seat before the hearth. The burning wood crackled as he stared into the flickering blue and orange flames, his mind a whir of turbulent thoughts over what had happened to Elizabeth when he left. Who had written the letter and why? And Henry wasn't fool enough to believe her supposed love for him had ensured her father write and demand he return. Elizabeth was hiding something. But what?

He gritted his teeth, scowling.

Soft footsteps sounded in the foyer, and he turned toward the door. "Lord Muir, I wasn't expecting you to call." Henry stood, clasping his hands behind his back. "I apologize for my intrusion, but what I wish to discuss cannot wait."

Elizabeth threw him a confused glance before walking to the bellpull. "Tea?" she asked.

"Thank you, yes."

She walked to the nearby settee and sat, her ease and graceful movements tinged with an edge of wariness, and his suspicions grew.

"What was in the letter you sent me, Elizabeth? The one that I supposedly refused?"

She paled before determination seemed to straighten her spine. "It was nothing other than a request for you to return to marry me. I foolishly thought myself in love." She fussed with her gown, blushing furiously, a trait she did often when telling fibs. "But I've told you this already, so I'm a little confused by your visit this morning."

"Was it because you lost your virginity to me and your

father thought it best that you marry the man who deflowered you?" It was the only reasonable truth he could think of. Another husband could've been mortified, humiliated should he realize that his wife was not as pure as he'd thought on their wedding night. Some men could've demanded an annulment if so offended by the realization. It was a just cause to ask for his return.

At her continued silence he stood, pacing before the hearth. "You were supposed to wait for me in any case. Did you not tell your father that before writing?"

She laughed, the sound cloaked with nerves. "You are reading into my actions more than you ought. Father did know of my ruin, as I said, but he also believed that I loved you, as I did. There is nothing more than that. It was a foolish impulse of an immature young miss."

"Don't force me to ask your grace, Elizabeth, for I will if it's the only way to find out the truth." Their gazes locked, and a flicker of fear passed through her eyes before she blinked and it was gone. "I cannot tell you what you wish to hear for what I state is the truth. Ask Papa, his recollection of the time will be the same as mine."

"My uncle did not send the letter nor did he reply to one from ye father. So someone else has played us fools, and we need to find out who that 'someone' is."

She stared at him, her piercing viridian eyes filling with fear. "There is something that I must tell you, Henry, but I'm not sure as to what to do about it."

He came and sat across from her. "What is it?"

"I suspected your uncle would write and state he did not know of our missive. The reason I suspected such is because..." She took a calming breath, meeting his gaze. "Because Lord Riddledale only a few days ago stated to me quite openly, and with not a little glee, that he knows of our tryst beside the lake and then last night at

Lord McCalter's he admitted to having the letter Father sent you. He confiscated my father's missive and replied as your uncle, all due to his intent to have me for himself."

Henry's world tipped off-kilter and he stared, dumbfounded at her. He would kill that bastard. "I'll gut the English mongrel."

She clasped his arm, her eyes beseeching. "You mustn't go near him. It'll only make things worse, and I do not see what we can do about the situation."

"I believe there is a legion of things I can do about the situation." Kill him came to mind. Maim him and then kill him…slowly. "I will talk to the marquis."

"He's threatening me, Henry. He's declared he will go public with our scandal should I not marry him."

He met her gaze, shame flowing through his veins that he'd left her to face such a fate. How many weeks had he seen the pompous ass sniffing about her skirts? And all that time the bastard had been threatening her, waving her father's letter as a threat to do as he dictated. "He's demanding ye marry him?"

She looked away, her eyes glinting with unshed tears. Henry wanted to pull her into his arms, comfort her as he should have done the moment he returned from America. Damn Riddledale to the cesspit.

"He is. I have not agreed to his demands, but I see little option other than to give over to him if he will not give it back. I may be a widow, seemingly above reproach, but I'm not willing to allow such a scandal to ruin the future chances of my sisters. If the ton read the letter, along with the story of what Riddledale saw us doing at the lake, my sisters would be tarnished with the same brush: as a light-skirts, an easy conquest, a whore."

"Ye're not a whore, and nor are ye marrying Riddledale."

He would meet him on a field of honor and rid the world of the pest before such an atrocity occurred.

"Well I certainly don't wish to, but unless we secure that letter I see little else I can do. I will not allow him to tarnish my family's name."

"Does ye father know of this?" Surely the duke could have sway with Riddledale. To anger the Duke of Penworth was no trifling matter and certainly not something to be taken lightly.

"I informed my brother as Papa has not been feeling too well, and I don't want to upset his constitution with this distressing event." She paused. "This may surprise you, but he recommended I tell you of these developments. Not that I expect it will change the outcome of this atrocious situation, but at least there is some chance that we can thwart Riddledale's plan. If we work together, that is. I just don't know which way to go about it yet."

She stood, and he followed. Taking his hand, she gazed up at him, and once again he was transported back in time to their youth, when there were no worries of reputation or honor. Just life and its possibilities.

Henry pushed a stray curl from her cheek and slipped it behind her ear. She shut her eyes, her delectable lips opening on a sigh. Henry swallowed, debating whether to lean down and kiss her to the point where threats of scandals were nothing but a vapid thought not worth their worry.

"At least I now know why you never wrote me. I wrote often, but never received a reply. Who do you think is working for Riddledale under your father's employ? We must find out and deal with him or her severely."

Elizabeth nodded. "It seems Lord Riddledale has been privy to all incoming and outgoing correspondence for our family for some time. To steal private letters is contemptible but hard to prove. It is our word against his. And now that we know for certain that your uncle did not send the letter and that no letters from you were ever received, Josh can take action into which servant have wronged us."

He pulled her down to sit beside him, taking her hand. "We have to get the letter back." Henry frowned at the thought. He may be Scottish, but he wasn't raised to be threatening or to pay his way out of bad situations. "We need to get into Riddledale's home, his library in particular.

The letter must be there, I'm sure. They are a prize to him, so he would keep them close at hand for safekeeping. We need to steal them back."

Elizabeth clasped her neck, her eyes going wide with realization. "Steal? From his lordship? I know we used to banter about as children, but Henry, we are not thieves of the night. He'll catch us for certain."

"No' if we play him right." He rubbed his jaw. "Riddledale has a sister, correct?"

Elizabeth nodded. "Yes, Lady Emily."

"She's a debutante this year, I understand. And requiring a coming-out ball…"

"Yes, that's right." Elizabeth's eyes widened when she understood where his mind was going. "And I suppose we'll sneak into his library, find the letter, and be on our way?" Her voice dripped sarcasm, and he raised a brow.

"That's exactly what we'll do." He took her small gloved hand and kissed it gently. "I'm sorry for letting you face his lordship on your own. I should've known from your reaction to him last evening that he was up to some sort of trick. We will face him together from this point on, and we will best him at his game." He paused, thinking of all that they'd lost and through no fault of either of them. "I cannot allow ye to marry him, lass. You shall not give over to such a fiend."

She smiled, but the gesture didn't reach her eyes. "I know, and I'm grateful for your help. I just hope your plan works."

She paused, her thumb sliding over the top of his hand. "I will tell Josh of our idea and see if he'll help us as well. I'm sure he will. Riddledale has never been a favorite of his."

"Ye brother likes someone less than me. I feel blessed."

She laughed, and the sound flowed through him like warm honey. Their gazes met, and again an urge to protect the woman before him seized him. She was as innocent as he was in the sick game Riddledale played, and no longer would he allow her to be the man's toy, to be pushed about and threatened at will.

He pulled her into his arms and kissed away the small frown marking her brow. She relaxed into his hold, and he reveled in the feel of her against him, her soft muslin gown and pliant body as he stroked her back.

She looked up at him, her eyes giving away the emotion she would not voice, and need roared through him. Without giving her a chance to pull away, he leaned down and kissed her lips, the lightest brush that stoked a small burn that had simmered for weeks into a raging inferno.

Her hands slid up his arms and clasped about his neck. Her tongue, tentative at first, soon matched his, her fingers tangling into his hair and pulling him close. Need he'd long suppressed made his blood flow hot and heavy in his veins. There was no hesitation in their embrace, only want for more of the same delectable kiss that consumed them both.

Hard footfalls sounded in the foyer.

Elizabeth sprang away from him, her gaze wide with alarm. "You should probably leave, before…before any more of this"—she gestured between them—"occurs."

Henry grinned, running a finger across her reddened, well-kissed lips. "What if I said I wanted to stay?"

"Then I would say you cannot." She threw him a feeble smile. "Think over what you wish for me to do with

Riddledale, and I'll do it. And once we've secured the letter, I think the magistrate should be notified of his thievery."

"Due to the fact we're also becoming thieves, perhaps we'll leave the magistrate out of this situation, but Riddledale will be dealt with and severely. Ye have my word on that."

"I want to be there when you mete out his punishment." Henry laughed, standing to go. "Ye're not turning into a savage are ye, my lady? Your brother will be calling you a Scot soon if you're not careful."

She grinned. "There are worse things to be called, I'm sure."

CHAPTER 7

*H*enry strode down St. James, the bow window of Whites coming into view before the club itself. Since leaving Elizabeth, and with the shocking knowledge of Riddledale's threats, he'd been looking for the bastard. His lordship needed a good uppercut to the jaw and whatever else he could mete out.

He strode into the gentleman's club hall, peering into the two morning rooms on either side. Gentlemen looked up in surprise at his haste but went back to their drinks and gossip.

Walking into the second hall, he took the stairs two at a time to the first floor landing and entered the coffee room, which ran the full length of the front of the building. It was there that he spied the scoundrel, lazing in a chair, one leg crossed over the other, smoking a cheroot as if he had not a care in the world.

Blaggard would be lucky to live out the day.

Fury unlike any he'd ever known threatened to consume him, to ensure he did something foolish like break the black-mailing ass's neck. He strode toward him, taking a deep breath to calm himself a little. It didn't make an ounce of difference.

Out of the corner of his eye, he spied Elizabeth's brother watching him with interest. He ignored the man and settled across from Riddledale, waiting for him in silence to look up from his paper that sat in his lap. The obnoxious fop turned a page, and only then did he meet Henry's gaze.

"To what do I owe the pleasure of your company, Lord Muir?"

Henry steepled his fingers on his chin lest he strangle the felon. The image of a gasping Riddledale, his face red with lack of air, brought a lift to his lips. "I've watched ye of late, your courting of Lady Newland, and I'm here to know what ye intentions are."

Riddledale scoffed, folding his newssheet and placing it on the table. "You are not Lady Newland's keeper. She's her own woman and able to choose whom she marries. I think I've made my intentions quite clear to her ladyship."

"Ah, but what ye forget to mention is that you've given Lady Newland little choice." Henry paused. "I know of the blackmail, Riddledale."

Riddledale met his gaze, his brows raised. "So she told you of what I know. Of how you rutted like a pair of animals outdoors, not even bothering with a blanket." He laughed. "I know the Scot's are savages, but even I thought you'd treat a lady better than that."

Henry ground his teeth, knowing part of what he said was true. They had made love outdoors without a concern for niceties, but they never rutted; their joining was the opposite of meaningless sex. It was loving, a joining of two souls made for each other. "Talk in such a way again, and our duel will take place here and now."

"I'm a good shot, and willing to take my chances against you." Riddledale shrugged. "And what I say is the truth, we both know it. Now, was there anything else you wished to discuss?"

"Ye will not marry her. Not now, at the end of the season, or ever."

Riddledale waved his words away. "You forget yourself, Lord Muir. You have no choice. I have stated my case to the chit, and she will agree. Surely you do not want to see her siblings ruined, their hopes for good matches lost."

"Of course I do not wish to see Elizabeth's siblings dishonored, but nor will I allow a woman I care for to sacrifice herself to you. Why can ye not do one honorable thing in ye life and walk away?"

"I find Elizabeth, the delectable Lady Newland, quite to my palate. I want her, have always wanted her, and now, due to what I know, I shall have her."

"If it's money ye want, name your price."

Riddledale contemplated Henry's suggestion for a moment, and a spark of hope coursed through him. Did his lordship require blunt? Was Elizabeth's inheritance playing some part in his decision to have her? "No amount is too much," Henry added.

"You will not buy my silence, Lord Muir. Elizabeth will be adequate enough."

"She's isn't a horse for sale at Tattersalls. The Worthinghams have been friends of yours for years. You are neighbors. How can ye threaten her in such a way and have little care of it?"

"It is easily done, for I have wanted her a long time. Yes, she is rich, her dowry a nice addition to my coffers, but she's the prize that I long to have writhing beneath me in bed, her sighs rasped against my cheek when she feels my desire."

Henry wasn't sure what came over him, but in a moment he had Riddledale beneath him on the floor, the man's eyes widening in shock. Henry's fist connected with the bastard's jaw, again and again, he ground his knuckles into the flesh of a gentleman who had no right to such a claim. Shouts sounded about them, and no sooner had he bloodied the fop's nose than he was wrenched backward.

He shook his captors off and felt the snarl on his face as he gazed down at Riddledale, who was searching for a hand-kerchief in his pockets. He righted his jacket, his breaths labored. "Think about my business trade, my lord. It would be beneficial for ye to have a happy and long life, instead of the opposite should ye refuse."

"Come away, Lord Muir."

Henry turned at the familiar voice and noted Elizabeth's brother standing beside him, his eyes wary but also without judgment. The others moved back to their seats now that everything seemed settled between the men. Muffled laughter and betting could be heard above his own rapid heartbeat.

"I should demand a duel, you Scottish whelp. How dare you strike an English marquis?"

Henry scoffed. "Quite easily. And I'd be glad to show ye again if ye believe I have a care as to what you think."

"Muir, come away."

"Yes, do go, Lord Muir." Riddledale waited for a footman to right his chair and then resumed his seat. "I hope you'll honor us with your presence at my wedding. Since we're such good friends, it would be a shame for you to miss it."

Henry took a step toward him, ready to kill him this time, and his grace grasped his arm, his hold unshakable. "This isn't finished, Riddledale. It would be unwise to crow too loudly too soon."

Riddledale laughed, wincing at the cut on his lip. Henry smiled at his discomfort. "But I will in any case. Good day to you."

Henry stormed out of the room, needing to distance

himself from the man, the urge to follow through on his desire and rid the world of the blaggard overwhelming.

Worth caught him on the stairs. "You cannot act like a man without a care. If not for your own self-respect then pull it together, man, and do it for Elizabeth."

Henry turned and leveled a cold stare at Worth, lest he tell him to behave like a good little boy again. "I beg ye pardon?"

"You heard me. A brawl. In Whites? I know you care for my sister, but you risk her reputation with actions like this. She's told you of the letter, I see. I'm surprised you're taking it so well."

"Yes, I know Riddledale knows of what transpired between Elizabeth and me before I left for America. I'll not allow him to threaten her into marriage."

"Is that all she told you?"

Henry paused, frowning. "What else is there to know?" Elizabeth's brother shook his head, stepping back. "No, nothing, that's the lot of it."

Henry glared, the niggling thought that he was still missing something of importance scratching beneath his skull. Worth bid him good day, and Henry hailed a hackney cab. What he really needed was a stiff whisky and time to plan their scheme to get back what Riddledale had stolen. No matter whom Elizabeth chose to marry, if anyone, she would choose for herself, not others, and certainly Riddledale would not make her decide under duress. She deserved so much more than a contemptible marriage that would bring her nothing but heartache and sadness.

CHAPTER 8

Some days later, an express from Dunsleigh put the whole London home in uproar. Within an hour, Elizabeth and her family were on the road to Surrey, the horses traveling at breakneck speed to ensure their speedy arrival, if they did not tip over, that was.

Elizabeth looked at her mother, whose pale lips and reddened eyes spoke of a concern they all felt but refused to discuss. The hours seemed to drag, and the passing landscape appeared to stay the same. The repetitive clop of the horses' hooves marked the time, and should her prayers be answered, they would arrive home by tomorrow.

If only to say good-bye.

A little after lunch the following day, the carriage rounded through the gates of Dunsleigh. Their mama didn't wait for the servant to open the door, but jumped out when the coach had barely stopped rolling and hastened up the steps to go inside.

Elizabeth let her grieved sisters step down before they proceeded indoors. Josh greeted them in the hall.

"How is Father?" Elizabeth asked, handing a footman her bonnet and pelisse.

"He had a turn three nights ago. His valet sent for me immediately, and I rode up posthaste. When I noted the seriousness of the condition, I sent for you all in town. The good doctor has just left."

Elizabeth placed a comforting arm around Alice, who'd started to sob. "And what did he say?"

Pain crossed her brother's features, and her stomach clenched in fear. "Father doesn't have long... It's his heart apparently. A seizure of some sort has damaged it beyond repair."

Elizabeth turned at the sound of another carriage barreling up the drive and pulling to a stop in a cloud of dust. Relief washed over her when she recognized the occupant. Elizabeth walked to the door and welcomed Isolde, who ran up the steps. Elizabeth gave her a quick embrace before her sister pulled off her gloves and handed them to the footman.

"Is Father in his rooms?"

"Yes," Josh replied, escorting Isolde to the stairs. Elizabeth followed and was met by their mother who was exiting the ducal apartments.

"He wishes to speak with each of you," their mother said, then turned to her second eldest child. "Isolde, you may go first, but not too long, my loves. He's very tired."

Elizabeth swallowed the lump lodged in her throat and watched her sister walk up the stairs and turn toward their parents' apartments. They followed and went to wait in the upstairs parlor. Elizabeth sat on a window seat that overlooked the gardens, gardens her mother adored pottering around in, driving the gardener to distraction with all the roses she loved to plant. Dunsleigh held so many wonderful memories, of how their parents used to stroll the lawns, hand in hand, while Elizabeth and her four siblings ran before them, playing and laughing at who knew what.

To know that their father would not live to meet any more of his grandchildren severed her soul in two. How would they all go on without their dearest Papa? She wiped away her tears and awaited her turn, tried to prepare herself to speak with her dear father one last time.

A short time later, Elizabeth entered the ducal apartments and paused on the threshold. Instead of the gloom she had expected, drapes pulled in mourning, a fire burning in the grate, her eyes had to adjust to the well-lit space. Every curtain was open, allowing the beautiful spring day to bathe the room in all its grandeur.

Elizabeth walked toward the bed, smiling. "Papa?"

"Ah, my dearest Elizabeth," he said, his voice hoarse. "Come sit by me and let me look at you."

She sat and felt her smile wobble as she fought to control her emotions. The strong, unstoppable father she knew had aged into an old man overnight. Dark circles sat beneath his eyes, his breathing was labored, and his pallor a deathly gray. Elizabeth bit her lip to stop herself from crying, yet with every moment she could feel herself losing the battle.

"Now, now. None of that. It can't be helped, no point crying over it."

Elizabeth laid her cheek upon his chest and welcomed the sound of his beating heart, wanting it to remain so forever. "How can you sound so calm?"

He sighed and ran his hand through her hair. "I've had a good life. A full and happy life. I have no complaints. I'm prepared for what's to come next."

She hugged him. "I'll miss you." Her words muffled against his bed shirt.

He chuckled. "I'll miss you, too, but I'll see you again one day in the very distant future."

Elizabeth smiled. "I love you, you know that, don't you, Papa? And I'm sorry I've been so much trouble for you all."

"I love you as well. And you were never a burden to me or your mama. People make mistakes, do silly things in their youth; you were never loved less because of it." He clasped her hands, catching her gaze. "But there is something I wish to discuss with you."

Elizabeth sniffed and searched out a handkerchief. "You do?"

"Yes," the duke said, passing her his handkerchief instead. "I don't want you to remain a widow. You're so young, with much to offer. Please do not hide behind Newland's name and grow old before your time. Promise me now you'll at least try to find someone worthy of your love."

Elizabeth frowned, hating that she couldn't grant him the favor he wished. "I cannot promise the impossible, Father."

"You can and you will."

The thought of Henry flittered through her mind, and her father's request didn't seem so impossible really...and yet, Lord Riddledale and his wicked imaginings and threats soon pushed the happy idea away.

Her time with Henry was past; they were friends again, yes, and he had promised to help her best Riddledale, but marriage to him? Although the thought raised goose bumps over her skin, she couldn't let herself think such a thing and be disappointed once more. The first time he'd denied her had nearly broken her heart, even if not of his fault. "I'm incapable of love, and there is no one I feel remotely loveable toward." The lie twisted her stomach into knots, and yet the words spilled out, wrong and awkward.

"Come, my dear, that is a lie if ever I've heard one." He threw her a mocking gaze and Elizabeth's cheeks heated.

"I know who you're hinting at, Papa, and you can stop. We've agreed to be friends and nothing more."

"Bollocks, Elizabeth. You may lie to yourself, but you will not lie to me." Her father sat up a little. "When Henry lived here I had my suspicions of your growing friendship. I knew Henry was determined to secure his future by any means possible, and I understood when he left for America. I have since learned that his uncle, no matter how rich and powerful in America, was not a man to be trusted. It was one of the reasons why Henry's late father banished him from his home in Scotland. I believe Henry has been duped in some way, and I've written to him regarding my concerns. Henry was an honorable man, and would've married you, I'm sure... had he known of the baby."

It was nothing that Henry and she hadn't come to realize themselves. "You are right, Henry was tricked and so were we, but it wasn't his uncle." She paused, wondering how to tell her father what she must. The words seemed to lodge in her throat. Her father coughed, growing paler than the first flurries of winter. "Father, do you want me to call the doctor back?"

He waved away her concerns. "No, no need for that. Now," he said, taking a sip of water. "What were you saying?"

"Henry wrote to his uncle, and he has denied any involvement in keeping our letter from his nephew. Henry is now looking into who else could've worked against us in such a vicious way."

"Henry will get to the bottom of all this trouble, and it pleases me greatly that his uncle has let past hurts lie and not meddle in the lives of two innocent people who deserve no censure, but it leaves me to wonder who it was that wronged you both."

She shrugged, not willing to let him know the truth that would undoubtedly upset him. Her father had always liked Riddledale—to know the man was a blackmailing, arrogant ass wasn't something he needed to know during the last days of his life. Henry and Josh would help rid her of the pestering fool, and that was enough. "Henry will find out. You know how much Scottish men love chasing down English villains."

He laughed. "You are right there, my dearest."

Elizabeth shook her head, loving her father's easygoing manner, no matter that he was a duke. First and foremost, he was always their papa. She took a calming breath. "Thank you, for everything, Father. You have always been so generous and loving. I'm truly blessed to be your daughter. I love you so much."

He pulled her against him, rubbing her back as the tears finally let go. "And I you. Forever and a day. Now off with you, and live a full and happy life for me, and please send your mother in on your way out."

She smiled through her tears and stood to leave. After one last glimpse of her father she walked from the room, knowing she'd never see him such again.

---

*E*lizabeth stood silent and subdued as her father's coffin was carried into the family mausoleum, his final resting place after the public service her mother and sisters hadn't attended in a nearby town's church.

Rain slid down her face and dampened her cloak, making it heavier than usual. Elizabeth welcomed the wet, for it masked the tears that would not stop. Her father was gone, and there was nothing anyone could do to change that horrible fact. Her brother, now the Duke of Penworth, stood at her side, his face as pale and drawn as the rest of them.

Isolde pulled her close, and Elizabeth welcomed the support. How would they go on without their dearest papa? The loving, caring man they adored could never be replaced.

The priest exited the mausoleum, their mother following behind.

Elizabeth's gaze was pulled across the grounds to the dark, hooded cloak that was the only beacon of light on this cold, somber day. Henry stood watching her, water dripping from his hat, his visage one of concern. She knew he wanted to come to her, give her comfort, and right at this moment, nothing in the world would feel better than Henry holding her close.

As the old metal doors closed, entombing their father, Henry strolled their way. He bowed. "I'm so sorry for your loss, Lady Isolde, Lady Newland. If there is anything I can do, please send word. I am at ye disposal anytime you should need it."

Elizabeth met his gaze, wanting to reach out and touch him, to take solace in him. "Thank you, Lord Muir."

Isolde squeezed her arm a little. "I'll wait for you in the carriage, dearest."

Elizabeth watched her sister walk away, before Henry held out his hand to escort her to the carriage. "I will not keep ye long in this atrocious weather, nor on such a sad day, but I have thought about Riddledale and wish to speak to ye regarding him."

"I have been thinking, too, but with Papa's death, I'm not sure when I'll be back in town. I will write to you and let you know if you wish."

The carriage loomed before them quicker than she liked. Henry placed his hand over hers, its warmth sending heat to course up her arm. "I am sorry about his grace. He was the best of men, and I was always fond of him. I wish I could..." He frowned. "I wish I could offer more comfort to ye in this troubling time of yours."

"You being here today is comfort enough. Thank you." He helped her into the carriage, shutting the door. He stood back, his arms held behind his back, and she pushed the window down, not ready to leave him yet. "You are more than welcome back at Dunsleigh, if you're not returning to London immediately."

"I'm afraid I must return to town. I have business to attend there." He bowed. "Good day, my lady."

The carriage moved away, and Elizabeth watched Henry for as long as she was able. It could be weeks, months even, before she traveled back to the capital to be able to see him again.

"Henry is smitten with you, and if I'm not mistaken, he's more in love with you than when he left for America."

"He wasn't in love with me before he left, we were the best of friends who—"

"Gave yourselves to each other in the most intimate of ways."

Heat stole over her cheeks at the reminder, not to mention Elizabeth knew Henry cared for her, more than she'd ever hoped. "You shouldn't speak of such things, Isolde. We're friends."

Her sister threw her a disbelieving look, which Elizabeth chose to ignore. She would write to Henry about Riddledale as soon as they returned to Dunsleigh, and they would go on as normal. Perfectly acceptable, non-kissing normal acquaintances.

*W*eeks passed and gradually the steady stream of local gentry and family started to abate after paying their respects over the passing of the duke. Their mother, who seemed more lost over the following weeks, found such visits tiresome and emotionally draining, and Elizabeth was glad when they finally stopped altogether.

Elizabeth strode through the front door after her morning ride and stopped as the aroma of roses wafted across her senses. Unease pooled in her stomach as she caught sight of the footman walking into the library with a pretty blue box with matching ribbon in his hand.

"Who is that for, John?" Elizabeth asked, stripping off her gloves.

"You, Lady Newland. It has just arrived."

Elizabeth walked over to the footman and took the parcel. After pulling off the blue ribbon, she lifted the lid and looked inside. She had to concede the blood red rose was very pretty, but highly improper. She checked under the flower and noticed, yet again, the absence of a card.

The awful thought crossed her mind that Riddledale was home at his estate adjacent to Dunsleigh. The thought of him this close, lying in wait until he could start pushing for a marriage, sent revulsion through her body.

"Thank you, John." Elizabeth entered the drawing room and sat beside Alice, who was reading a book. She took the rose out of the box and laid it onto the open page.

Alice chuckled. "Ah, I see Lord Riddledale is still courting you."

Elizabeth pursed her lips in disgust. "So it would seem, although I find it's in poor taste, since it's only been two months since Father's death. He should know gifts should not occur during such a time or at all." Alice nodded in agreement. "We'll not tell Mama. It'll only upset her more." Alice looked thoughtful, laying her book in her lap.

"I will not, I promise you, but what are you going to do about him? He seems determined to have you as his future marchioness."

Elizabeth fought not to grimace. She would never marry him, and Henry would help her gain that end. "He's absurd, but I'm certain that in time he'll move on to another victim."

Once they had the letter in their possession, Riddledale wouldn't be able to crow about what he knew, for who would believe him without proof, and he would hopefully give up pursuit.

"I heard Mama saying that Josh is going to invite Lord Dean down for a week or so." She twirled the rose about in her fingers. "He's due to arrive by luncheon tomorrow. I fear your Lord Riddledale will not appreciate the competition."

"Lord Dean and I are friends and nothing more, and as to what Lord Riddledale thinks on the matter I don't give a fig." Elizabeth mulled over what she'd once thought she could feel for Lord Dean, and realized it was nothing but ordinary. Having Henry back in her sphere, attentive and with as much honesty as they'd once shared, Lord Dean paled against the vibrant Scottish earl.

She'd certainly never had the reactions that she endured whilst around Henry. Just the mention of his name made her stomach flutter in trepidation and anticipation. No other man had ever made her feel what she felt whenever Henry cast his determined, heated gaze on her.

"If not Lord Dean, then who have you set your cap on, may I ask?" At her silence, Alice prodded her in the ribs. "Well?"

"No one at all."

Alice frowned. "But I thought you liked Lord Dean. He was courting you at the start of the season. Has his ardor cooled?"

Elizabeth nodded, knowing the truth of her sister's words. "You know I've had lots of suitors since Newland, but I'm not looking for marriage, Alice. I have little Samuel to care for and raise." Who, she reminded herself, was due to wake up from his nap and would be awake for a play very shortly. "A husband is not a priority of mine."

"You're very young to stay a widow forever." Her sister's

words reminded Elizabeth of her father's only weeks ago and her promise that she'd at least try to find happiness in her future.

"If, and that is a stern if, I were to marry again, I would not settle for less than the deepest, heart-pounding love."

Alice sighed. "Well, I'm sorry for Lord Dean, but the decision is yours, of course." She sat up, pulling out a letter from her reticule. "Oh, I nearly forgot to tell you, we received a letter today from Isolde."

Elizabeth was thankful for the turn of conversation. "You did? What did she say?"

"Just that she is staying in London only another week before traveling back to Avonmore in Scotland. She writes that Lord Muir is rumored to be courting Miss Andrews. You know, his American cousin."

"What?" Elizabeth winced at the panic prevalent in her voice. "What did she say exactly?"

Alice nodded, her eyes bright with her sister's interest in the matter. "Only that he's been attentive about town with the chit." She paused, throwing her a speculative gaze. "I didn't think you liked Henry in that way. I know you're friends again, but…this seems to bother you. Why?"

Elizabeth stopped listening, having started to pace before the hearth. Why would Henry court his cousin? His kisses, his mannerisms, his statements were not of a man who was interested in another. "There is nothing romantic between Henry and me." Elizabeth pushed away the thought of their kiss and her unashamed lie. Oh yes, nothing romantic at all. "I do believe in this instance Isolde may be wrong. He's simply being attentive and ensuring his guests enjoy their time in England."

"And you trust his word after all that has happened between you?"

"I do." She nodded, realizing that she did indeed trust

117

Henry again, more than anyone else. At her sister's continued confusion, Elizabeth disclosed the truth of the situation with Henry and what had transpired to keep them apart. Alice sat in stunned silence before she glared, her hands fisting in her lap.

"I hope you'll serve Riddledale his comeuppance. How dare he interfere in matters that did not concern him. And trying to make you marry him. Why, I'll never be polite to the man again."

"You must continue on as you did before. I don't want him to suspect of any plan to get the letter back. When I return to town I'll try to persuade certain friends to sporadically suggest to Riddledale that he ought to hold a coming-out ball for his sister—as far as we know he's not looking to hold one for her. It's at such an entertainment that we intend to make our move and hopefully, all this mess can be put behind us."

Elizabeth stood and walked to the windows that overlooked the side gardens, the green vista of endless lawns always a comfort, but what she needed to do was leave for London. It was time to take back what was rightfully theirs and be rid of Riddledale and his threats. She looked over at the rose, strode toward it, and threw the blasted thing into the fire. "I think I shall return to town." She would deliver Samuel safely back to Newland Estate and then carry on to London.

Alice sighed. "I guess this is where I offer to stay and keep Mama company so you may travel to London?"

"Would you, dearest? That would be most helpful, and maybe in a week or two, with both Isolde and me in town, perhaps Mama will allow you to come up for a visit. Of course you'll not be able to attend balls, but we may be able to attend the theater one evening."

"It doesn't signify since the season is almost over, but

once you're settled, I shall ask Mama." Alice picked up her book again. "When will you leave?"

"Tomorrow, I think. There is a lot I need to discuss with Henry, and I cannot do it here." She walked to the bellpull and rang for a footman. "And with any luck, by the time the season comes to a close, we'll be well rid of Riddledale and will not have to suffer his presence in our lives anymore."

Alice nodded. "Now that is the best of news." Elizabeth laughed. "I agree."

CHAPTER 9

With not much else to do, due to their mourning period, Elizabeth rode daily with Isolde in Hyde Park, a much- needed outing for them both. They cantered down the row, the smell of leather and the sound of pounding hooves always a soothing balm.

At the end of the track, they slowed their horses just as a party of three rode onto the row. Elizabeth had written to Henry asking him to meet her here by chance, and he'd not disappointed her. It seemed too long since she'd seen last.

She urged her horse abreast of Isolde's as they walked toward Henry and his cousins. He looked up when he noticed her; the small grin only for her to see left a fluttering in her stomach. Elizabeth smiled at each of them, but the glower from Miss Andrews said more than words that their meeting in the park wasn't ideal for the woman.

"Good afternoon, Lord Muir, Mr. Andrews, Miss Andrews," Isolde said, as they pulled up their horses.

"Good afternoon," Henry replied. "A lovely day for a ride, is it not?"

Elizabeth shifted on her seat, impatient to get the niceties over so she could speak with him alone. "It is a lovely day, and I'm glad to see you're showing off our lovely park to your cousins, Henry."

He caught her gaze and, like an unseen force, Elizabeth couldn't look away. His eyes lit with mirth. "Are you staying in town for long?"

"Isolde leaves next week for Avonmore, but I'm staying for the foreseeable future. I'll return to Newland Estate after the season."

"How are you enjoying the season, Miss Andrews? I heard it said that you're to settle here for some time. I can only assume, by such news, you like our country." Elizabeth marveled at how Isolde could smile at someone who glowered back at her.

Much to her shock, Miss Andrews rolled her eyes with a decided sniff. It reminded her of Lord Riddledale, and she decided to dislike the American a little more because of it.

"England is tolerable, although the weather could be more congenial," Miss Andrews said, looking anywhere but at them.

Elizabeth cleared her throat, the thought of cutting the woman here in the park with a serious setdown flittered through her mind. She wouldn't do it, of course. For all of Miss Andrews's faults, she was Henry's cousin and guest.

"Well, perhaps on your next visit the gods will grant us better weather." Elizabeth steadied her mare when it shifted beneath her, the animal itching for another run.

"My brother and I would like to travel to Scotland soon. I find I've had my fill of London."

Elizabeth raised her brow. "I'm not sure if Lord Muir has told you, Miss Andrews, but Scotland is by far less congenial than England with its weather. Even in summer it's likely to be cold. I do hope we do not scare you back to your homeland." Miss Andrews's eyes narrowed, and Elizabeth smiled, knowing she'd vexed the little minx. Good. With any luck, the viperish woman would scurry back to America instead of Scotland.

Miss Andrews shrugged. "I will see, will I not?" Elizabeth patted Argo when she pawed the ground. "I'm sorry to desert you, but I must take my horse for another run. Lord Muir, would you care to join me? I know how much you are fond of riding."

*enry clicked his tongue and followed Elizabeth onto Rotten Row's track. "I won't be a moment." He threw the words over his shoulder, not wanting anyone else to join them. He lived to be alone with Elizabeth where no one could interfere with their chats.

"How are ye getting on back in town? I had heard the dowager has taken to her rooms at Dunsleigh. Is this true?" Elizabeth sighed, watching two gentlemen canter down the row. "Yes, unfortunately it's true, but I'm sure, given time, she'll become better. My parents were a love match, as you know, and it's hard when you lose someone you do not wish to be parted from."

Henry couldn't agree more. He watched her; a slight frown marred her brow, making her look sad, and the urge to hold her, comfort her, was strong. But within a moment Elizabeth seemed to shake the sullen thoughts away and said, "Father is gone, and as much as that pains us all, we must move forward just as he wished. And as for moving forward, did you receive your invitation to Lord Riddledale's ball?"

Henry nodded, having not thought after his run-in with the blaggard in Whites that he would be invited. Luckily, his lordship had thought better of slighting him, not that Henry wasn't fool enough to know Riddledale would be less than pleased when he received his acceptance. "I have. A most fortunate turn of the cards."

"Yes," Elizabeth said, her eyes full of laughter. "I thought so, too. Lady Emily is a lovely young woman, and it's quite unfortunate she was lumped with such a baboon of a brother. The ball will be a perfect opportunity for us."

The words "opportunity for us" brought up a whole different scenario that Elizabeth and he could partake in at the ball. Of stolen moments away from the ton where he could kiss the delectable lips that haunted his dreams every night, long legs clasped about his waist in the throes of passion, of sighs and decadent kisses.

He cleared his throat. "Yes, it'll be our only opportunity to gain entrance to his house. It's a most welcome that his lordship has decided to throw a ball for his sister's coming out."

Elizabeth laughed, the sound a balm to his soul. How he'd longed to hear her laugh, to make her as happy and carefree as she was as a girl. "I agree. The ball is perfect timing."

"I will ask for the supper dance and take you in to eat, and after a quick repast we'll sneak out to search his library."

"You don't think his lordship would keep the letter in his bedroom? I should hate to be caught rifling through his things in there. I'd be made to marry him on the spot, and that would never do."

"If the letter is not in the library, then that will be, of course, our second option, but I'll go alone, and you can keep watch if you like." He wiggled his brows and she chuckled. "Unless you want to come into the room with me; if caught it would be I who would have the honor of your hand."

She grinned, blushing a little. "Very amusing, Lord Muir." She paused. "But you never know, maybe if we are successful with our plan we ought to offer up our services to Bow Street?"

Henry threw back his head and laughed. "If being a lady

of leisure and an earl does not work out for us, perhaps we could." He paused, realizing they had come to the end of the track. "Do ye wish to race back?"

Her eyes glowed with a competitiveness he knew well. "We're not allowed to gallop on the row. You're being a bad influence, Henry."

"Ye have no idea, lass," he said, winking.

Her eyes widened at his words before she kicked her mount, sending her forward and away from him at a blistering speed. He heard her laughter as he chased after her. Her horse Argo was fast and ate the distance of the track quickly, and it took him some time to come abreast of her.

She looked delectable, hair askew from the speed, her cheeks a light rosy hue. They pulled their mounts up together, both of them laughing.

"I think I won," she said, gasping for breath.

Henry laughed; it was he who had won, for if she would only open her heart again to him, he would be the richest man on earth. "This time perhaps, but I hope to spar with ye again, my lady."

She nodded, turning her horse to where her sister sat with Henry's cousins under a copse of trees. "I look forward to it, my lord."

CHAPTER 10

"*I* cannot believe it. He has sent another gift of flowers." Elizabeth held out the morning glory to Isolde. "I don't know why he continues to harass me in such a way. He's a veritable ass." She growled and sat beside Isolde on the settee, looking up at the painting of her parents that hung above the hearth.

"He's asked to marry you and is now, probably due to his threats, trying to woo you the old-fashioned way." Isolde threw her a consoling smile. "Don't let it irritate you so, my dear. They are only flowers, after all."

In disgusted outrage, Elizabeth looked over at her sister, who sat embroidering a cushion. "How can you be so calm over it? Without even mentioning he's trying to blackmail me into marrying him, we're in mourning. How could he be so inconsiderate?"

The door to the drawing room opened, and Elizabeth turned to watch their butler walk in. "I'm sorry to disturb, Lady Isolde, Lady Newland, but you have a visitor who insists on being seen."

"It's still morning, Peter," Isolde said, looking at the

mantle clock. "Who is it that has called?"

Elizabeth too noted the time before she turned her attention back to the butler. John stood still, his wiry frame clearly uncomfortable at having to ask if they were at home in the first place. An inkling of unease crept over her and, when the butler announced none other than Lord Riddledale awaited entry, Elizabeth couldn't hide the shudder of revulsion that ran down her spine.

"Thank you, John. Please advise Lord Riddledale we shall see him quickly, and please come back in five minutes to escort his lordship out."

John bowed. "Yes, my lady."

Isolde's eyebrows rose. "Very well, I agree he is pushing the boundaries of society's rules just a little." Isolde held up her hand before Elizabeth could speak on that exact point. "I understand, dearest, your concern. However, let us see what he has to say for himself first before we send him to the gallows."

Elizabeth bit her tongue and fought not to roll her eyes as Lord Riddledale waltzed into the room. He seemed to take in all the grandeur and comforts the room held and approved it all with a decided sniff. Elizabeth's eyes narrowed at the money-hungry rogue, his desire for all things well-to- do obvious with every salacious look he bestowed on her family's fine things. He came to stand before them, wished them a good morning, and then sat in the wingback chair across from them.

Elizabeth remained silent as Isolde smiled in welcome.

"It is kind of you to call, Lord Riddledale. Pray what has brought you out so early in the day?"

He laughed and tweaked his nose. "Ah, yes," he said, laughing out loud. "I know this isn't the correct time for visiting, but since we are country neighbors and friends I thought you wouldn't mind such an etiquette slip. I have come to pass on my condolences once more to your family over your father's death and ask if Lady Newland would accompany me for a ride in the park tomorrow afternoon."

Elizabeth felt her eyes widen at his request.

Condolences in one breath and a declaration of intent in the other.

The way this man went about was in poor taste. She may throw convention aside sometimes and do as she pleased, but Lord Riddledale knew how devoted to their papa they were. During this time of mourning, none of them would step out of line. His lordship's wits were obviously muddled. "I'm sorry, my lord," Isolde said. "But we are not permitted to drive in the park with gentlemen while we are in mourning."

He waved her sister's comment aside with a flick of his hand. "No need to stick to convention when we're all old friends. And I saw you in the park yesterday with Lord Muir, so surely my invitation is also agreeable."

"I'm sorry, my lord, but the answer is no. And yesterday in the park we only happened upon Lord Muir and his guests. It wasn't intentionally arranged." Isolde stood. "And it is probably best, since we're alone, that you take your leave. I do not mean to be rude, but it is wrong of me to have even allowed you enter, as we're unchaperoned."

Lord Riddledale huffed out a breath. "But surely at your age, Lady Isolde, there is no need for a chaperone. Say, what are you now, four and twenty?" He turned his piercing stare toward Elizabeth. "And you, Lady Newland, are a widow. Perfectly acceptable me being here."

Perfectly acceptable by society's standard still didn't mean they wished him there with them. Her sister blushed at the insult to her age, which was completely incorrect, and Elizabeth's temper got the better of her, but before she uttered the words "prig" and "get out," her sister spoke.

"Thank you for reminding me, my lord. That was very

gentlemanly of you," Isolde said.

"Always a pleasure, Lady Isolde." Riddledale smiled, completely unaware of any wrongdoing. His lordship stood and bowed. "Lady Elizabeth, might I be so bold to remind you I'm waiting for your answer to my question. I should like it soon, as my patience grows thin."

Elizabeth also stood, standing almost eye level with the man. "You shall have it by the end of the night of the ball you're hosting for your sister."

He preened. "Very good. I look forward to the event with even more zeal." His gaze raked her body in a most disturbing manner, and her fingers twitched, wanting to scratch out his eyes.

He was slimier than a toad, and becoming more so with every passing day. Then, much to her horror, he picked up her hand and kissed it, his wet lips meeting her skin along with the light touching of his tongue. Elizabeth ripped her hand away, wiping it on her dress. "Good day to you, my lord."

Seemingly unfazed, Lord Riddledale smiled, leaning in close enough for only her to hear. "I'm so pleased to have you back in town, my dear. I have missed you."

Elizabeth glared, not bothering to reply to his words as she watched him leave. When the door closed, Elizabeth rounded on her sister. "He. Licked. My. Hand."

Isolde stared, unable to form words at that very moment. "I noticed," she said at length. "He wasn't good at hiding his…tongue."

Elizabeth threw her hands up in the air. "What am I going to do? He's beyond measure." Elizabeth wiped her hand against her gown again, shuddering.

"He seems most determined. I hope you and Henry are able to get that letter back so this dark cloud looming over you can clear."

How she hated the man at that very moment for treating her like something that could be bought, like a horse or a treat. "I'm determined to succeed. I'll not let that man," she said, pointing toward the window, "ruin my name and drag my family, including dear little Samuel, through the mud."

The door to the room opened once again, and Elizabeth wondered who else wished to call at this time of day. "A message has arrived for you, Lady Newland."

Elizabeth sighed and swiped the card from the silver salver. Her hands fumbled with the seal when she recognized the script. Dismissing the butler, she sat, wanting to read the missive immediately. When opening the parchment, a single violet sat atop the written words, just a small gesture that oddly meant more to her than a whole posy of hothouse blooms Riddledale thought to send.

"Who is it from, my dear?"

Elizabeth reread the note before folding it away. "Miss Duncannon. She has invited me for tea to discuss her travels. She's returned from abroad, you know."

"Oh, I didn't know you were friends with Miss Duncannon," Isolde said, picking up her embroidery and packing it away in a small basket beside her chair.

Elizabeth nodded and strove not to blush. "Yes. She writes often." She refused to react to her sister's disbelieving stare and instead slumped back in her chair with an air of aloofness.

Isolde stood. "Well, I'm going upstairs for a bit. I'll see you at luncheon."

Elizabeth smiled. "I will see you then."

Moments later Elizabeth sat alone and reopened the note. The little purple bloom's scent wafted up and intoxicated her heart when she knew it should not. She looked to the neat flowing script and a smile quirked her lips.

E,

The violets await, abound the track that lead
directly to me. Meet me there, one-of-the-o'clock.
I'll be waiting.
H.

Elizabeth folded the missive and headed upstairs to her room. Thoughts of what she should wear bombarded her mind, the green or blue riding ensemble, hair up or down? No sooner had she had the reflections did she dismiss them. She was not a young girl anymore; to act like a love-sick fool would not do at all, and Henry certainly didn't need more encouragement; he'd been forward too oft as it was.

They were friends, and they were working together to best Riddledale, so of course they needed to meet, but to flutter about and take too much interest in one's dressing was too much, even for her.

She picked the blue riding gown.

---

*R*otten Row had fewer horses as the weather started to turn, the wind whipping the leaves across the grounds in swirls. Elizabeth sat atop Argo. Her groom Tony, only a short distance away, occasionally checked her location before looking back up at the sky.

The echoing of hooves sounded through the woods, and Argo shifted beneath her, sensing another horse approaching at high speed. Elizabeth looked to where a single rider emerged from a copse of trees and smiled.

Henry.

She took in every detail of him as he rode toward her. The masculinity hidden under tight riding breeches, shirt and jacket that made her skin prickle in awareness knowing what was underneath the garments: a treasure trove of muscle and bronzed skin.

Nerves pooled in her belly when she thought of how they would proceed as friends if that was all they would ever be to each other. The last time such closeness had formed, a tryst beside a lake had ensued, hot and fast, delectable kisses that left one breathless and aching with need. Not to mention the heated kiss they shared only weeks ago. She shook the thoughts aside, not needing to remember what Henry looked like devoid of clothes or his mouth ravaged by her own. She was a widowed woman, a mother; her priorities should be elsewhere...but as he approached, his hair askew, all thoughts of staying strictly platonic with the gentleman present seemed too difficult.

Much too hard.

"Good afternoon, lass."

The words of acknowledgment and the use of his Scottish term made her stomach clench. She shifted in her seat as warmth spread through her limbs. "Good afternoon, Lord Muir."

Henry brought his horse beside hers. "Lord Muir? Surely ye can call me Henry. We're friends in arms, after all, are we not?"

Tongue-tied, Elizabeth nodded, not sure if her words would come out as a squeak. Seeing him again, alone, only the two of them without family present—who had the uncanny ability to listen in on one's conversation—left her as nervous as she was during her first ball.

She took a calming breath. "Of course I'll call you Henry if you wish it."

He smiled, his eyes alight with pleasure. "I do." He paused, frowning up at the sky. "I didn't think you'd come."

Elizabeth had had her own misgivings on Henry arriving as well. Not about to state that, she clicked her tongue to move on. "Yes, the weather is turning, but I thought it best if we spoke."

"I wanted to let ye know that a close friend of mine who's also related to Riddledale, poor man, has drawn a layout of his lordship's house for me. I would hate for us to get lost and end up under the stairs in the dark."

Elizabeth met his gaze and realized that, although the words were said as a lark, his dark hooded gaze burned with intent. She shivered under the intensity of his eyes. Oh yes, staying strictly friends was going to be troublesome if not impossible. "That is wonderful news. I would never have thought of that."

"I wished to be as organized as possible. We only need hope his lordship keeps the letter in the library where apparently from my source, his estate business is also attended to."

"And after we have the letter, what then? Will we confront Riddledale?" How grand it would be to throw such a triumph back at the blackmailing ass's face. To taunt him to try to ruin her family through a folly of hers that was none of his business in the first place.

"We will let him know the game is over, but that is all." Henry laughed, shaking his head. "I can see your mind is working in its devious way. We will not gloat, lass, if that is ye thinking."

She laughed. "La, you've turned into a bore since leaving for America. What happened to the Scottish fire that lives inside you? You may have dark hair, Henry, but even I know you're a true redhead at heart."

"You know me too well," he replied. They rode down the side of Rotten Row beside the metal fencing that separated the track from the walking path.

"I do need to confess something, which, although I'm not overly proud of, ye should know."

"What is it?" she asked when he remained silent, his brow

furrowed. And what was it? She hoped it didn't involve Miss Andrews and kissing her in New York. Elizabeth wasn't sure if she ever wished to hear about that.

"I confronted Riddledale in Whites and...well, there was an altercation."

Elizabeth snorted and then laughed. "You didn't. Henry, you really are a natural redhead." She reached over and clasped his long locks. The moment she touched him she knew it was a mistake. It left her longing to reach back, grab his nape, pull him across the small space that separated them and kiss him. Worse was the fact he leaned into her touch, taunting her to do exactly what she longed. Elizabeth pulled her hand away and gripped her reins. "What happened? What did you say to him?"

"I hit him, quite a bit in fact." Henry raised his brow at her amusement, shaking his head. "He deserved a good beating, mind, but know this, even if we fail at finding the letter, I'll not allow—and nor will your brother—ye to marry him. Scandal be damned."

The thought of marrying Riddledale sent a chill down her spine. To have him touch her intimately, kiss her on the mouth, was more revolting than the time Henry had made her try haggis. "We cannot fail."

A lone rider passed them, and they nodded in greeting. "Tell me, Elizabeth, how it was your marriage to Newland came about. I would like to know if ye would tell me."

Elizabeth swallowed, choosing her words with care. "After we received the letter we thought was from you, Father became concerned for my welfare. I was a little low in spirits, you see. He was friends with Lord Newland, and we were invited to stay at their country house for two weeks. Marcus, Lord Newland's son, was kind and attentive, and we became friends."

"You did not love him?"

She kept her gaze between Argo's ears, not confident enough to meet his gaze, which she could feel burning into the side of her face. "It wasn't that kind of love, but he was a kind man. We talked a lot during those two weeks I first came to stay there, and we became close. He offered marriage, and I accepted. He passed away in his sleep over twelve months later. The physician thought the injury he originally suffered falling from his horse may have triggered a bleed in his brain of some kind, but we will never really know for sure."

"I'm sorry, lass, for everything, but also for your loss. He sounds like he was a good man. May I ask how long ye were actually married?"

She nodded. "He was the best of men, and we were married almost two years give or take a couple of months." And Marcus had saved her, from the moment he caught her being sick behind a maze, he'd guessed her plight. Instead of shunning her, outing her disgrace and sending her packing, he'd offered her marriage, had offered her unborn child the protection of a name. And it had been an equal trade, since Newland himself had stated no one would look at him since his fall, which had injured his mind. "He deserved better than me."

She felt the touch of Henry's hand on hers, but she couldn't look at him. Shame washed over her along with anger. Should Henry find out the secret she still kept from him, it would devastate and break his heart, but to tell Henry of Samuel's existence would not do her child any favors, either. Henry could not claim Samuel, no matter how much he may wish to. And despite telling Marcus the truth, her deceased husband had loved the little boy beyond measure. By telling another of his true heritage, it seemed the ultimate betrayal to a man who had saved her from ruin.

She could not do it.

"There is not much that is better than you, lass." Elizabeth smiled, meeting his gaze. "You're a flatterer, Henry. I see that has not changed since you left."

"Ye're easy to flatter."

A strong gust of wind threatened her hat, and she reached up, clasping the rim. "I think we should leave. The heavens are about to open, I suspect." She cursed the weather having shortened their time. "I thought I might ride out to Richmond Park tomorrow and sketch the more natural landscape there. Would you care to join me?"

Henry nodded. "If the weather permits, I'd like that. What time would ye like me to meet ye at Richmond?"

"Eleven? Would that be suitable?"

"More than suitable." Henry looked up at the gathering clouds just as a lone droplet of rain hit her cheek, followed by a rumble of thunder.

"I had better leave. Isolde will be worried with the storm coming in." She turned her horse and started toward her groom. "Tomorrow then?" She threw the question over her shoulder, smiling at finding Henry's gaze locked on her.

"Tomorrow, my lady."

Elizabeth turned and rode off, marveling at the way Henry was able to make the words my lady seem like a statement of intent instead of the salutation it was meant to be.

Flirt indeed.

*T*he storm ravaged London; branches scattered through the streets, leaves and litter lay everywhere the eye could see. Elizabeth stood at the front drawing room window and noted the time. It was still early enough to cancel, but something stopped her from sending a missive to Henry.

She had to admit, she didn't want to abandon their outing. The impromptu idea to visit Richmond and invite Henry was too good an opportunity to abandon. Wet grass was a poor excuse to miss a few hours in his company, and the wind had settled to a slight breeze, in any case.

She sent a note to the stable and notified her groom to be ready within the hour and then headed upstairs to change into her riding habit.

Richmond Park was abandoned when she arrived. Sitting on a wooden bench, she breathed deeply the freshness of the earth after the heavy rains. Birds pecked at the ground, hoping to find a juicy worm or two, and it wasn't long before the echo of horse hooves pounding the damp earth sounded behind her like the drums of an approaching army.

Within moments, Henry cantered into the clearing. She pushed aside the excited whir that stirred her body at the sight of him. With his hat clasped in his hand, his shoulder-length hair again looked disheveled and unruly, much like the man.

The horse skidded to a stop before her, and she smiled at the mirth and vitality she read in Henry's gaze. Elizabeth reminded herself yet again they were friends and nothing more. No, nothing, nothing more. "Good morning, Henry. Lovely day, is it not?"

He laughed, dismounting. "It's all the better for seeing you again, lass." He sat beside her, his grin infectious. "Ye survived the weather last night?" he asked, looking up at the sky as if it would open up once more and drench them. "I hadn't thought we would for a time."

Elizabeth smiled. "We did, thank you." She paused, looking out over the park. "Walk with me."

"Of course." They stood and followed a line of trees that sat beside a grassy meadow. Henry clasped her hand and placed it through the crook of his arm. She swallowed as with each step she could feel the muscles in his arm flex, just the slightest movement that left her breathless.

"Last night, after everyone was abed, I realized that of all the years we've known each other, I'm not at all familiar about your home in Scotland. Will you tell me about it?"

Henry shut his eyes, a wistful smile on his lips. "'Tis beautiful. The castle has been in my family for six hundred years. It resides at the base of the highlands, where the mist can obscure it from view as if it were never there. The smell of heather meets your senses every morning. The loch, not far from the house, is as blue as the sky. My grandfather nearly lost it all due to gambling and living beyond his means in England. My father inherited an estate on the edge of bankruptcy. When he passed away and I became earl, I realized I only had a few years left to turn the family's fortune around before we lost it all."

Elizabeth nodded and watched a squirrel try to carry a walnut up a tree and realized, in a way, it was what Henry was trying to achieve—security for his family and home in the highlands. Of course he loved his home as much as she loved Dunsleigh. Should crippling debt ever threaten her family's estate, Elizabeth knew her brother would do anything in his power to keep Dunsleigh theirs.

"Why did you not tell me of this before you left England? I mean, we knew you were in need of funds, but we never assumed it was as bad as that."

"Pride, I guess. Few out of the family knew of the predicament I faced. I never even told ye father all of my woes, as I knew he'd try to help me."

Elizabeth hugged him closer to her as they strolled. "Father would've tried to help." She smiled at the memory of his kind heart. "And rightfully so, he was your guardian, after all."

"Aye, I know, but I wanted to earn my fortune back, and

thanks to some hard work and sound investments I've achieved that goal before it was too late."

Elizabeth looked up at him. "I know your return to London was a little turbulent with me, but I'm proud of you, Henry, and you should be proud of yourself as well."

His gaze captured hers, and again awareness shimmered between them, wrapped about her like a cloak, and dug up a need that she'd long thought buried.

"I am proud and, above all else, relieved I'll not be the earl who lost the estate." He pulled them to a stop, turning her to face him. "I know we've not spoken of this for some time, but surly ye must know that my feelings toward you are unchanged, have never altered, in truth."

"Henry." She sighed. "I'm not looking to marry again."

"I worked for three years, harder than I've ever worked in my life, and with the sole hope that when I returned we would wed, as we planned. I still wish that, above everything else."

She couldn't reply; to crush his dreams seemed too cruel a blow. And she didn't want to face the cold hard truth that Henry's dreams were still what she desired as well. To give voice to such a truth could never be locked away again. It had taken all her strength to wrestle her heart into a box, and that was where it would stay.

"When I first arrived at Dunsleigh I know I took delight in teasing you mercilessly. You were a lass easy to annoy." He chuckled. "But after a time we became the best of friends, and when of age I knew what I had to do to ensure I won ye."

Tears smarted in her eyes, and she blinked to clear her vision. How she wanted him to stop, to not say another word, but at the same time she wanted him to keep saying these wonderful things, declarations that filled her with an emotion she'd not thought to ever feel again.

"I fell in love with ye, lass. I still love ye."

Elizabeth stopped breathing, her gaze riveted on the ground at her feet lest she topple over. Henry had always been honest to a fault and, it seemed, he still was.

"You shouldn't say such things," she whispered.

"I want to show ye my home. I want ye to be the woman who wishes me good mornin' and good night every day. I want ye and no one else." His eyes beseeched her to agree, to step once more into the abyss of the unknown and take a chance. "I don't want to be just ye friend, lass. I want all of ye. I always have."

The longing in Henry's voice tumbled the fortress she'd erected around her heart. "This is madness," she said, her heart thumping hard against her ribs. Tears spilled over her cheeks, and he wiped them away.

"We will deal with Riddledale and his threats, I promise ye, but let me court ye, let me show ye once more I'm trustworthy and capable of keeping ye heart safe."

He stepped close enough that she became aware of his scent, of sandalwood mixed with something that was just him, intoxicating and safe. The scent pulled her into the past, of stolen kisses and wicked words. This was madness, but what a delicious madness it was. "Henry, so much has happened. So many things are different since you went away. I don't want to hurt you again." And if he found out about their son, hurt would be the least emotion he would feel. She was walking a fine line that could break at any moment.

He picked up her hand and kissed her fingers. A sharp bolt of desire coursed through her blood, and her heart tumbled for the Scot once again.

"You will not. 'Tis impossible for ye to do so."

Elizabeth swallowed the guilt that rose within her at his words.

If only that were true.

CHAPTER 11

*E*lizabeth looked over her shoulder onto Bond Street as a pricking of unease slithered down her neck. She watched the busy crowd of shoppers but couldn't see anything to raise her suspicion. And yet, for some absurd reason, the notion that someone was watching her, following her, would not dissipate.

She came to the door to Hatchards, her favorite book-seller, and motioned for Tippy, her maid, to follow her inside. Elizabeth breathed deep the delightful smell of leather and paper as she walked toward the nearest window. Looking outside, she took in the street and noted a large man wearing laborer type pants and a grimy linen shirt leaning against a wall across the way. Such a gentleman wouldn't normally catch her attention, but that his consideration was fixed on Hatchards—not an establishment he looked to visit often—was odd.

"Tippy, do you know who the man across the street is by any chance? The big one, leaning against the milliner shop." Tippy leaned past Elizabeth and looked to where she pointed.

"No, my lady. I've never seen him before." She turned back to her expectantly. "Should I know him?"

Elizabeth bit her lip and frowned. "No. I don't believe you should. I just wondered, that's all."

Tippy went to pick some books of her own to read, while Elizabeth stayed at the window and watched the burly fellow. He seemed content to stay where he was, but why a man who looked more suited to the bowels of London would be interested in a bookshop was strange. Just as strange as the notion the same man was possibly following her.

With a resigned sigh, Elizabeth went about looking for something to read.

A little while later, pleased with her assortment of books, she stepped from the shop, pulling on her gloves with a false air of calm. Her body, on the other hand, was coiled tight with nerves. Within her peripheral vision, the man leaned away from the wall and made a show of looking about the street. Maybe he was following her, but why?

Elizabeth looked over at him and took in his every detail. She studied, with blatant curiosity, his features and dress. If he were following her, Henry and Josh would question her about him, and she needed to remember what she saw.

The man, not expecting her to pick him out of all the people on the street, shuffled about and then took off down a lane between the stores. Elizabeth marked the direction he went and watched him until he was out of sight.

She headed for the family carriage parked a little away, wondering who would need to spy on her. Not that he was a competent spy, in any case, but it was absurd. She'd certainly never done anything to warrant such attention. She stopped at the thought, and her maid let out a little yelp at having nearly run into her. Unless Lord Riddledale had taken it upon himself to keep tabs on her every move. It was not without warrant, and she certainly wouldn't put it past the unrelenting gentleman to act so high-handed.

The man's audacity had gone quite far enough.

Upon arriving home, Elizabeth found a letter waiting for her. The unease that pricked at her earlier jabbed her innards. The writing wasn't from anyone she knew, and there was no forwarding address. She walked to the library and shut the door. After ordering some afternoon refreshment, she sat and broke the seal. Somehow she knew she would need the tea and its calming remedies upon reading the note.

She was not wrong.

My dearest Elizabeth,

As you know, my deepest desires are for us to marry and soon. It pains me that you've made time for others and not your future husband, but never the one to complain, I have a little titbit that should persuade you to follow my decree.

In light of my inability to wait for you, I have decided to announce our betrothal next week, and should you fight me on this, I will be made to show Henry the letter and the news that it contains of your disgrace and of your child.

It is time, my dear, to let the world know you're mine. Write me and tell me how much you're looking forward to being my wife.

Yours always,

R.

Elizabeth tore the note in two and threw it into the fire before realizing what she'd done. She grabbed the poker, hoping she could pull the parchment from the flames, but it was too late, and the fire licked the note to ash before she could stop it.

Slumping back on her haunches, she cursed her temper to Hades. Damn it, she should have kept it. Henry would wish to read anything Lord Riddledale sent her. The thought pulled her up short. She couldn't show Henry the missive. He would know all her lies, all her disgrace against his person. He would hate her.

No, Josh was due to arrive in London any day, and she would tell him of the missive and see what he could do to stop his lordship from announcing a betrothal that had not, nor ever would, occur.

"What are you doing on the floor?"

Elizabeth whirled toward the door, where Alice stood pulling off her gloves and hat.

Elizabeth stood. "You're in town? Have you come to stay?"

"Of course. In fact, all of us have come up to London. Mother wished for a little distraction from Dunsleigh. We arrived when you were out at Hatchards. I've just been out for a walk." Alice paused. "What's the matter?"

Elizabeth swiped at her cheeks as her sister's comforting arms enfolded her. "I received a letter from Lord Riddledale. He's going to announce our betrothal next week, and I haven't even agreed to marry him. He says if I do not, he'll allow Henry to read Papa's letter and allow Henry to know of Samuel."

"Where is Samuel, is he in town?"

"No, he's at Newland Estate. Why?"

"And I think until all of this is sorted he should stay there." Alice paused. "Tell me Elizabeth, does Henry know of your son?"

Her sister's words made her feel ill. "No. I cannot tell him of Samuel or the real reason why I married Newland. He'll never forgive me." It didn't matter who had deceived them—when Henry found out about a child she had kept from him, that he would never have his rightful father's name…such a scenario wasn't worth thinking over. It was all a nightmare.

"And you wish to be forgiven by Lord Muir?"

Elizabeth swiped at her cheeks. "I fear I like Henry more than I should. As you know he's been helping me thwart Riddledale, and the plan should work if luck is on our side, but I cannot tell him the truth. I just cannot."

Alice rubbed her back, joining her on the floor. "Josh is due in town tomorrow. We shall seek his council and see what he can do." She paused. "You're still planning on looking through Riddledale's office when he holds his sister's coming-out ball?"

"Yes, that is the plan."

Her sister nodded. "Even if Josh can only delay his announcement until after the ball, which I'm sure he can be persuasive enough to achieve, it will give you time to get the letter back and be done with this mess."

Alice pulled her to stand and pushed her toward a nearby settee. "You look as white as a ghost. I hope you're not fretting over this and are looking after yourself properly."

Elizabeth thought over her sister's words, all of which she'd not thought of herself. Maybe she was panicking more than she ought, and therefore not seeing as clearly as she should. "I will try better not to worry over things until they occur." She patted the cushion beside her, needing to change the subject if only to keep her sanity. "Come, sit, and tell me about Mama. Is she doing better?"

Alice filled her in on their mother's lifted spirits and what they planned to do while in London. Although balls were still out of the question, other than Riddledale's, of course, they would attend some private dinner parties and musicals with their closest friends.

Elizabeth welcomed the opportunity of distraction, but her mind churned with impatience for Josh to arrive so he could deal with this latest threat from Riddledale of which Henry could never know—all these lies and secrets, the evading of truth. Even if it was with the best of intentions, or little choice, she wondered if she should not just state the facts, lay her head upon the block, and let the ton do their worst with the executioner's ax.

---

*E*lizabeth's brother leaned over their father's mahogany desk and played idly with the blue felt blotter. Over the weeks since their father's death, she had to concede that Josh had matured, eased into the position of duke with grace and forthrightness. Their father would be proud.

"Do you have this letter from Lord Riddledale? I wish to read it."

Elizabeth shook her head, annoyed at herself again for throwing it into the fire in a fit of temper. "I was so angry I burned it. I'm so sorry, Josh, but what I recited to you is word-for-word what Lord Riddledale wrote."

Josh stood and strolled over to the liquor cupboard. Again she was reminded that the brother she knew had turned into a duke, a man. His shoulders seemed broader, and so they should be with the weight of the title he now carried. "Why did you not tell me his harassment of you was worsening?" He rubbed a hand over his jaw. "Now I'm glad Lord Muir bloodied his nose at Whites. The fop deserved a good walloping."

She nodded, agreeing wholeheartedly. "Yes, Henry is quite angry about the situation, but Josh, he does not know exactly what Father wrote in the letter. Should he find out about Samuel…"

Josh swallowed the contents of his drink before pouring another glass. "Which leaves Lord Muir innocent of any crime other than ruining you at Dunsleigh. Do not think for one moment I've forgiven him for that."

"Henry never received the letter, so he doesn't know I've borne a child. And you forget there were two consenting people by the lake that day, brother. I knew what I was doing, and you cannot wholly hold Henry to blame for what occurred."

"Hell, Elizabeth." Josh ran a hand through his hair, slumping back into his chair. "If this becomes public knowledge it'll ruin the family. It'll ruin your son."

She nodded, knowing only too well what was at stake. "I know that. Don't you think it's all that's occupied my mind for the last few weeks? Riddledale has been constant in his longing for me, his words have bordered on obscene, and yet all the while I know he knows about my ruin, my child. I don't want to be blackmailed into marriage." Elizabeth looked toward the windows and watched the bustling square beyond, the carriages, the people.

"Lord Muir knows more of your concerns than I. Why did you not tell me Riddledale has brought up Samuel's parentage?"

Elizabeth cringed at the hurt she heard in her brother's tone. "I should have, but the time never seemed right. Henry returned. Father passed away. Everything's been such a muddle. I panicked. I'm sorry."

"Elizabeth, that is the most absurd thing I've ever heard anyone say." He took a deep breath, his nose flaring with distaste. "We're family. I may be a duke, the head of this household, but you're my sister, married or no, you are and always will be a priority in my life, and what Riddledale is about is..." He paused. "Well, he ought to be called out, that's what. I'm surprised Muir didn't call him out at Whites. It seems he certainly deserved to be."

"Henry has told me a little about what happened that day."

"Muir beat him to a pulp, and rightfully so."

Elizabeth leaned back in her chair and bit her lip, wanting to laugh at the image of Riddledale being tackled in Whites. "Yes, I know."

"Words were seldom, fists were not." He steepled his fingers beneath his chin. "And now what to do with the marquis. Tell me, what is the latest with this plan you've concocted with Muir?"

Elizabeth stood and moved over to the window, watching the traffic travel around the square. She absently played with the velvet drapes while she told Josh of their idea to steal the letter back and therefore remove any notion of blackmail. "He intends to announce our betrothal in the papers next week. You must speak with him soon. If he does such a disastrous thing, well, I'm not sure what we'll do."

"I'm meeting Lord Riddledale tonight, in fact. I believe he thinks it's to arrange the marriage settlements."

"What is your plan?"

"To allow him to think that is the case. We'll let him believe you're thinking of his request, if only to give Lord Muir time to acquire the letter…as for your involvement in that plan, I forbid it."

She felt her mouth pop open. "You forbid it? I think you forget, Josh dear, that I'm a widow and quite capable of making my own decisions." Her brother stared at her, and she refused to give way on this.

"If you're caught with Lord Muir—"

"What of it? I'm not a debutante. I'm a widow, which no one could raise anything other than an eyebrow over. If I were caught on top of the desk, however…"

Her brother's eyes flared, and he raised his hand, halting her words. "Really, Elizabeth. Do be serious. If this story gets out about you and Henry, being caught in Riddledale's library will not look promising if we're trying to alleviate such a rumor and, just to spite us, Riddledale releases Father's missive."

Her brother had a point, but still, Henry needed her help and, if only to be a lookout for him that night, to ensure he was able to search uninterrupted, she would risk it. "I will be helping him. So if you can speak to Riddledale, hold off his ridiculous threat, we'll do our best to put an end to all this mess. Do you agree?" They stared at each other before her brother sighed, slumping back in his leather chair.

"Very well. Not that I like it, mind, but I agree to your plan."

"Excellent." Elizabeth sat back down, smiling. "One thing I wanted to mention was Lord Riddledale did seem to think on Henry's offer of money. Do you think his lordship being so set on me is due to lack of funds?"

"I've not heard he's in any financial difficulties, but I'll put my man of business on it and see what he can find out. And if I offer him money to go away there is always the chance he'll continue to bleed us of funds, and I refuse to be his bank. No matter what strife he may cause."

She nodded. "I agree. Please let me know as soon as you can how your meeting with him goes." And then she would seek out Henry and tell him. She fleetingly wondered where he was and what he was up to. What events he planned on attending over the next few weeks, all of at which she would not be present.

A knock on the door sounded, and their butler bade entry. Josh called him into the room.

"I'm sorry to bother you, Your Grace, but Louise our parlor maid was coming back from an errand and happened upon a missive two blocks from here. She picked it up to see who it was addressed to, hoping to find its rightful owner, and recognized Lord Muir's name and address."

"Pass it to me please, John." Elizabeth took the note, frowning. "This is the letter I sent Lord Muir. Why would it be on the ground?" Elizabeth could hear the butler shuffling behind her, unsure if his presence was needed. "John, can you please fetch my maid Tippy."

"Of course, Lady Newland."

Their old retainer backed out of the room, and she looked at Josh. "Surely Lord Riddledale is not still stealing our mail?"

"He wouldn't dare."

Elizabeth started at her brother's ire. "Do not for one moment think he's incapable of doing such a thing. He's the worst of men." No better than a lowbred whelp who stole and ruined people's lives.

"If the mail is still being circumvented through him, someone here is working for him."

A cold shiver ran down her spine. Her brother was angry and rightfully so, and so was she. With the turnover of staff in large estates like the ones they had, Elizabeth had just assumed that the person helping Lord Riddledale two years past had changed employment. But maybe she was wrong. Was the marquis still screening all their correspondence? "I thought it had stopped, but for this letter to be found so..." She chewed her bottom lip. Maybe it was an innocent mistake by a maid and she was too scared to own up to the error of losing her letter.

Another discreet knock sounded before Tippy, her maid, walked into the room, her gaze a little frightened. Elizabeth stood and went to her. "Tippy, I wanted to confirm that you placed the missive I gave you yesterday afternoon on the salver in the front hall."

"I did, my lady."

"Do you know who takes the letters from there to their

destinations?" His grace asked, smiling a little to put the servant at ease.

Her maid froze like a frightened mouse before a cat. "No, your grace, I do not."

Their butler cleared his throat. "If I may, your grace, I believe I know who took the note."

"Who?" Both Josh and her asked in unison. "An upper housemaid by the name of Kate."

Josh leveled the butler with a cold stare that Elizabeth had often seen on her father's face. Wow, he really was the duke.

"And this maid is not before me, why?"

The butler shifted on his feet, a light sheen of sweat forming on his brow. "She's gone, your grace. Packed up her room and left this morning, or so the kitchen staff said. I think it's safe to say whatever she was about was not in this family's interest."

Josh glowered but nodded. "Thank you for your assistance in this matter. You're both dismissed."

Elizabeth waited for the door to close before she spoke. "So it would seem Riddledale's still rifling with our business. It's almost too radical to believe."

"Yes," Josh said, his voice thrumming with anger. "And I will deal with his lordship in due course over this. I cannot believe a man would act in such an underhanded way. And all to procure a wife. It'll be a miracle if I keep my countenance at today's meeting."

"I'm sorry for all this trouble, truly, Josh. But we will best him. I promise you."

He chuckled, but it was without mirth, only revenge. "I hope so, sister. I do hope so."

CHAPTER 12

*D*inner at the Kinruths' home was a delightful diversion for an evening out. Her sister, Isolde, had come to know the family well when living at Avonmore in Scotland, since they were her closest neighbors for miles around.

Once seated, Elizabeth was pleasantly surprised to be beside Henry for the dinner. Footmen entered the room, all wearing the same dark maroon livery and severe blank stares as they went about the table with their occupation.

The first course of oysters was placed before them, and Elizabeth couldn't concentrate on the seafood, but only on the man seated to her right who seemed to take up all the available air in the room.

His presence, his undivided attention toward her, left her as breathless as if they'd swam a race across the pond at Dunsleigh as they had as children. He was such an attractive gentleman, his presence commanding her absolute notice, and over the years they'd been apart he'd grown into a handsome, confident man who left her a little discombobulated and not always as sure of herself as she'd like to be.

"This is a novel experience, Lord Muir. Not something I would have thought possible only a few weeks ago," Elizabeth whispered, leaning toward him.

His knowing chuckle rumbled through her and made her hands shake. She stole a sideward glance and devoured every hard line and muscle she could see. Her hold on the silver cutlery tightened as his smile drew her attention to his mouth. Lips that she'd kissed, wanted to kiss again...devour.

She swallowed and looked away.

"I'm glad we're no longer estranged." He sat back, placing his mouth closer to her ear. "Have I told ye how beautiful you look tonight, lass?" The hair beside her neck tickled with the air of his breath.

Elizabeth bit her bottom lip, praying she wouldn't blush. A devilish part of her reveled in the fact she was finally feeling something again, after years of feeling nothing at all. But a dinner party was hardly the place for flirtation, although she suspected Henry was well on the way to making a sport of this evening. "You had not, but thank you, that's very kind, my lord."

"Henry."

Elizabeth smiled and turned to fork the first oyster into her mouth, conscious of Henry watching her every move. She took great pains of making the most of pulling the oyster slowly from her fork, closing her eyes, and humming her enjoyment in the slimy little thing's texture.

He shifted in his seat, pulling at his cravat a little. "Ye seem to be enjoying ye meal." He raised his brows, and she grinned.

"I am. Immensely so."

"Are ye always so vocal when ye eat? I don't remember ye being so." Henry finished off his last oyster, the laughter in his gaze making her smile.

"I'm only vocal about things that I'm passionate about." *Now who was flirting?*

He shook his head, his attention snapping to her lips. "And you're passionate about oysters. You used to hate them."

Elizabeth placed a third in her mouth, the salty, slimy feel of it against her tongue making her stomach roll, but teasing him was so much more fun, and she could stomach some oysters to gain his undivided attention. "There are a lot of things you don't know about me anymore, Henry. I don't mind seafood now, although you're right, I used to hate oysters."

"Liar." He laughed, waving over a footman to gain his attention. "Please bring Lady Newland the second course. The oysters are not to her taste."

Elizabeth watched as her plate was swiftly removed and soon replaced with a delicious lobster soup. "Thank you. You've saved me from an uncomfortable night of stomach pain."

"Ye're very welcome, lass."

At the sound of his deep, rumbling voice, she met his hungry gaze and realized it had nothing to do with the food before them. The hum of conversation dissipated around them, and she fought to gain her breath. Henry's suit, cravat, and highly starched shirt gave him the airs of a gentleman, and yet his hair, longer than it ought to be, the prickling of stubble across his jaw, the solid, muscular shoulders that belonged more in Gentleman Jackson's fighting saloon than at a dinner table, went against the sublime effect of his attire.

His gaze snapped to her lips, the muscle in his jaw flexing. Images of them together at the lake, their last day together, assailed her mind so that she could almost feel the cool grass beneath her dress, the raspy breath of Henry as he said her name over and over as they... The clearing of her brother's throat pulled her back to reality.

Josh threw her a scathing look across the table before he turned back to his meal, jabbing at his soup like he held a fork instead of a spoon. She felt the loss of Henry's attention like a stab to the heart when he returned to his meal.

"I purchased a new curricle last week. May I call on ye tomorrow and take ye out in it?"

Elizabeth masked her delight at his invitation. She told herself again, such things were what friends did together, but it was a falsehood. She reveled in the fact Henry wanted to spend time with her. Wanted her all to himself just as she wanted to have him all to herself as well.

"I would like that very much." Their gazes held, and she lost herself in his blue eyes as dark as a swirling sea. "Thank you for asking me."

"My pleasure."

The words my pleasure rolled off his Scottish tongue and she shivered, her body aching in places she'd never thought would ache again. Heat bloomed beneath her gown and she took a sip of wine to hide her embarrassment. Her brother watched them, his eyes narrowed and darting from Henry to herself and back to his food.

Elizabeth knew what he was thinking, and he had every right to, for she was thinking the same. She'd been married, after all, and the marriage bed, although nothing like the pleasure she felt at Henry's touch, was not abhorrent with Newland. Quite the opposite, in fact, and there was some-thing about sleeping with a man that Elizabeth had the niggling feeling there was a lot more to enjoy, to sample, and experience.

She grinned down at the third course of braised turkey and seasonal vegetables. They were toying with each other, something they hadn't done in eons. For the first time in an age, Elizabeth felt happy, alive again in the presence of a man, and it was an intoxicating, delightful sensation that one could get used to.

———

*T*he female party gathered a short time later in the drawing room for card games and music. Elizabeth sat with her mother and waited for Josh to join them. Her eyes stole to the mantle for the millionth time. They would leave soon and still the gentlemen hadn't joined them.

Having not had the time to speak to Josh about his meeting with Riddledale, Elizabeth was impatient to find out how it went. As for the dinner tonight, Riddledale hadn't sought her out or been inappropriate, which gave her an inkling of hope that her brother had succeeded with his request, and Riddledale was holding off his threats.

Elizabeth stood and walked to the terrace doors, seeing that the bright moon sprinkled the garden with dappled silver light. The peaceful tranquility of the grounds was the complete opposite to her nerves, which would not settle until she knew Josh had been successful with their plan. Looking about the room, she noted no one taking any heed of her whereabouts and slipped out onto the terrace.

The cool night air made her shiver in her silk gown and the smell of coal smoke masked the sweet-smelling flowers that lined the garden beds. She walked along the flagstones toward the darkened part of the terrace and leaned over the railing, looking up at the moon.

"Are ye well, lass?"

Elizabeth stifled her scream and clasped her chest. "Henry." She sighed, her heart hammering hard against her ribs. "You must stop startling me. I'll scream one day." She chuckled a little to break the tension thrumming between them. "What are you doing skulking about outdoors?"

"I know when ye're lying, and ye are now." He joined her at the balustrade and leaned against the stone. "Something is on ye mind. Tell me what it is."

Only you. Us. The dreadful secret I still keep from you... They were so close she could feel the warmth of his body down her side, and she shuffled a little closer, wanting his heat to enfold her, to warm her. "It's nothing really. Josh has some news that I'm hoping is good. I thought to have known before arriving tonight, but I've yet to talk to him."

Henry frowned, contemplating her words before he said, "Does it have anything to do with Lord Riddledale?"

She looked up at him sharply, wondering if he'd noted anything during after-dinner drinks. "What made you ask that?"

He raised an eyebrow, looking at her in disbelief. "Our lives at present seem entwined with the fellow, so one does naturally assume. Also, ye brother and his lordship were ill at ease with each other just now. It made me suspect somethin' had occurred between them and not to Riddledale's liking."

Elizabeth turned to face him fully, hope blooming in her heart. "Did he?" She nibbled her bottom lip, fighting a smile. "Did they speak at all? Or were they avoiding each other?"

"They spoke, but greetings only." Henry let out a rueful laugh. "I almost felt sorry for Riddledale. Ye brother seemed less pleased with him than he was with me, and that's something I dinna think anyone else could accomplish."

Elizabeth laughed, shaking her head at Henry's attempt at a joke. She ran her hand down his lapel without thinking. "Nothing will ever persuade me to feel sorry for Riddledale, but I'm glad to think that you and Josh may be friends again one day."

*F*riends? Henry didn't think the Duke of Penworth would feel friendly toward him if he knew what thoughts Henry was currently occupied with.

His delectable lass seemed to realize her hand was scorching its way down his chest, and she pulled it away quickly. She went to leave, and he clasped her arm, pulling her up against him. The action made her gasp, and he wanted to hear such sounds, and more, wanted to feel her heat, her heart, everything against his.

The softness of her arm marked him like a burn, and he reveled in her touch before propriety made him rethink his seduction of her. It was probably a wise decision for Elizabeth, as he'd already flirted enough with her throughout dinner to set tongues wagging. Touching her on a darkened terrace was risking their reputations and his self-restraint just a little too far. Being a gentleman would only keep her safe to a point…

"What was ye brother going to disclose to ye tonight?" He wondered at her continued silence, but stopped himself from pushing her on the subject. His mind raced with the possibilities. Had Lord Riddledale threatened Elizabeth further? Had the fiend tried his wiles on her? His fists clenched at his sides; imagining such horrors was beyond endurance.

She sighed, her face clouding with frustration. "Josh had a meeting today with Lord Riddledale. His lordship had threatened to announce our betrothal in the papers, which I have not agreed to. He's gone mad, I'm sure." She paused. "Josh was going to try to make him see sense that in pushing me on the subject of marriage through such threats would not secure my affections in the matter. We need the letter in our hands before Riddledale loses all patience and acts on his threats."

Henry's teeth clenched at the thought of Elizabeth

married to the bastard just to escape scandal marring the family. At the thought of someone else laying claim to her, touching her in the way a husband ought to touch his wife, with reverence, care, and pleasure, was enough to pull a red haze over his eyes.

"It would seem by Riddledale's less than pleased visage that his grace got his way with his request. And I promise ye, lass, we'll take back the letter that is rightfully ours, and we'll be free to go on with our lives in whatever way we wish."

She looked back over the garden, giving him a view of her perfect profile. Sweet nose, full lips, eyelashes that were long enough to see blinking in the moonlight.

"I'm hopeful this is what occurred." Her usually smooth brow marred for a moment. "Josh is displeased and knows everything about our plans and what Riddledale has been about these last weeks."

"Riddledale will not be the victor in this war, Elizabeth." She met his gaze, her teeth working her bottom lip. His attention snapped to the delectable sight even knowing he didn't need to be distracted by her person right at this moment. "Sometimes I want to forget London, the ton, and even my family and return to Newland Estate and live in peace, where no one will bother me or care what I do."

Henry reeled at her words. Running his hand over his jaw, he wondered what could possibly pull her to an estate that was no longer hers. Yes, she'd married Newland, but that was as far as the relationship went. "Why would you return to Newland Estate? Surely whoever was next in line to take up the viscountcy has done so."

She paled, her gaze snapping to his. "He's learning all that he can at this time, but it's no small undertaking, and the heir has a lot to learn, as he is very young."

"And so ye will be free to marry whomever ye choose? To live as ye please without any threats from Riddledale?"

"Yes. Well," she paused, "I certainly hope that's the case." She sighed, turning back to face him fully. "It's complicated, Henry, and I never thought to marry again, as I said before."

A twinge of regret pierced him, knowing that was true, but it wasn't something he'd allow. Elizabeth was too young to give up on life, to not love as he knew she was capable of loving. "No more talk of Riddledale for tonight. He's taken up enough of our time for one evenin'."

She seemed to shake herself from her thoughts, smiling. "I agree." They both looked up at the night sky, the bright moon high above them. "Do you remember when we would lie out under the stars and try to count them all, or see what animal shapes they could be made into?"

"I always came up with the best animals; all you could ever see were cats."

She laughed at his teasing. How he loved the sound, and he knew, down to his very core, it was something he'd always strive to hear.

"I'll have you know they were always different breeds of cats, not one and the same."

"Is there really a difference?" Her eyes sparked up at him with amusement, and he chuckled. "I have missed our friendship, Elizabeth."

"And I you, even if I was terribly mad at you to begin with. But I know now it wasn't your fault." A sad smile tilted her lips. "Friends?"

He nodded, stepping closer than he ought. "Always, lass."

Elizabeth met his gaze as the lightest touch of her fingers laced around the lapels of his jacket, seemingly flattening them further against his chest. Desire, hot and demanding, coursed through him. Damn, he wanted her, wanted to taste her sweet lips that had haunted him for all of the time he was away. And damn it, he wanted her to feel, to see without words, that he wanted a future with her that involved more than friendship. "Is my attire not to ye liking, my lady?"

The slight shrug of her shoulder brought his gaze to appreciate her delicate bones, the gown of lace and silk that shone silver in the moonlight. "I find your attire quite pleasing, but I've yet to see you in a kilt."

He laughed, having not expected such a reply. "Furthermore," she continued, "your brogue has lessened since you've traveled abroad. You sound more English than ever these days."

"Would it please ye if I slipped back into me Scottish accent, lass?"

"Very much so."

Henry had to lean in to hear the whispered words, so softly were they spoken. She looked up at him, and the longing he read there eroded what little restraint he had left. Unable to deny himself, he took her lips in a searing kiss—a kiss that was neither sweet nor beckoning, but hot, demanding, and full of overwhelming need.

He groaned as her tongue thrust against his, her hands sliding up the lapels of his coat to clasp about his neck, pulling him hard against her, their closeness never close enough. Heat drove between his legs, and once again they were back at the lake, young and carefree, devouring the other with hands, grinding bodies that created the most exquisite torture, a wet, conflagration of touch and taste that was never enough.

He lifted her to the terrace railing and caught her gasp with his mouth. Her feminine moan, music to his ears, had him harden. The lacy silk gown was cool beneath his fingers as he pushed her legs apart, wanting to be closer still. Elizabeth lifted her leg a little, wrapping her foot about his knee and urging him forward.

A warning voice at the back of his skull thrummed that

what they were doing was wrong, scandalous, against the rules. From their past actions, he should know better, damn it; so should Elizabeth, but as her lips took his, demanded more, her hands clutched tight against his neck, he knew he'd lose the battle within himself to keep away, to step back and beg forgiveness for such an action.

Perhaps he really was a savage.

She broke the kiss, staring up at him with a look of awe that he knew his own mimicked. "We're not supposed to be doing this. Friends do not go on in this manner," she said, grinning a little.

The terrace doors rattled, and he stepped back, quickly helping her off the railing. Not that Henry would care if they were caught; he would marry her tomorrow if only she would say yes, but he would not force her hand. He wanted Elizabeth to come to him of her own free will, no coercion or due to society's demands.

"You should return indoors," he said, letting go of her hand. "I'll go around the front and enter from the foyer doors. We don't need another scandal dogging us." Even in the dim light Henry could make out the rose-colored blush blooming on her cheeks. Hell, she was beautiful, a perfect English rose.

She nodded. "Yes, you're right." She looked as if she would leave, but instead she took a step toward him, reaching up to fix his cravat. Once more his body ached to touch her, to give himself one more memorable imprint on his mind of what she was like within his arms.

"Good night, Henry."

He bowed, watching as she walked away. "Good night, my bonny lass."

Elizabeth turned at the terrace doors and smiled before going indoors and taking his heart with her, just as she always had.

CHAPTER 13

The following morning, Elizabeth halted at the library door when she caught the sound of raised voices inside. She hesitated, then, curiosity getting the better of her, stopped to listen. Their butler came from the breakfast room and bowed when he noticed her.

"Who's in there with his grace?" she asked.

The old retainer cleared his throat. "The Earl of Muir, my lady."

As more arguing ensued, Elizabeth ignored the butler's disapproving eye and put her ear to the door. They were arguing—that was obvious—but over what, she couldn't discern. With Henry being here, it obviously involved her and perhaps the despicable Lord Riddledale. Her hand hovered above the handle before thinking better of the sudden intrusion, and she knocked.

A curt, "Come in" was all the reply she received before entering.

"Elizabeth, leave."

Elizabeth shut her mouth with a snap at her brother's curt command. She ignored him and closed the door. "What is going on in here?" she asked, watching as her brother glowered at Lord Muir. "Your arguing can be heard in the foyer." She raised an inquiring brow and waited for a reply.

"Nothing that concerns you," Josh said, a muscle ticking at his temple. "Now if you don't mind," he said, gesturing toward the door.

Elizabeth shook her head and sat beside Henry, and his closeness, the sight of him again, left her breathless. "I've been meaning to catch up with you in any case, as I wanted to know how you got on with Lord Riddledale yesterday. We never had a chance to speak last eve."

Henry smiled at her a little, and her stomach flipped. Keeping her gaze locked on Henry, she asked, "I hope you enjoyed your evening, Lord Muir?"

He grinned wickedly, his eyes holding unknown pleasures still to be had. "Very much so, Lady Newland."

"I'm glad." She turned back to her brother. "Well, what did Lord Riddledale say, Josh?"

"It was exactly what I was asking," Henry stated, crossing his legs and making himself comfortable in the chair.

"I'm under no obligation to discuss family business with you." Josh jabbed a finger in Henry's direction.

She sighed and clasped Henry's arm lest he launch himself across her brother's desk and have at him. "I entrusted Henry with my worries over Lord Riddledale, as you well know. We've spoken of this, Josh. There is no need for such rudeness. If you have anything to inform me of from your meeting with his lordship, then please tell us, and stop this nonsense." She made a point at looking at them both. "I expect you to get along, no more bickering between us. We're all adults, and we all know the truth of the situation."

With a barely leashed growl, Josh picked up his quill and twisted it between his fingers. "Riddledale has agreed to hold off announcing your farcical betrothal until after his sister's coming-out ball, even though I did point out to him you've not yet agreed to such an understanding."

"Nor will you ever," Henry quipped.

Her brother nodded. "Our conversation was amicable until I told him I couldn't give my blessing to such a union if you were not agreeable to it."

"How did he react?" Elizabeth wasn't sure if she really cared. Riddledale could go hang.

Her brother thought over his reply for a moment before he said, "He was adamant there would be a wedding, or scandal would follow you about for the rest of your life. He would declare all that happened between you and Henry, and he would have the letter Father wrote Henry printed in The Times."

Coldness, unlike any she'd ever experienced, slid down her spine. Should the ton find out about Samuel, should Henry find out, her son would be ruined, no matter that Lord Newland loved him from the moment he laid eyes on the boy. "We cannot allow that."

"I did find out something that was of interest and could give us hope. I wanted to see the letter. If he's so adamant in using it against us, I wanted to know if it really existed still. Riddledale pulled the missive from his desk and showed me, like he was showing off his best pointer hunter."

"So you had this meeting at his London home?" Henry asked, meeting her gaze quickly.

"I did. In the library," her brother said, looking confidently sure of himself.

Hope blossomed in Elizabeth's chest. And if that is where Riddledale kept the missive at all times, their chance of success had doubled, no tripled. They already had the layout of Riddledale's home thanks to Henry's friend, and now they knew for certain the letter was in London. "This is good news."

"The ball is to take place in two weeks. It's to coincide with the ending of the season." Josh ran a hand through his hair, making it stand on end. "I will help keep Riddledale from his library during your search. The more we can do to thwart him, the better all our lives will be."

"Thank you so very much, Josh." She stood, walking around the desk to lean down and give her brother a kiss and quick hug. His cheeks turned crimson, and she smiled at his apparent embarrassment.

"Yes, well," he said, patting her arm still clasped about his neck. "One does what is required of one in these situations." She pulled back a little, tears blurring her vision. "So it wasn't because you love your sister?"

He grinned, shaking his head. "No, never that." He laughed, the sound more carefree than she'd heard in an age.

Henry cleared his throat. "Thank you, your grace, for all ye've done. I'm relieved that our course is set and looking to be a success."

Elizabeth caught Henry's gaze as he stood to leave. She walked over to him, and he caught her hand, slipping a small note into her palm before bowing.

"Thank you for all your help, Lord Muir. We're appreciative of it."

He nodded. "Always a pleasure, lass." His tone brooked no argument, and her heart stuttered. How easy it would be to fall for the handsome rogue, to wake up and fall asleep every day for the remainder of her life within his arms.

Her brother muttered under his breath something about killing an earl, and she stepped back, breaking the spell between them. "Well, if we're to go on from here with normalcy, I had better take myself upstairs. Victoria wanted me to accompany her to an afternoon tea."

"Do you wish for me to accompany you?" Josh asked. "I had planned on going to the club, but if you think

Riddledale will attend, I'm more than willing to partake in tea and cake.

Elizabeth shook her head at her brother's offer. "There is no need. I've yet to see him at such an event. I'm certain Victoria and I will be well enough."

Walking to the door she cast Henry a speculative gaze as the footman helped him into his jacket, the note burning a hole against her palm. He winked and left without saying another word, and her heart no longer felt her own. How she longed to live the life she'd always dreamed of with Henry, to love and be loved unconditionally.

But what of her child?

Henry still had no idea that she'd even borne a son, nevertheless that it was his. Samuel was already uncannily familiar in looks to Henry and it would not be long before he suspected that the child was never Lord Newland's. Not to mention, Elizabeth couldn't keep such a secret from the man she loved. It would be an impossible cruelty that would wear her down and triumph.

And then their marriage would be over before it even began, and Elizabeth had no doubt Henry would hate her. Hate her more than she already hated herself.

———

A short time later, Elizabeth, along with Victoria, sat in the family carriage, making their way to Belgravia to an afternoon tea. The carriage lurched sideways as it turned Hyde Park Corner, and Elizabeth laughed as both their reticules slid off the seats and landed with a thud on the floor.

"Do not trouble yourself, I shall get them," Elizabeth said, bending down to pick up their purses and gasping as a loud boom rang out within the streets. The piercing sound of a woman's scream sounded outside, and both she and Victoria looked out the window to see people scattering inside shops and away from the road.

"Was that a gunshot?" Elizabeth clutched at the seat as their driver picked up speed, turning through the streets and seemingly heading back toward the direction they'd come.

"I think you may be right." Victoria frowned, her eyes wide with worry. "Why would anyone be firing a gun in central London?"

Elizabeth shrugged, having no idea herself why such a random, bizarre thing had happened. No sooner had their outing started, was it over? Their driver pulled up before the family townhouse and sent the tiger up to the front door to rap the knocker. Elizabeth helped Victoria alight from the carriage just as Josh rushed from the house, his face uncommonly pale.

"Are you well?" he asked, looking over them like his prized mares. "Your tiger informed me you were shot at." Elizabeth stole a quick glance at Victoria. "We heard a gunshot, but that was all. No one was shooting at us." Elizabeth turned to the driver. "Tell my brother he's misinformed."

Josh pushed past them, striding to where their driver stood looking at the carriage. "Then why, pray, is there a bullet hole in the carriage, if no one was shooting at you?"

Her heart missed a beat as she looked at the perfectly round hole just above her window. Had the bullet only been a little lower and had she not leaned over to pick up the reticules… "We didn't know…" She swallowed, feeling lightheaded at the thought. "I'm sure it was an error. Why would anyone shoot at us? We haven't done anything."

"Why indeed." Josh ushered them indoors, striding toward the library where it seemed he expected them to follow. They did, both of them sitting before the hearth while they watched their brother pour a large glass of whisky, drink it, and pour two more, handing them each one.

"Do not overthink this, Josh. I'm sure it was an accident. Some adolescent being silly with a new toy."

Worry etched her brother's face, making him seem older than his years. "I cannot help but overthink the situation." He ran a hand over his jaw. "Surely for all of Riddledale's pressure he would not threaten a woman's life with such a cowardly act. I cannot believe this of a marquis. Someone must have fired off a gun, the bullet going astray, just as you said."

"You suspect Riddledale?" Elizabeth hadn't even thought of the gentleman, but then she remembered the burly man whom she'd caught watching her at Hatchards, and the idea didn't seem so dismissive. "I do believe at times Riddledale has had me watched. When at the bookstore last, I caught a burly man in tradesman attire watching me. When I noted his interest, he fled."

Josh looked almost wild, and she cringed at having forgotten to tell him.

"Why did you not inform me of this? Damn it, Elizabeth, is there anything else that I do not know?"

She shook her head. "No, nothing, and I've not seen him again, and so… I should've told you, I'm sorry." Elizabeth bit her lip, casting a look at Victoria who didn't look well at all. "You don't believe because we're fighting him on his threats that he wishes me harm?"

Victoria gasped. "Oh no. Surely not."

"Perhaps you ought to lie down, V. You do appear a little shaken by the events." Elizabeth took her hand, and touching snow would've been warmer.

"I do feel a little faint," Victoria said, her voice holding a thread of fear.

"I will have a tisane sent up to you," Josh said, ushering her to the door.

Once Victoria had left, Josh sat across from her, the muscle in his temple flexing with every second of silence. He was rattled, and that was one emotion her brother rarely was.

"I don't understand why Riddledale would go against your agreement, and so soon after your discussion. It makes no sense. It mustn't be him."

Josh scoffed. "I think your assumptions were correct, even though to admit such pains me to say so. He has a maggot in his head." He cringed. "It's too coincidental not to be his lordship. He's making it plainly clear if he cannot have you, no one shall." Her brother met her gaze and grimaced. "But we'll not be able to prove it, of course. It'll be our allegation against his word yet again."

"Have you ever heard of a carriage in central London being shot at before? I know I certainly have not."

Her brother shook his head, frowning. "Of course not. Maybe in the bowels of London such an occurrence would happen, but not in Mayfair."

The front door slammed, and raised voices sounded in the foyer before the library door flew open. Elizabeth turned to see Henry, his gaze flicking over the room, before landing on her, his shoulders slumping in relief.

"How dare you intrude at such a time? You may leave." Josh's voice brooked no argument.

Henry strode toward her, his smile melting away her fears over what could've been. "I came as soon as I heard what happened. It's already all over London that ye carriage was shot at. I had to see…"

His words trailed off, but Elizabeth didn't need to hear them to know what he was going to say. *I had to come see that you were not injured.* "Our carriage is indeed sporting a bullet wound, but I am not, and neither is Victoria, who was with me. We're fine."

"If you do not leave and now, Lord Muir, I may feel inclined to place a bullet wound in you."

Elizabeth met her brother's eye, her glare forcing her sibling to stand back. "Brother, please," she said, turning back to Henry. "Thank you for coming and checking on us."

"Always, lass."

Josh growled, pouring himself another whisky, mumbling something under his breath Elizabeth couldn't hear.

A sharp knock sounded before their butler entered. "Your grace, Mr. Johns, the driver of the carriage, would like a word with you. Should I summon him to the house, or would you prefer to see him at the mews?"

Josh downed his drink and glared at Henry. Henry, oblivious to her brother's annoyance, or not bothering with it, kept his eyes on her, making her hope Josh went out to the mews so she could have Henry alone to herself.

"I will go to the mews." He picked up his discarded jacket from the back of his chair and pulled it on. "I want to have a look at the carriage. The door is to stay open. I will return shortly," Josh said, throwing Henry a pointed stare.

Elizabeth grinned and, once alone, turned to face Henry. "Thank you for coming, but it wasn't necessary. As you can see I'm fine." She gestured to herself.

"I was in Whites; they've reinstated my membership." He grinned. "Laird McCalter informed me of ye predicament." Henry swallowed, a small frown marring his otherwise perfect brow. "May I speak candidly, Elizabeth?"

"Of course."

Henry seemed to gather himself before he said, "I've never known such fear as I had when I heard what happened to ye. It consumed me, and I had to see ye. To make sure you were well."

"I'm more than well, but thank you for caring so much. That's very sweet."

His gaze smoldered and the longing near overrode all decorum in her. "I've always cared, lass."

Forgetting or no longer caring where they were, the open library door, the servants, everything, Elizabeth watched as Henry dipped his head and captured her lips with his, a light feathery touch that made her toes curl in her slippers. His hands settled on her hips, and she wrapped her arms about his neck, closing the small space that separated them.

He broke the kiss, his gaze ferocious with serious intent. "I cannot live my life without ye."

She shuffled even closer. Such actions were wicked and not at all responsible, but she no longer cared. "Then don't." His eyes widened, and she didn't give him a chance to respond before she kissed him again, this time with just as much need and hunger as he. Henry required no urging and deepened the embrace. Elizabeth gasped as a multitude of emotions coiled through her. With relentlessness he urged her on, teased and taunted her with the slide of his tongue, a nip against her lip. It was beyond wonderful, and only reinforced the thought that making love to a man could be more than she'd ever known.

Leaning into him, her nipples pebbled against her soft cotton shift and, with each movement, heat pooled at her core. Henry's clasp against her hip slid toward her breast, and the slow glide of his touch maddened her. Too slow, too little when she wanted everything now, to be as they once were, two souls that created a whole.

Her breath hitched as the slightest touch skimmed her breast and, needing more, Elizabeth tried to move, to make his hand clasp hers as she wanted, needed. "Henry," she sighed, biting her bottom lip and loving the fact his attention was fixed on her mouth.

"I've missed you and me," he said, taking possession of her mouth once more. Elizabeth whimpered through the onslaught of emotions he'd always been able to bring forth. How she'd missed him and the feelings he'd always evoked. He brought her to life with a touch, a look, a smile... Somehow he'd always managed to intoxicate her soul with his love.

"Henry..." Elizabeth met his gaze. "Don't stop."

───────

*H*enry pulled back and watched as Elizabeth's emerald green eyes darkened and swirled with longing. For months he'd wanted to see such a look in her eyes, and it was an elixir to his soul to finally have it aimed at him.

"We're in the parlor, lass," he said, playing with the buttons along the back of her gown, wishing he could pry each one open, slide the garment off her, and ravish her, here and now.

She chuckled, playing with his cravat. "I'm fully aware of where we are."

Henry gathered his wits, resting his forehead lightly against hers. Elizabeth's words were logical but not heartfelt. Should he wish it—and he did, very much so—he'd only have to lay her down on the settee, lift up her silk skirts, and seduce her a second time. Make love to her a second time.

His heart beat frantically in his chest. Never had he wanted a woman as much as he wanted Elizabeth right at this moment. With willpower he'd not thought he possessed, Henry set her back and placed some distance between them. "I promise ye we'll discuss you and me in more detail. But first," he said, a serious edge to his words. "Did ye read my note?"

She nodded. "I did, and I will meet you there tonight."

His finger stroked her bottom lip before he let his hand drop to his side. "Good, now, tell me everything you can remember from earlier today. Anything you think may help us in finding out who did this to you and Lady Victoria."

Elizabeth nodded; her brow furrowed as she recounted the tale in full, even including the burly man she'd noted. They spoke for some time, her memory becoming more vivid with each line of questioning. It was only when she wilted a little, tiredness taking its toll, did Henry stop.

"It will be difficult to charge Riddledale with such a crime, and I'm loathsome to think a man would stoop to such a level all because he could not get what he wants." He paused. "You look in need of more tea and rest. I will wait here until your brother returns. I wish to discuss this further, in any case, and get his thoughts on the matter."

Elizabeth nodded. "I think I shall take your advice and have a little lie-down. It's been quite an eventful day."

The butler knocked on the door. "Lord Muir, his grace wishes to see you in the library if you please."

"Of course. I will be there forthwith."

Henry turned back to Elizabeth and his mind was torn at the delectable sight she made. Her lips, swollen and well kissed, made him ache to do it again, made him want to forget someone was trying to threaten her and keep them apart. But then to ensure the future he envisioned, he must stop Riddledale and his maddening schemes. "I will see ye tonight then?"

"You will," she said, straightening her gown. "I look forward to it."

Henry ran a hand through his hair as he watched Elizabeth walk from the room. He soon followed and made his way toward the library. The door was ajar and, knocking once, he entered, noting a man he'd never seen before sitting before the duke's desk.

His grace looked displeased, but Henry wasn't sure if it was due to his presence or what had happened earlier. Probably a combination of the two. "Lord Muir, this is Mr. Gribbles. He's the Bow Street runner I've hired to look into the incident today."

Henry shook the wiry-framed man's hand, then sat. His grace rattled off the day's events, as the runner noted the information down on his small piece of parchment.

He listened to the numerous gifts Elizabeth had received over the past months, the sly comments and outings, the threats Lord Riddledale had bestowed. Henry shuddered at how close Elizabeth had come to death. That right at this moment, had that bullet strayed a little lower on the vehicle, the life he wished for, the future he'd so carefully planned with Elizabeth, would be nothing but a lost dream.

Anger coursed through him at the thought of losing her, of her being the victim of some fool's obsession and jealousy. He'd be damned if some pompous English bastard like Lord Riddledale would take her away from him, ruin his life and one that, deep down, he knew Elizabeth wished for as well.

"The gentleman you mention, if indeed the culprit, may try some other nefarious way in which to gain her hand," the runner said, tapping his pencil against his notebook.

Henry pulled himself from his thoughts. "And what do you intend to do about it?"

The runner took a deep breath, his lips pursing with the action. "He seems, to me, to be a coward by nature, if his actions over the last months are anything to go by. It first involved benign courtship. Flowers and love notes. His ability to gain her heart has failed, and so he has turned more devious by using threats and demands toward the lady involved. And now we see he has changed his tack once more to remove the young woman altogether, so no one can ever have her," the runner said, pausing.

"None of Lord Riddledale's plans have worked to secure Lady Newland to be his wife. To me, the marquis is not of sound mind and may try another way of seeking his revenge against your sister, your grace. I will place an associate of mine to keep watch on Lord Riddledale and his daily routine. I do believe the henchman your sister spied is who's carrying out these latest attacks."

Henry nodded in agreement, the man's summary of Lord Riddledale's character ringing only too true and what they had come to surmise as well. Riddledale had always been a jealous fop and a coward to boot. From the first, Henry had never liked the marquis, had not liked his slyness, which was as slippery as an eel; his mannerisms and temperament ran as hot and cold as an English summer. He would have his revenge if it were the last thing he did on this earth. How dare the bastard have a lady's carriage shot at? Henry didn't believe for a moment it was anyone else but Riddledale who'd orchestrated the attack.

"This will, of course, come at a cost..."

The duke sat back in his chair and raised his brow. "Hire anyone and as many as you need for the task. I'll not have my sister or family threatened in such a way again. Money is no concern."

The runner stood and bent into a deep yet awkward bow. "Thank you, your grace." The runner strode out the door, closing it behind him with a formidable click.

Henry stood and walked over to the desk. He leaned over the inlaid mahogany and met the duke's disdainful glare. "I wish for Elizabeth to be my wife. And today, right here and now, I'm formally asking ye for her hand. I care not how ye answer, but she will marry me and only me."

The duke glared, standing and placing them at equal

height. "What makes you so sure Elizabeth will even have you? You may be what some would deem friends, but I've heard whispers of your close association with Miss Andrews. And I do not care to see my sister hurt a second time, Lord Muir. She deserves much better than you."

Henry's jaw clenched. "I suppose ye deem her more suitable for ye pretty English friend, Lord Dean. She'll not marry him or anyone ye believe fit. She's mine, has always been mine."

"Thomas!" the duke called out, ignoring his words. Henry turned as the old retainer walked into the room a moment later. Henry eyed him with humor. If the duke thought the old codger was strong enough to throw him out on his ass, he would soon find out otherwise.

Henry chuckled. "I'll be back tomorrow to call on Elizabeth. And I will give ye until then to come to terms with my proposal. I wish your sister to be my wife, and should she agree, she will be by season's end. Good day to ye, your grace."

The duke looked past him, and Henry strove not to react to the cold, aristocratic bastard. He reminded himself the duke loved his sisters, would protect them and see them happy over anything else. And he would eventually come to accept Elizabeth's happiness as his wife.

"Please show Lord Muir to the door, Thomas. He is leaving."

Henry smiled, knowing the gesture was more like a snarl. "Your grace." He left without causing a scene and let out a frustrated breath when he stepped onto the footpath. He glanced toward the second floor windows where Elizabeth hopefully slept and then headed back to Whites to collect his horse. In his haste to make the Worthingham's London home, he'd left his mount behind.

His hastened strides ate the short distance to the gentleman's club and it wasn't long before the bow window in St. James came into view. Thoughts of how to keep Elizabeth safe tumbled about in his mind. The unhinged marquis would not get away with such a folly. He would pay for his callous acts. And he'd also place his own man on the case, to ensure the runner did carry out all he'd promised the duke, and to keep Lord Riddledale under careful scrutiny.

Henry was so close to winning Elizabeth's heart once more, he wouldn't lose her to anything or anyone. Their future would be a happy one. Nothing else was an option.

CHAPTER 14

*T*he sound of the carriage wheels on the gravel road went some way in lulling Elizabeth's nerves, before they rocked to a halt before Theatre Royal on Drury Lane, and her calm demeanor vanished. Elizabeth sat patiently while her family—except Isolde, who had decided not to attend— alighted from the carriage and awaited her on the cobbled footpath. The front of the theater was ablaze with light, the sound of voices spilling out onto the sidewalk. The street sconces, with their smoky hue, gave the night an air of mystery and clandestine pleasures.

It had been so long since they'd been out in the capital. Their father had been a jovial man who'd not wanted his children to go into full mourning, and even though they missed him every day, they would honor his wishes and continue on as best they could.

They made their way through the front entrance of the building, past the tall circular pillars and into the buzzing throng of the saloon. Elizabeth nodded to friends she hadn't seen in some weeks as they made their way to the ducal booth on the second floor, ushered to their seats by a footman dressed in red and black livery.

Victoria, Alice, and their mama sat in the front row, Josh and herself behind them.

Elizabeth pulled a spyglass out of her reticule and looked about. She spotted an actor peeking from behind the stage curtains as the orchestra made final adjustments to their instruments. Her mama turned and commented on the abundance of theatergoers and Elizabeth agreed, there were certainly many here tonight. Why, the gallery before them was almost full to capacity, conversations and laughter deafening and making speech challenging as they waited for the play to begin.

Elizabeth looked along the boxed seats and wondered if Henry had arrived. She spied Lord Dean and smiled in welcome when he bowed from across the multitude of boxes separating them. She supposed he was nice, a well-known, likeable, and trusted friend to her brother, and handsome, too, but he was not for her. Maybe Alice or Victoria could perhaps gain his heart.

Her attention moved past Lord Dean's box, and her excitement vanished in an instant. She stifled an unladylike retort at seeing Henry seated beside Miss Andrews, the lady's brother notably absent. Elizabeth focused her spyglass and watched them as best she could without being obvious, which she hated to admit, was probably quite obvious. They conversed, their enjoyment in each other's company apparent to any who noted their presence.

Nausea pooled in her stomach when Miss Andrews laid her hand on Henry's arm in a beguiling way, her eyes merry and full of admiration. She looked away when Henry sat back, looking about the theater himself. She masked her features to indifference and watched the stage, refusing to look back in Henry's direction. She bit her lip to stop the sting of tears. Why had he come with Miss Andrews when he'd wanted to meet her here?

Thankfully, the play began, and darkness covered the overwhelming emotions seeing him closeted with the miss was doing to her composure. What was Henry about? Of course, they were his cousins, but that didn't explain Mr. Andrews's absence. Did Henry not understand what his being in a box alone with a woman of equal birth meant to society? What he was silently declaring to the ton? Elizabeth sighed in relief when the theater curtains drew back.

By the time the first act was complete, Elizabeth's neck was stiff from her refusal to look anywhere other than the stage. A footman came in and lit the sconce on the wall as the actors prepared themselves for the second half. Elizabeth turned and smiled as a string of guests came to make their addresses.

All declared how happy they were to see the Worthinghams back in London. Elizabeth tried not to react every time the curtain pulled open, but her heart refused to listen and jumped with the hope that Henry would appear. Lord Dean, always the gentleman, called and, irked by Henry's slight, Elizabeth played up to his pretty compliments and smiles, and even allowed him to kiss her hand. She was starting to wonder if she, too, had bats in her head like Lord Riddledale.

When the bell sounded for everyone to take their seats, Elizabeth sat and fixed her skirts. She cast a look at Henry's box, and relief poured through her like a balm when she noted him sitting behind Miss Andrews and her now very present brother beside her.

Perhaps she'd been too hasty in judging him. Again…she mused, feeling a little guilty. Looking past Henry's cousins, she started when her gaze locked with his. His eyes burned with something that resembled longing and definitely anger sparking behind his level stare.

Unable to tear her gaze away, she took in his finely cut suit, the starched white shirt overlaid by a silver embroidered waistcoat, and a perfectly tied cravat. Her hand clenched into a fist, her fingers ached to untie the knot about his neck, to run her hands through his hair, pull him to her lips and kiss him as they had only days ago in the seclusion of her family's home. To make him hers and no one else's.

No Miss Andrews. No one's.

He nodded his head toward the exit before getting up and leaving the box. Elizabeth looked at Josh, relieved to see him so engrossed in the play, he'd have no idea what she was about to do.

"I'm feeling a little warm. I think I'll go and use the retiring room for a moment. I'll be back shortly," Elizabeth said, going to stand.

Josh frowned, studying her quickly. "Should I come with you? I don't think it's safe for you to go on your own."

She waved away his concerns. "That's not necessary. No one will attempt anything foolish at the theater where anyone could see them. I'll be back soon. I want to sit and have some fresh air. There will be servants there. I'll be secure enough, I promise." And with Henry beside her, she'd never feel in danger.

Her brother didn't look convinced, but the laughing crowd soon pulled his attention back to the play. "Very well, but be as quick as you can."

"Of course." Elizabeth stood and left the box quickly, walking behind the stalls that were filled with the upper ten thousand who owned London. As she made her way to the stairs that led to the foyer below an arm shot out from a small room between the boxes and dragged her into the darkened space.

She stifled a gasp, for a moment thinking her brother's fears that the assailant would strike her here had come true, before the whispered voice she knew as well as her own breathed against her ear. "Are ye trying to make me jealous tonight, Lady Newland?"

Elizabeth pushed him away so as to see him a little better and liked the fact she'd made him as crazed as he'd made her. It certainly wasn't fair if she was the one forever wondering what he was doing, thinking, who he was with.

"I don't know what you mean."

He looked at her incredulously, and she knew he didn't believe her. "I think ye do." He pulled her close, the thin material of her dress hardly a barrier between their bodies. Her breasts pushed hard against his chest, and she felt her blood warm at the contact. Again, she ached in places she wanted him to touch, willing herself to have some decorum, restraint. But when his hand idly rubbed up along her spine, then down to clasp her bottom, her resolve fractured.

"What are you up to, Henry?" her words but a whisper. He grinned.

"I want to kiss ye sweet lips and seduce ye to sin with me."

Heat rushed through her body at his words. Henry tempted her, more than she liked to admit, more than she thought ever possible between a man and a woman, but her mind urged caution. They were at the theater in a room surrounded by the ton who thrived on scandalous on-dits. Not to mention they'd been down this road before, and it had ended in disaster. Well, not completely, she mused. She did have a son who was everything to her.

"We shouldn't, Henry. Not here."

He allowed no other words as he kissed her with such passion, such longing, she was soon swept up into the firestorm of need and belonging. His kiss was hard, demanding, all too consuming, and she knew deep down she ought to pull away, to make him stop and see sense, but instead of pushing him away, her hands clasped the lapels of his jacket and held him close.

The palms of his hands slid across her cheeks, holding her as his lips supped at hers as if giving him life, taking what they sought for sustenance and longing for more, to be more with him. The man in her arms consumed what little self-control she possessed, and she gave up the fight to see sense, to remain guarded, and succumbed to the passion.

Even after all their time apart, Henry knew how to kiss her. His teasing, beckoning lips seemed so right, his hands over her body, holding her tight against him made her long for his touch elsewhere, everywhere. She wanted to feel what he showed her the other day, to forget all the pain that had been between them for so long, and just enjoy.

He walked her backward until her legs hit something solid. She gasped through their kiss when he lifted her, his hands clasping her skirts and sliding them up her legs to pool about her hips. Henry stepped between her legs and need seized her.

The words make love to me flittered through her mind and with them a tremble of fear. What they were doing was wrong, against the rules. Against her rules, but she couldn't stop. Didn't want to, if she were being brutally honest.

Henry broke the kiss as he boldly removed a slipper; his large, warm hand left her skin burning as he wrapped it about her ankle, the touch tempting her to sin. He lifted her leg to sit against his hip, and she used it to pull him toward her. He stared at her a moment, understanding dawning in his eyes of what her action meant. His gaze was ferocious with need and layered with emotions she herself was only now coming to understand, to admit to herself.

"I want ye so much, Elizabeth."

The lightest touch of his hand feathered across the skin on her hip. Elizabeth bit her lip, waiting for him to touch her where she ached most. He took her lips in a searing kiss as his hand finally ran over the thatch of curls at her core. His fingers ran across her sex, delving into her body with rhythmic strokes. She gasped, clutching at him as if he were the only thing keeping her on earth.

Wanting to make him as crazed for her as she was for him, Elizabeth slid her hand down his chest and felt along the hardness in his pants. He groaned, not shying away from her touch, but pushing against her clasp. Without heed, she touched him, enjoyed that she was able to make her highland earl as excited as she.

"What are you doing to me?" she gasped against his lips, never wanting him to stop the delicious sensations he was bestowing on her.

"Making love to ye in an unconventional way."

The words, whispered against her neck, made her shiver. He shifted and pushed her further along this wonderful road of desire. Toward a pinnacle Elizabeth could not yet reach, but was maddened to climb.

"But I thought… Should you not…" She moaned when his thumb skimmed her sensitive bud, tipping the axis of her world.

He chuckled and nibbled the sensitive skin beneath her ear. "Not tonight, lass. Not here. But for now this will have to do."

Yes. For now, her mind screamed. Having now sampled what the touch of a man could do, her life would never be the same. And nor did she want it to be. Their one time together in their youth was nothing like this kaleidoscope of sensations she struggled to comprehend and endure without screaming out his name in pleasure. The first time between them was fast and awkward. Nothing like this. This feeling that he evoked in her, made her wish to climb against him and demand more.

No longer was Henry the awkward youth on the cusp of adulthood. Now he knew how to touch a woman, how to please and bring pleasure to the female form, and she reveled in it.

"Henry," she gasped, as relentlessly he stroked, kissed, marked her as his, and then it happened. A release, the pinnacle that was only moments ago so out of reach bloomed through her, and she cried out as shivers of delight stole throughout her body. Spasm upon spasm brought forth pleasure unlike any she'd ever known, and she shattered in his arms.

The sensations were exquisite, left her breathless, and wanting more of the same.

Henry muffled her cries with a kiss, taking her lips and allowing her pleasure to subdue, ebb and flow away just as his kiss softened, comforted, and eventually stopped.

"I had no idea." Even Elizabeth could hear the wonder in her voice.

They stared at each for a moment before he stepped back, righting her gown and helping her to stand. "How pleasurable it can be between us every time I touch ye." His answer was matter-of-fact, straight to the point, and without guile.

Elizabeth felt heat steal up her neck, an absurd reaction after what he'd just done to her. "And every time we're alone, will you promise it will end in such a way?"

Henry chuckled, kissing her softly. The scent of sandalwood and something else she could not name intoxicated her senses. Elizabeth breathed deeply, wishing they never had to leave the small room that held nothing but very fond memories now.

"I certainly hope so." He grinned. "I would do anything for ye, lass. I will always want to please and make ye happy. Your pleasure is mine." He stole a look over her gown, stepping back seemingly pleased with what he saw. "How do ye feel?"

Elizabeth sighed. "Boneless. Like my legs have turned to jelly and my mind wishes to sleep."

Henry laughed. "Then my work here is done. Now come, I must get you back to ye family before ye're missed. We've been gone too long as it is."

Elizabeth nodded and walked to the door. What they'd done she shouldn't have allowed, but Henry had only to touch her and her resolve vanished like a breath of air. "When will I see you again?"

He lifted her hand and kissed it quickly. "I'll be in the park after dawn if you're up for a ride." He opened the door and looked along the corridor.

Elizabeth nodded; the thought of being alone with Henry, even if only at Hyde Park, was what she wished. "I'll be there." She stepped into the corridor and started toward her family box. "Good night, Henry."

"Good night, lass." His whispered words floated up behind her, and she smiled.

---

*E*lizabeth woke early the next morning, her body expectant, her mind abuzz with thoughts of the night before. She paused while doing up the buttons on her riding jacket and wondered when she'd ever felt so happy. In truth, likely not since the day she'd lain with Henry at Dunsleigh or when she'd given birth to their son, Samuel.

Wanting to make the park after dawn, she left a hastily scrawled note for her maid before almost running to the mews to have her horse saddled. Argo snickered in welcome, lopping his head over the stable door, while Tony, her groom, looked less than pleased to be braving the chill of the

London morning to accompany her. But the ever- faithful groom mounted his own horse and followed her into the morning throng of traffic. Elizabeth weaved her way through parked carts of market sellers and shop deliveries before turning into Hyde Park.

At this hour the grounds were almost vacant of life, bar the few early morning riders like herself. Elizabeth made her way toward Rotten Row, marveling at Hyde Park's beauty this early in the morning. The smell of horses and trees made her long to be home at Dunsleigh, the many mornings she'd ridden out with Henry across the meadows at full gallop, each of them betting the other to jump a hedge grove, fallen tree, or stream.

Seeing Henry, her heart flipped at the wicked grin on his lips. She took in every detail, his tight-fitting tan breeches and blue riding jacket that brought out the color of his eyes and the devilish glint that was only for her. A secret under-standing that only they had.

Today more than ever he resembled the man she'd once adored. His unshaven jaw boasted a night's worth of stubble. His hair looked wind tossed and beckoned her to run her hands through it. She wanted to steal him away to some-where secluded, allow him to kiss her senseless, make her his as she had an inkling her heart had always been.

Elizabeth smiled as he came to a stop before her. "Good morning, Lord Muir. How fortunate to meet you here this morning."

Henry chuckled and drew closer still. "How fortunate indeed." He winked, and the breath in her lungs expelled. "Do you wish for a run or would ye prefer to ride at a more leisurely pace?"

Elizabeth masked the telltale shiver that his husky voice brought forth. Maybe her hopes of being kissed senseless was a possibility after all. She caught a disapproving glance from her groom, and her wayward thoughts were put to heel. "A leisurely ride I think," she said, unable to hide the disappointment in her voice at having her groom with her.

---

*H*enry led the way into a bank of trees. It was a beautiful morning, made even more so by the company he kept. Memories of last night flooded his mind when her knee brushed his. He looked at her, a smile quirking his lips when she met his scrutiny.

"You are well this mornin'?" he asked.

The lightest blush rose on her cheeks and Henry knew what his question had reminded her of. Of her locked in his arms, her masked moans as he brought her to pleasure, her shivers and trembles of ecstasy. He swallowed, urging his blood to pump at its rightful speed, not a gallop.

"I am very, very well, my lord."

Henry chuckled, and they settled into an easy pace. The paths led them through wooded and lawned areas, yet Henry saw none of the park's beauty, only Elizabeth's. "Did ye enjoy the remainder of the play? I thought ye looked a little flushed and distracted." He paused. "I must admit, it couldn't hold my attention, as I was quite preoccupied." And never had he been more distracted then he was last night watching Elizabeth walk away. He'd wanted her with need that frightened him. The sooner she agreed to marry him, the better they all would be.

Elizabeth smiled, but something in her eyes gave him pause. He pulled up his horse and she followed his suit. "Is something wrong, lass? Has Lord Riddledale pressed upon you again?" He wouldn't put it past the bastard; he was capable of anything, the blaggard.

Elizabeth shook her head, a tendril of golden hair

bouncing against her cheek. "No. Lord Riddledale has kept away, thankfully, but there is something on my mind."

Henry watched an array of emotions flick over her face before she masked her features and turned to face him. His stomach knotted, wondering what it was that could make her so serious all of a sudden.

"I need to be honest with you, and I'm afraid of what my honesty will cost."

An inkling of foreboding settled about his shoulders, and he rolled them to dispel the tightness. "What is it?"

She lifted her chin, biting her sweet bottom lip. "As you know our past has been...well, not the easiest, to say the least. A lot has happened between us. Our interlude, you leaving for America, Riddledale stealing our correspondence, and now blackmailing me to marry him."

Henry reached for her hand when her voice wobbled. How he hated himself for hurting her, even if unknowingly. "Go on," he said.

Elizabeth frowned. "I hated you for not coming home. I couldn't believe you had dismissed our request after all we'd shared. But then I married Newland, and I was content, happy even for a time. There is something you need to know about our marriage, Henry." She paused, looking out over the park, not able to meet his gaze.

Never had Henry seen her so unsettled. "Ye're making me nervous, lass. Stop choking on the words and tell me."

"I'm nervous." She laughed, but he could see the tension radiating from her. What was it she was trying to say? He slid off his saddle and pulled Elizabeth from her mount. Heedless of who saw them, he pulled her hard against his chest. "I'm sorry for everythin'. If I could change the past, I would. I would never have left ye had I known how much ye wished for us to wed. But please tell me ye know why I left. That I wanted to provide for ye, to give all that I could to my bride, and not rely on her dowry."

Elizabeth wiped at her cheek, and he cursed knowing he'd hurt her so much. "I know why you left, and I do not think any less of you for it. But some things do change, and I had quite a momentous change in my life upon marrying Newland."

The sound of thudding hooves came up the track. They turned to watch the rider look about and then, spotting them, galloped toward them as if the devil himself was after his life. The rider gave Tony the missive and after reading the address quickly, handed it straight to Elizabeth.

"For me?" Elizabeth took the letter, and he noted the moment she tensed. Breaking the seal, she read it quickly, her eyes widening with alarm. "I must go."

"What's happened?" He looked at the missive and watched as she sought her saddle. "No, it's news from home. I must return to Newland Estate. Today, without delay."

Henry clasped her leg, helping to put her shaking foot into the stirrup. "Why, lass?"

She swallowed, tears brimming in her eyes. "My son, Samuel, has become ill. He lives at the estate. I would normally bring him to town, but I didn't this year since we now have a nanny." She shook her head. "I must go. I'm sorry."

Henry stumbled back, shocked into silence as he watched Elizabeth gallop through Hyde Park and toward Mayfair. She had a son? With Newland? She was a mother?

How had he not known…?

In a daze, he mounted his horse and set for home. He couldn't actually remember the ride back to the townhouse, but entering his home, the presence of his cousin Richard, seated in his library at ease, aggravated and relieved him at the same moment.

"Ah, there you are. I was hoping to catch you. What are your plans for the next few days? Amelia wishes to travel to Bath, and we were wondering if you'd be up for a trip?"

Henry slumped into the chair behind his desk, only half listening.

"Henry? Are you well?"

Richard waved a hand before his eyes, and he pulled himself from his thoughts. "She's a mother."

His cousin chuckled, grabbing the chair near the desk and pulling it closer to lean on the mahogany wood. "Who's a mother?"

"Elizabeth." He paused. "Lady Newland. She's a mother."

Richard's brows rose. "She is? When did you find this out? She's not spoken of a child before?"

No she had not, which was odd. Had he been a father, it would be all he'd speak of, he was sure. To have little bairns was one of life's greatest gifts. And finding out Elizabeth had a child did not lessen her in his eyes, quite the opposite in fact, but they were friends. Were supposed to be friends, in any case, so why had she not told him? "Today, in the park just now. She's returned to Newland Estate as the boy is ill." A knot formed in his stomach at the thought that someone Elizabeth loved beyond any other was not well, was sick enough that his mama was called home. It didn't bode well.

His decision snapped into his mind and he walked to the fire surround and rang for a servant.

"What are your thoughts?"

"Apologies, my friend, but you'll have to take Amelia to Bath yourself. I'm headed for Wiltshire."

"Wiltshire?"

"Aye, Newland Estate." If he could give her solace, a friend's support during such an ordeal as a sick child, then by God he would be there for Elizabeth this time. He would not fail her again a second time around.

"Did she ask you to go?" Richard poured him a whisky and, walking over to him, passed the crystal glass with the fortifying amber liquid inside. "I fear you're being hasty."

"No, she did not, but I'm going, and that's all there is to say on the subject."

Richard raised his glass in salute. "Well then, I wish you luck, Muir."

Henry smiled. "Thank ye."

CHAPTER 15

*O*nly a few days later Henry arrived at Newland Estate. His carriage pulled up before the two story homemade of Bath stone; its warm golden glow in the afternoon light was as welcoming as the woman who occupied the house.

A young man came running from the side of the home and helped his driver steady the gray matched pair after a day's hard ride. Henry stepped from the carriage, eager to see Elizabeth, to offer aid and anything else that could help the boy become well.

The front door opened, and a liveried footman stepped aside to allow him to enter. "I'm here to see Lady Newland." He bowed, ushering him toward the front parlor.

"If you'll wait here, my lord," the servant said, opening the door to the room that sported an abundance of settees and tables, the windows overlooking a pretty vista of lawn and willow trees to the side of the house. "I will summon Lady Newland immediately."

Henry strolled into the room and walked about, taking an interest in the small painted images of different family members over the years that sat atop any available surface. A large portrait of whom he assumed to be the late Lord Newland sat above the fire surround, his blond hair almost as light as Elizabeth's, but where she had a golden hue running through her long locks, his lordship had the tinge of red.

Footsteps sounded in the foyer along with Elizabeth asking the servant who had called. Henry felt a small twinge of guilt he'd not given the man his name when she received no answer to her question.

The door swung open, and she entered, no longer the woman who danced at balls with little care of the world around her, of perfectly coiffed hair and impeccable dress. Now stood a mother, a woman who ruled the house in which he stood, a woman in a plain white cotton afternoon gown with a pink sash. Her hair sat against her shoulders, an abundance of sun-kissed gold, and he lost the ability to speak at the beautiful vision she made.

"Lord Muir." He heard the surprise in her voice. "What are you doing here?"

He stood with his hands clasped behind his back lest he reach for her, pulling her into his arms and giving her all that he could, his heart, his everything. "You're a mother." It wasn't his best reply. In fact, he supposed he was still shocked by the notion of her having a child.

Elizabeth raised her brow, smiling a little. "Yes, I am. I have a son, Samuel." She turned as a butler stood in the door, clearing his throat a little. "Smithers, if you could have tea brought in and some sandwiches, I'll have my lunch in the parlor today." The servant bowed and left as quietly as he'd arrived.

She walked toward him, sitting down on the settee. "How is it you're here?"

He sat also, taking her in as if he'd not seen her for weeks instead of three days. "I wanted to see if your child is well or at least on the mend."

Her face softened at the mention of her son. "He's much better now that I'm here. I think he wanted his mama, and I'm perfectly happy to leave London to come and care for him. He's only two, you see, and this is the first time we've been apart."

"You took him last season to London?" It was unusual for a woman of rank to do such a thing, but the daughters of the Duke of Penworth had an unconventional upbringing. They had been raised almost wild at Dunsleigh, running, swimming, picnicking at will, and their parents had adored such activities for their children. None of them was high in the instep.

"I did, although he was much smaller then and didn't fuss a lot. But as a toddler, he's looking for more stimulation now, playing outdoors, riding on his pony, swimming in the lake when it's hot enough, of course. I didn't want him to miss out on all that to be in London with me for the season. I find town tedious, so I imagine he would, too, very much so."

"I'm glad he's feeling better. When they called you home, I imagined the worst."

She laughed, nodding as the tea tray arrived. The maid set it out before them on a small table and Elizabeth poured, handing him a cup along with a selection of sandwiches.

"I did also. I thought I was going to lose him, but upon arriving here, his fever had broken, and he was up in bed again, happily playing with his favorite teddy bear and small soldiers."

"I'm glad to hear it." He paused, feeling a little absurd having panicked so much on her behalf. "I'm sorry to intrude. Had I known the boy was well, I would never have—"

She reached out, clasping his hand. "I'm glad you've come. Thank you for caring enough to be here."

Their gaze locked, and a shiver of awareness ran through him. "I shall take my leave after luncheon if you're agreeable."

"If you wish." A frown marred her brow. "You're more than welcome to stay, Henry. The house is large enough for company, and as I've written to my family assuring them of Samuel's wellbeing, I'll be here alone for the next week or so. I would love to have another in the house if you're able to stay."

"We'll be alone, lass."

The words, heavy with intent, longing even, hung between them. Should he stay, it would take all his effort to keep his distance from her, and by God, he didn't wish to. He wanted her like he'd wanted no other in his life. It had always been like this between them, a need that surpassed everything that ever impacted them.

"I know." She shrugged, the action bringing his gaze to take in her slender shoulders, the rise of her breasts against her gown. "I'm a widow, not a debutante, and if we're discreet about your visit, no harm will come of it."

Henry swallowed, shifting on his chair, wondering if she was aware of what her words sounded like. A proposition...

"I would be happy to stay and visit with ye, lass."

She smiled, taking a bite of her sandwich. "It's settled then. I'll have a room prepared for you."

---

*L*ater that day, Elizabeth brought Samuel down to meet Henry. Nerves pooled in her stomach at the thought of a man about to meet a boy he'd never know was his son. She checked her little boy's gown, stalling as guilt over keeping Samuel from Henry pierced her soul.

She was being cruel, and yet, if she did not continue with the farce, Samuel would be termed a bastard and Henry, no matter how much he may wish to declare the boy as his, could not enable him to inherit his Scottish estate. And blast it all to hell, but had Riddledale not impinged on their lives, none of this would have happened. She blinked back the sting of tears for a future lost, lifted her chin, and entered the drawing room.

Henry sat before the fire, a brandy in his hand, as he'd taken his after dinner drinks in here with her. It was such a homely situation, a man and woman, cooing over a child brought down before bedtime. It made her heart ache at the loss of such a life.

Henry stood when she entered the room, his attention on Samuel who wiggled against her hip and patted her cheeks with his little hands. She put the boy down, and he walked over to Henry, looking up at him with curiosity and awe.

"Hello." Her son waddled over to the chair and climbed up, playing with his teddy.

Henry smiled and sat. "Hello. It's lovely to meet ye, Samuel."

Elizabeth came and sat beside her son, watching as his chubby hands clasped and moved his toy about on his lap. How she loved this child, would protect him from anything or anyone who tried to hurt him. "He's just started lessons on deportment. He's not very good." Samuel looked up at her, and she grinned.

Henry laughed. "He'll get there, and no doubt you'll have him well looked after during his lessons."

"Of course. Lord Newland knew of a local family who had a daughter who had gone to school specifically to become a nanny, and she's the sweetest girl. Samuel adores her."

He leaned back in his chair, crossing his legs, and

contemplated her. "Do you like being a mother? I must admit, it never even occurred to me that you would have a child."

Elizabeth cuddled into her son, reveling in his warmth beside her. "When I first fell pregnant I thought my life was over."

"Over? Why would you think such a thing?"

Her eyes widened, and she swore at her slip. "Only that we'd just been married and already I was increasing. It was quite a shock." The lie felt thick in her throat, and she hated having to say it to him. He watched Samuel, smiling at the little boy, and she hoped he could not see the similarities between father and child, which, over the past year, had become more apparent.

Even now, the cowlick in Samuel's hair, just above his right temple, was in the same position as Henry's. The little cleft in his chin, his blue eyes, and long eyelashes. Not to mention Samuel had ebony colored hair while she and Newland were both light in shade.

"Newland would have been happy. I understand he was in an accident during his early life."

"Yes, he fell from a horse and never fully recovered." Elizabeth didn't want to elaborate. The fact that her husband had told her he was unable to lie with a woman after his fall due to severe spasms that attacked his lower back still brought shame. After all he'd given her, the security of his name, a father for her son, she'd not been able to please him as she would have liked.

A scratch at the door sounded, and Samuel's nanny walked in. "Excuse me, Lady Newland, but it's time for his lordship to go to bed."

Samuel jumped up on the chair, clasping Elizabeth about the neck, smacking his lips against her cheeks. She laughed.

"I love you, too, my little boy. I will see you in the morning. Sweet dreams."

"Good night, Mama." No sooner had she given him a big hug than he jumped down and ran toward his nanny, his small legs working hard to move quickly. Henry bade her son good night and smiled at her as the door closed behind them.

"He's a lovely lad. Ye must be so proud."

"I am proud of him. He'll be a good lord and an honorable man."

"Just as his father sounded to be," Henry said.

She nodded. "Yes, just as his papa was." *And is.*

CHAPTER 16

The following morning not a breath of wind sounded outdoors, and if the glow behind her green velvet drapes were any indication, the weather was faultless.

Elizabeth rose, pulling the curtains open and marveling at the beauty that was Newland Estate. Her room afforded her the most pleasing vista to wake up to, and an overwhelming urge to show Henry her home, to enjoy what little time his visit to Wiltshire would bring, filled her with excitement and expectation.

Ringing for her maid, she dressed quickly and ordered Samuel's nanny to prepare her son for a picnic breakfast. She caught the cook and servant staff before they had laid out the breakfast room and instead had them pack a basket for an impromptu breakfast outdoors.

She found Henry walking into the breakfast room, which faced east to capture the morning sun and was always warm and welcoming, even on a cold winter's day. "Good morning, Lord Muir," she said, taking his arm. "We're to breakfast outdoors this morning, so follow me."

He looked down at his buckskin breeches and coat. "Should I change into something less formal?"

Elizabeth took the opportunity to run her gaze over his attire; his breeches were certainly cut well and optimized what Henry had to offer beneath all that cloth. A blush stole up her cheeks, but she didn't relent. He was attractive, one who in turn found her to be also. She would take her fill as much as she could while he was here. "You're dressed perfectly fine. Samuel will be down shortly. We can wait out front if you like."

He ushered her toward the door, and they stepped into the morning sunlight, the air warm and fragrant with summer flowers.

"This is spontaneous, lass. Do ye have a special location we'll be breaking our fast this mornin'?"

"I do, it's only a short stroll away, and a place Samuel loves to play." The sound of her son giggling as he came down the stairs with his nanny made her smile. He was such a happy little boy, had a love for life, and she was thankful his fever wasn't as bad as she'd first thought. The unimaginable horrors she'd faced on the way back to Newland Estate thinking he may have been sick enough that she'd lose him had been too much to bear and not anything she wished to experience again.

Her son ran out between them and onto the gravel drive, his nanny following close on his heels. Elizabeth followed, watching him play with his nanny, squeals of laugher bursting from his little lungs.

"You adore him; it's written all over ye features." Henry smiled at her. "And Newland Estate makes ye happy."

"I am, I must admit. Being here with Samuel always makes me so. When I return to town next week, I'll be bringing him with me. The season is coming to an end, in any case, so he'll not have to spend too much time in town."

They walked toward a lake to where the servants had set up a small picnic for them. A large woolen blanket was spread out upon the grass with a large hamper and a bottle of wine beside it.

"Wine for breakfast, lass. Are ye Scottish?"

Elizabeth laughed. "An oversight, but if it's supplied, one must not waste such an opportunity." They sat as a kitchen servant served up their breakfast and, even with champagne instead of tea or coffee, it was delicious.

Samuel walked off toward the lake, and his nanny followed, both of them sitting beside the bank and watching the water flow over the shallow rocks along the edge.

"There is something that I wish to say, lass. Something I've wanted to say for quite some time."

She turned and met his gaze. He was serious, and she hoped above hope that what he was about to say was what she wanted to hear, had wanted to hear from the first moment he'd walked into the ballroom at the beginning of the season.

―――――

*H*enry took her hand and kissed her palm. She shivered, and the urge to make her react to him so, to always be aware of him, urged on the declaration that had been burning in his gut for weeks. "I want this, lass. I want this kind of life with ye more than I want to draw breath, and that's the truth."

Her hand tightened around his. "I know you do, Henry."

Her reply was not what he'd been expecting. He'd thought she'd want him to stop speaking, to stop the declaration of love he wanted to shout to the world.

"From the moment we met, I knew we were meant to be.

I loved ye from the moment you called me a vexing, meddle-some Scot and I'll love ye until the day I die."

Tears pooled in her eyes, and she sniffed. He handed her his handkerchief, glad this time her tears were accompanied with a smile. "I want this too, Henry. So much it aches, but there is too much happening in our lives at present. I have Samuel. Riddledale is threatening me. I'm not sure if it's the right time for this,"—she gestured between them—"to begin."

"It's already begun, lass." He shuffled closer, moving the basket out of the way. "If I stay here with you until ye return to London, I'm not sure if I can keep my distance from ye any longer, even if I wanted to."

She shook her head, grinning at his words. "We cannot do that," she stated, adamant.

"We're consenting adults. You're a widow, not a debu-tante, as ye said yourself. What's to stop us?" Nothing that he could see.

"Henry, are you asking me to sleep with you?" Her eyes widened and her cheeks blushed a little.

"I'm in love with ye, Elizabeth. I want to marry ye, and if there is any way in which I can win your regard, win your heart, I'll do it. I want ye, in every way a man can want a woman, and I'll not give up on my plight just because it's frowned upon by the English ton."

An excited thrum ran through him when she didn't dismiss him directly. He wanted to show her what they could be together, and over the next week he would prove to her he was determined to succeed.

He looked out toward Samuel and smiled at what the little boy and his nanny were doing. "I want to be the boy's father, his guide in taking on Newland Estate when the time comes. I want to raise him, love him as he should be, just as you do, for I love ye, and all I care about is your happiness." Tears ran down her cheeks, and she bit her lip. She cast a glance at her boy, and he discerned the moment she'd made her decision. "Should we get the letter back from Riddledale, and his threat is removed, I will marry you, Henry."

"Aye?" He clasped her chin, lifting her gaze to his. "Ye will marry your Scottish barbarian?"

"I will and gladly so." She paused, clasping the lapels of his coat. "I love you, too, more than I ever imagined I could." He took her lips in a searing kiss, the giggles of the nanny and Samuel lost as he declared his love, his promise, through a kiss that left him as breathless as Elizabeth.

"We will best Riddledale, and then we will marry and return to Scotland. You're everything to me, lass, and today ye've made me the happiest of men." He kissed her again. "Come to my room tonight, promise me ye will."

Elizabeth bit her lip, a coquettish look in her eyes that drove him to distraction as much as her reply did. "I promise."

---

*B*lackness surrounded Elizabeth as she stepped from her bedroom door, looking out at the long passage to ensure no servants were about. The night held no moonlight, and the windows running the length of one side of the passage were inky black, the only image her reflection in candlelight, an eerie figure much like a ghoul.

She pulled her pelisse close about her, shivering a little at trepidation and expectation. At the end of the hall, only a few rooms away, Henry waited for her... She wondered what he was wearing, was he before the fire, lying on the bed, standing by the door in wait. She bit her lip, wondering if he was shirtless, naked...

Continuing on, she passed the staircase and came to the next set of suites that they kept for guests only. Candlelight flickered beneath the third door along the passage, and she paused before it, taking a deep, solidifying breath before opening it and stepping into the room.

He sat before the fire, a contemplative look on his face. He leaned on his knees, seemingly lost in thought as he watched the flames lick the wood in the fire. The smile he bestowed on her washed away all her nervousness. This was right; nothing ever in her life had felt so correct.

"Ye came, lass. I thought you may have changed ye mind."

Elizabeth went and stood before him, stepping between his legs and laying her hands upon his shoulders. His muscles flexed under her grip, and she was reminded of his strength not just of mind, but of stature. "I said I would." She grinned at him, leaning down and kissing him quickly before she lost her nerve. His eyes flared with heat, and her breath caught in her lungs.

His hands slid along the backs of her legs, and her knees shook. "Ye tempt me more than you ought. I want this to be the start of forever for us. I want ye to remember tonight with nothing but awe."

"I already do."

He pulled her down onto his lap, and Elizabeth straddled his legs. They touched, their most intimate of places rubbing with wanton desire that left her breathless. He kissed her cheeks, her lips, her chin, making his way down her throat, leaving her a shivering mess of desire in his arms.

He pulled back, looking at her with such love her heart gave a hard thump. A small lock of hair fell over his brow, and she pushed it back, wanting to see his beautiful soul that shone through his eyes.

"I love ye so much, Elizabeth, that sometimes I think I'll go mad with it."

His words warmed her heart, and she knew at that moment, to the center of her being, that what they were doing was right. She wiggled closer, wrapping her arms about his neck. "And I you, Henry. I missed you so much when you went away. I don't ever want to be separated from you again."

He placed a finger against her lips, shushing her words. "None of that. We'll not speak of the past, only the future and all the wonderful things we'll do together as a married couple and family."

He cradled her face with his hands, her eyes smarting with tears. "I don't remember you ever being so romantic, Henry. I could get used to you being this way."

He laughed, waggling his brows. "Aye, I believe it stems from me mother's side of the family. Father, on the other hand, had not one romantic bone in his body." He paused, kissing her lightly and leaving her needy for more. "And I want to please ye, always." His breath rippled across her skin like a sensual caress.

Elizabeth took the lead and kissed him, let him know with her touch, the slide of her tongue against his, that the time for talk was over. She wanted him, here, now, to be joined with him as she'd always wanted to be. How they always should have been.

Henry pulled her close, his hands delving into her shift and yanking it up to her waist, pulling it off and leaving the night air to kiss her skin. The scorching look he threw her body left her tingling, a feeling of power coming over her that she'd brought this Scottish laird to his knees.

"Touch me, Henry."

"I'll do more than that, lass." He growled, his hands sliding up her waist to clasp her breasts. Henry dipped his head, kissing one puckered nipple; the feel of him caressing her in such an intimate spot was utterly delightful and all too addictive.

Elizabeth let her head fall back, wanting to enjoy what he

could do to her. She ran her hands over the taut muscles along his spine, loving how his body felt beneath her hands, but it wasn't enough. She wanted him as naked as she was, to see his delectable muscular frame that had haunted her dreams ever since, as a young woman, she'd become aware of him.

"I should move us to the bed, and yet, I cannot. I have to have ye, here, now."

She clasped his face, making him look at her. "There will be many more opportunities for the bed, and I find myself quite comfortable where we are."

A low growl resonated deep in his belly, and he pulled her close. "Do not tempt me, lass."

She wrapped her arms about his neck, feeling through his clothes what her presence was doing to him. A wicked smiled quirked her lips. "Do I tempt you, Henry?" The fact she had such power over him, made this beautiful, strong Scottish man honey in her hands, was an exhilarating elixir.

"Ye always have."

He went to kiss her, and she averted her lips. His gaze captured hers, and she knew his eyes were a mirror into her own soul, a soul that longed to be touched, to feel, to love again. She grabbed his hand and placed it between her legs, sighing at the rightness of his touch.

"I know it's scandalous of me, and something that I should not do, but I want you more than anything in this world." Elizabeth grinned as his gaze turned molten when she flicked open the top button of his waistcoat. "Make me yours. Please…"

*H*enry swallowed and strove for calm as each button down his waistcoat deftly popped open. The creamy white flesh of her breasts rose and fell with each breath. Her mons teased his cock and threatened his promise to not act the barbarian and take her without heed or care.

"Are ye sure? Once we start, I dinna think I'll be able to stop." She paused, and Henry read the determined glint in her eye. He dumbly watched her, having never imagined a woman could consume him fully. To have her in his arms once more, promised to him, was a dream he'd not thought possible when he'd first returned from America.

She leaned up and kissed him, the scent of jasmine lingering on her skin. "I've never been more sure of anything in my life. We're alone, and we're to marry. What's to stop us?"

He pulled her against him and kissed her hard. She gasped, and he made use of her acquiescence as he stroked her tongue with his, over and over, until she squirmed on his lap, her need for him as much as his for her.

It was easy to divest himself of his clothes, and Elizabeth was more than helpful in getting his waistcoat, shirt, and cravat off. She threw them to the floor with abandon, as he himself had thrown her shift. When her hands clasped his frontfalls, Henry had to fight not to lose control before he'd even taken her. Her determined touch, her light strokes against his flesh, incinerated him and made him burn.

He pulled back to watch her as her hand slipped beneath his trousers, and she stroked his hardened flesh.

"Oh, lass, that feels so good."

A wicked smile quirked her lips, and he was lost. He ripped his frontfalls completely open, the sound of material ripping loud in the quiet room. Elizabeth giggled and gasped when he lifted her, placing her hot, wet, and more-than-ready core against his cock.

She bit her lip as he lowered her upon him. Henry breathed deep, clenching his jaw as her tight, hot core anchored around him. She was magnificent. To see her lips open on a sigh of pleasure and her eyes glaze over with wonder, would've tumbled him to the floor had he been standing. How he loved her, adored her, would cherish her for the rest of their lives.

Elizabeth ran a finger over his lips, watching him intently. "I love you, Henry." Her whispered words were the sweetest melody he'd ever heard.

"Blast it, lass! Ye would tempt an angel to sin." And he wanted to sin with her, whenever and wherever she'd allow. He took her harder than he ought, but by the sounds of her delectable gasps, her fingers that dug into his shoulders, her breathlessness told him she was more than accepting of the situation.

He knew the moment her orgasm was upon her. Her legs clasped him tight, her fingers clutched for support as she fought against a release that would consume them both. Henry clasped her waist, pulling her down on him hard, deepening their connection, giving no quarter, and she shattered.

Elizabeth shouted his name, and he stifled the sound with a kiss, pumping until his own pleasure pulsed through his body and they were left, breathless, joined and consumed in passion.

They stayed clasped tightly in each other's arms for a time. It was no difficulty to do so, but with the fire having burned down to coal, the cooling night air made its presence known. He stood, lifting her and carrying her to his bed.

She dozed, an odd, contented quirk to her lips as he joined her beneath the blankets, pulling her snug against his chest.

"I should probably return to my room," she mumbled, but not moving.

He clasped her tighter, kissing her neck. "In the morn will

be soon enough. I want ye here with me tonight and nowhere else."

Elizabeth turned her head and looked back at him. "Thank you."

He frowned. "For what?"

She clasped his arm tighter about her tummy and turned away. "For being everything I'd always hoped you would be."

Henry smiled. "We've only just begun, lass."

"Hmm," she said, sighing contently. "I love the sound of that."

CHAPTER 17

*T*he week they spent at Newland Estate was one of the most romantic and best times Elizabeth could think of up to that point in her life. Samuel took to Henry and his enthusiasm for life, for fun and laughter, and her heart swelled knowing that at least in some small measure, Henry would be a part of the boy's life, if not as his known father, but at least as the custodian of him. It was not what she'd wanted, but under the circumstances it was all that was possible and, should Henry know the truth, Elizabeth was sure he would understand. Someday...

They had traveled back to London together, not taking any heed of the fact. No more would she be scrutinized by the ton and their law or by Riddledale. They would gain the letter back and be done with the blaggard so Henry and she could live the life that should always have been theirs.

The night of Lord Riddledale's ball for his sister's coming out was one the ton would never forget. His lordship had outdone himself to please his sister and promote to the ton that he was a marquis to be reckoned with. The room was lit with hundreds of wax candles in gold and silver chandeliers that cast an abundance of light on the guests below, their jewels and gowns sparkling like hundreds of stars.

The parquetry floor, waxed to perfection, shone in the room, and small, scalloped-legged chairs sat before each window that had its own nook so not to take any space away from the gathered guests and the dancers beyond.

His lordship's London home was beautiful, oozed old money, but that was where the prettiness ended. The lord of the manor himself was as vile as a cesspit, and the sooner Elizabeth and Henry held what rightfully belonged to them in the palms of their hands, the better.

Her brother escorted Elizabeth and her three sisters to the ball and, finding other acquaintances of theirs, helped thread them through the guests to where they could watch the ton at play. The ballroom was full to capacity, the strains of a quadrille playing, the dancers laughing and moving about the room with enjoyment.

They had planned the night and how they would go about getting into his lordship's library to steal the letter. The first part of the plan was to assume the guise of guest, merely here for enjoyment and dancing. Keeping up the appearance of a guest, Elizabeth danced first with Lord Kinruth and then the second, a country dance with Viscount Boxley, both of whom were attentive partners, but they weren't the man she sought to see.

Casting her gaze over those present she was yet to see Henry, and her stomach knotted wondering if something had occurred to keep him from attending. And then a prickling of awareness shivered across her nape, and she turned to see the very man himself, the man she loved beyond anything she'd ever known, standing idly against the wall beside the terrace doors, his attention locked on her.

His roguish dark looks and height made him taller than most of the guests here, and her heart somersaulted in her chest at the sight of him. Heat pooled at her core, and she fought not to blush, remembering all the delectable things he'd done to her while in Wiltshire. All the exquisite touches that left her chasing after him for more of the same like the lovesick fool she was.

She'd acted quite the determined minx.

"Are you well, Lady Newland? I can take you onto the terrace if you're a little warm." Lord Boxley's words brought her out of her musings, and she shook her head, smiling. "No, I'm very well, thank you, but perhaps a drink would be welcome."

Lord Boxley obtained her a glass of champagne, gesturing to the crowd. "What a lovely turnout for Lord Riddledale's sister's coming out. Nothing like a celebration of coming of age."

Elizabeth listened with half interest. "Yes, quite." He escorted her to her sister Alice, and she took the opportunity to speak to a few guests while stepping toward a large potted palm she'd spied. The position gave her a good vantage point for watching Henry without being too obvious.

He was so handsome and sweet. He was everything one ought to look for in a husband, and by the admiring glances he received from the ladies present, she wasn't the only one who thought so. Jealousy pinched at her, but she pushed the stupid thought aside. Henry was hers. They'd promised themselves to each other. Nothing would tear them apart again. Ever.

"He is not for you, Lady Newland," a mocking voice stated matter of fact beside her.

Elizabeth fought not to lose her temper and flay the man alive before his guests. "What I do and think in my life is, and will always be, my choice, Lord Riddledale. You of all people should know this of me by now." Elizabeth moved to return to her sister, and a strong hand shot out and clasped her arm, ripping her back beside him. Elizabeth pulled at his hold without success.

"I see your Scottish earl has disappeared. What a shame my presence has caused you to lose sight of him."

Elizabeth looked to where she'd seen Henry last and frowned, noting him gone. She cast a look about the ballroom and couldn't see his tall frame standing out above everyone else. "Lord Muir is his own person. I do not own him, and he may go wherever he likes at a ball."

His lordship's chuckle sounded mocking. "I heard the gentlemen were partaking in billiard contests this evening. Perhaps there is a game afoot that you may be interested in."

Elizabeth pulled at his clasp once more and was relieved when he let her go. "I'm not interested in billiards." All she wished was to take back the letter that was hers by right and leave a home she never wished to see again.

He waggled his finger before her face, and she looked away. Never in her life had she known such an prig of a man. "Perhaps you ought to take an interest, my lady." He strolled away, throwing one last smile over his shoulder before disappearing from view.

Elizabeth frowned over Lord Riddledale's words. She looked about the room once more, trying to seek out Henry with little success. Disappointment washed over her and with it a dose of fear when Mr. Andrews, Henry's cousin, walked past without his ever-present sister trailing behind.

She chastised herself for thinking Miss Andrews was wherever Henry was. They were cousins, friends, even if Elizabeth couldn't stomach the woman for more than five minutes. But Henry loved and adored her. She would not allow Lord Riddledale's words over Henry's absence make her think the worst of a man she trusted beyond anyone else in the world.

Why then, only minutes later she found herself seeking

out this billiards room was anyone's guess. It was certainly not the niggling concern that Riddledale was trying to warn her of something. Never that. She was just interested in what the men were up to with their competition, and to see if Henry had partaken in such games and was enjoying the night.

———

*H*enry walked about the ball and talked with as many people as he could, talked of horseflesh, politics, Scotland, anything he could think of. He kept tabs on where Riddledale was at any one moment, of where his lordship's library was located, and if he'd had the room locked for the duration of the ball, which he had not.

Supper was not far off, and he was thankful for it. To watch Elizabeth swirl about the dance floor with another English toff would be too much even for him. But tonight they were both playing roles, to gain what they'd come here for, to best Riddledale at his own sick game.

Not for the first time tonight, the lure of her deep green gown of silk that brought out the fierce color of her eyes tempted him to pull her into a darkened room, slip it from her body, and enjoy each other as thoroughly as they had in Wiltshire.

Her golden locks, coiled high on her head, accentuated her cheekbones and sensuous mouth. The thrum that tonight was the start of their future pumped through his veins. From this night forward, Riddledale wouldn't be an issue in their life, and rightfully so. They would marry and return to Scotland, bring up Samuel to be a well-adjusted young lord and, God willing, have more children.

After seeing Elizabeth with Samuel, all he'd thought about was having children with the lass. She was a loving mother, and from her son's adoration of his parent, he wanted their children to have the same upbringing as well. She was perfect for him; she was, in fact, a woman without faults, and he adored her.

"Excuse me, my lord. This has arrived for you."

Henry pulled from his musings and remembered to thank the footman before breaking the seal of the missive. He frowned at the note, which sported only his first name and no address. He looked up and checked Elizabeth's location. She was still alone, her attention fixed on the dancing couples.

He read the missive quickly, the blood in his veins warming at the impending delight the words brought forth in his mind. He excused himself from the few gentlemen gathered around him and made his way to the private sitting room adjacent to the billiards room as asked within the note. Muffled voices of gentlemen and a few ladies sounded behind the closed adjoining door. Henry walked over to the fire, kicked at a smoking log, and prepared to wait for his guest.

At the sound of the door handle twisting, he turned; the lighted hall illuminated the woman before the cover of the darkened room shrouded her features.

"Are you lost, Miss Andrews?" he asked, having not expected her.

Her chuckle raised his unease. "No, far from lost, for I'm here...with you, and quite alone."

Henry watched Miss Andrews walk toward him, her steps reminding him of a lion's saunter while hunting its next meal. "You need to leave, Amelia. You're not chaperoned."

He stilled as she stood before him, her hand running down his chest. He caught hold of her hand and moved it away from him before she went any further with her touch.

Her eyes widened with hurt, and a pang of guilt pricked his soul. There was no denying Amelia was a beautiful woman and would make some chap a wonderful wife one day, but she wasn't for him. Only one woman would warm his bed, and it was not the lass standing before him.

"But I don't want to. You're here, as I knew you would be. Come, Henry, don't play coy with me now."

Henry stepped back, unsure why she would say such a thing. "How did ye know I would be in this room?" He frowned as she laughed louder than he liked with men so close next door. The last thing he wished was to be caught in a compromising position with Amelia.

"I received your note. I'm so happy you finally recognize your feelings for me." Amelia ran a finger along the lapels of his coat. "You must know I've wished for such an opportunity as this. For us to be together, to be alone for just a moment."

"My letter?" Henry paused, dread taking hold. "Miss Andrews, I never sent ye a missive." Henry watched as she visibly paled and, feeling for the poor chit, he escorted her to the settee before sitting beside her.

"You didn't?" A small frown marred her normally serene brow.

He shook his head. "No, I did not." He sighed, wondering what was afoot and who was playing games with them yet again. He could certainly take a good guess. "I fear we have both been tricked for I, too, received a note, but..." His words trailed off, not wanting to let her know of his understanding with Elizabeth. As it was he would hurt the lass, no need to rub salt into her wound here and now.

"But?"

"But it wasn't addressed from you."

She leaned back, sighing. "Was it from Lady Newland?" When he didn't reply, she clasped his hand, patting it. "I cannot deny I'm not disappointed in your choice, for I would've loved for you to have picked me as your lass, but one cannot change what one's heart feels." She paused. "I wonder who gave us the letters, then. Why play a trick on you and me?"

Henry knew of only one who'd love to see him married and safely away from his English lass. What ruse was this getting them alone other than the one of catching them in a compromising situation... "We should leave. Now."

Amelia's hold tightened on his hand, halting his departure. "Have you asked her to marry you yet?"

Henry chuckled at her infectious grin. "I have, and she's said yes. How did ye know of my affection toward Lady Newland?"

"I knew the first time I saw you with her that you loved her. I cannot deny I'm sorely disappointed, but I know when the game is up." Amelia smiled and, for the first time in all the time he'd known her, she truly looked beautiful, not spiteful or deceptive, but accepting of the situation, happy for him even. "I wish you all the very best, Henry. I know I have not been the nicest person when around your lady, but it was entirely due to jealousy, you see. I've acted shamelessly, and I'm not proud of it. I apologize, and I owe Lady Newland an apology, too."

"Thank ye, Amelia. I'm grateful for your blessing and friendship, but I should have told you my heart was taken long before ye feelings became engaged. It was wrong of me, and I'm sorry."

"May we still be friends?"

"Always," he said, leaning down and kissing her cheek, pulling her into a short embrace, a farewell between friends.

"*O*h, forgive me," Elizabeth said, unable to move from the threshold of the sitting room door, the light from the hallway casting the lovers on the settee in light. She willed her legs to move. To get herself away from where she stood, but the shock of seeing Henry embracing Miss Andrews left her incapable of doing either. Pain tore through her chest, and she stood there transfixed.

"Elizabeth!" Henry said, standing.

"I'm sorry. I was looking for the billiards room. I'll leave you now."

"No, wait." Henry came about the settee and reached for her hand. "This isn't what it looks like, Elizabeth. I assure ye."

Elizabeth wrenched her hand free, stepping away, the gulf between them opening larger than the Atlantic Ocean. "Isn't it? Perhaps you'd like to explain your situation then," Elizabeth stated, her tone icy.

A muscle worked in Henry's jaw, and she willed him to tell her what she'd just seen wasn't true. That he hadn't been sitting in a darkened room with only firelight, embracing Miss Andrews. She bit her lip to stop it from trembling.

"I'm sorry," he said.

"You've already said that." She looked at Miss Andrews, surprised triumph wasn't written all over her features. "It seems I should offer my congratulations on your forthcoming marriage."

"What? No, Elizabeth, ye've got it wrong." Henry shook his head, his eyes beseeching.

Elizabeth wished she could believe him, but she could not. "Are you telling me I didn't just catch you in a compromising position with Miss Andrews?" Elizabeth said, gesturing to the woman.

"No," he said. "Well, yes ye did, but it didn't mean what ye think."

Elizabeth laughed mockingly. It was either that or cry. "Really, and should I have married you, would all such liaisons I heard of or caught you in be viewed in such a way?"

Henry frowned. "Of course not. Ye're not thinking right." He swore and she started at the word. "Miss Andrews and I are nothing more than friends."

"Very good friends by the looks of it," Elizabeth stated.

"Please stop and just listen, lass."

Miss Andrews stood. "Lady Newland, really there was nothing in the embrace, it meant—"

"That will be all from you, Miss Andrews. I'm neither your friend nor do I trust your word. And as for you, Henry, well, I don't know what to think." Her voice sounded as dejected as she felt. She swallowed as the lump in her throat made it hard to breathe.

"Miss Andrews, if ye would leave us please, I wish to speak to my future wife."

Elizabeth huffed out a breath. "She needn't leave, I'll go."

Henry reached out and clasped her hand, pulling her toward him. "Ye will not."

Miss Andrews shuffled from the room and shut the door. Elizabeth watched in shock as Henry followed her to the door, the snip of the lock sounding as loud as a war drum.

She crossed her arms over her chest, hating the fact he was pulling such high-handedness with her. She was a duke's daughter, not some scullery maid.

He turned and leveled his displeased visage on her. "Come here, Elizabeth."

She didn't move, just stood there wondering how she could get to the door and through it with him standing in her way. "No."

"If ye do not I'll be forced to come to you."

His words thrummed with promise, and a little part of her

wanted to push him to see what in fact he would do should she not follow his order. Not that she intended to ever do as she was told. He'd picked the wrong woman to marry if he wanted a docile, obedient wife. Elizabeth paused at the thought. That was, if she ever married him after what she saw tonight. "I will not."

He stalked toward her, and she backed up with each step he took. The determination in his gaze elicited a shiver of awareness to run through her. A small table that abutted the settee met her bottom, and she clasped it for support with nowhere else to go.

"Nothing has ever happened, or ever will happen between me and Miss Andrews. I simply gave my friend a farewell embrace after declaring to her my love for you. Her affections were engaged toward me, but it was one-sided, and I should have been honest with her from the start on who I wanted for my wife."

"You told her about me?" It was pleasing to hear such words, but still, what was one supposed to think when one walked into a darkened room and found one's betrothed in a compromising position?

"I was given a missive, addressed from you, that I was to meet ye here. Miss Andrews received the same, but supposedly addressed from me. How is it ye're here, lass?"

She thought over his words, and anger coursed through her veins, scorching and molten. "Riddledale said you were playing billiards, and I should go view the game, but the way he said it, I suppose, raised my suspicions, my insecurities about us, and even though I wanted to trust you, I had to come see what his lordship was talking about. And so when I saw you—"

"With Amelia, ye assumed the worse," he said, finishing her words.

"Yes." He stepped up hard against her, lifting her atop the

table and settling between her legs. Her body warmed, and heat pooled at her core. "I'm sorry, Henry."

"I'm sorry, lass, for it looks like Riddledale has tried yet again to fool us and compromise me with another woman." Her eyes flared and she clasped his lapels. "We should leave. Should we be caught in such a situation, well, it wouldn't bode well."

Henry kissed her quickly, nuzzling her cheek and ear. She sighed, loving the feel of him so close to her again.

"Not yet. I need ye."

Elizabeth looked up and met his gaze. "Here? Now?" Even to her ears she sounded scandalized.

"Aye. We're betrothed, and who cares if Riddledale catches us, he would not dare speak of your…misdemeanor, as it were. It would not fit in with his plans for ye." He grinned, and his intent became clear.

"But what about the letter?" They couldn't leave it here; it was imperative that they gained it back.

"We'll continue on with our plan as agreed, but first I need to remind ye of something."

A warm strong hand clasped the edge of her gown, sliding it slowly up her legs. Night air kissed her skin and she reveled at being in his arms once more. Since her return to London she'd not slept well, her bed too big, too empty for one person. She'd dreadfully missed him sneaking into her room or vice versa, making love and being together until the wee hours of the morning. "And what is it that I need reminding of?"

He grinned, his hand brushing her mons and making her gasp. Elizabeth raised her legs and pulled him toward her, wanting him with a need that surpassed all else.

"That ye're mine and I am yours, and that nothing, not Riddledale or Miss Andrews, will change that. I love ye, Elizabeth, and I'll not lose ye again."

His eyes glowed with primal need and, unable not to taste the sin that he offered, she reached up and pulled him down for a kiss. He hauled her hard against him, wrenching her into a world of bliss. Absently, she felt him rip open his frontfalls before jerking her core against his hardness.

Their eyes locked as he slid within her, and she muffled a groan against his shoulder at the feel of him again, of the delicious friction he wrought on her body. There was no sweet surrender, no time to fall into pleasure, it just rocked into her, hard and fast, the actions frantic and edged with a promise that this was forever, and nothing else would suffice.

All she could do was hold on to Henry and try to keep up with their mutual need. Over and over again he took her, their bodies grinding, undulating, clasping to get closer, to enjoy more what being together like this did to each other.

Henry clasped her bottom, and the action heaved her hard against him, once, twice, three rigid strokes, and pleasure shattered throughout her body. He kissed away her gasping moans, his own cries of bliss muffled against her lips. Elizabeth held him close, her breathing ragged and her body weak and sleepy.

Distantly the sounds of the supper dance sounded, and Henry pulled back, helping to right her clothing and his. "Ye look thoroughly ruined." He grinned, a self-satisfied smile on his lips.

Elizabeth laughed. "I feel ruined." Ruined for anyone else. She wiggled off the table and checked her hair in a nearby mirror. "What now?"

"Now," Henry said, coming up behind her and wrapping his arms about her stomach. "We get ye letter back and announce to the world we're to marry."

She smiled at him as he watched her in the mirror. "I like the sound of this plan."

Henry nuzzled her neck, kissing it gently. "Me too, lass. Now, let's go," he said, slapping her bottom.

---

*W*ith a nod to Elizabeth's brother, the Duke of Penworth, their plan was set in motion. Henry watched as Josh headed toward Lord Riddledale to keep the man occupied while he and Elizabeth disappeared to look for the stolen letter.

Elizabeth had excused herself a few minutes before, citing a need to freshen up, and now it was Henry's turn to disappear for a time. He made his way through the throng of guests, walking toward the gaming room, which, from what Elizabeth's brother had stated, shared a door with Riddledale's library.

The room was full of gambling men, many of whom held expressions that were displeased and some outright terrified. He shook his head at their need for such sport. Gambling in any way was not for him, not after his grandfather had nearly lost the estate due to the habit that became an obsession.

He watched the games a moment before spotting the door he needed to get to. Strolling toward it, he casually leaned on its threshold before noting no one taking heed of his actions, so he slipped inside.

The room had only two candles burning and both were on the mantle. Henry shut the door quietly and snipped the lock, striding toward the fireplace and taking both candles over to the desk. He ducked as the other door to the room opened and closed quickly, the lithe, delectable form of his future wife making him sigh in relief. He stood, and she started before walking over to him.

"You scared me," she whispered, giggling a little. "Apologies." He smiled, twisting back to the desk with turned golden feet. "Come, I need ye to search Riddledale's shelves over by the mantle." He pointed to a large cupboard filled with paperwork, scrolls, and books that looked like journals. "And I'll search the desk."

"The letter will be in Father's writing, if you can remember his script."

"I believe I can." He tried the drawers and found every one of them locked. Searching for the key, he noted Riddledale kept his desk organized and nothing like the cupboard that Elizabeth searched through that was a mess of gargantuan proportions. "It may be in a tome, so shake them to see if anything falls out."

Other than a quill, inkwell, blotter, and bronze letter racks, not much else was on the desk; certainly no key shone out like a beacon. Henry kneeled and felt along the wood under the desk, searching for a hidden compartment where one would hide a key. His search proved fruitful when a small silver key fell onto the floor.

"I've found the key."

Elizabeth came over to him, kneeling beside him. "Unlock both sides, and I'll search these drawers."

Henry did as she bade, and they both looked through the abundance of correspondence. His lordship had many IOUs in his possession. Henry grabbed a piece of parchment and noted down as many names as he could of to whom Riddledale owed money. Should their plan fail tonight, there was hope if he bought all of Riddledale's debt that he could barter a deal out of threat of financial ruin against the man. Either way, from tonight, the dark cloud that Elizabeth had been living under would end.

"I cannot find anything. Maybe he carries it around with him." She slumped back on her haunches, and he continued to sift through the mail.

"I would not think so, and ye brother stated he'd seen him get it out of a drawer." After more thorough searching and his frustration rising, Henry had to concede Elizabeth may be right. The letter wasn't here.

He stood, taking in the room, trying to think where one would hide correspondence. His gaze stopped at a lady's gold filigreed rosewood traveling case sitting on a table beside a large globe of the world. Would Riddledale hide gentlemen's correspondence in a woman's desk? It was certainly not the usual place one would look if searching for something related to a man…

Henry strode over to it, conscious that their time was running short. They'd been in here too long as it was.

"What are you doing, Henry?" Elizabeth whispered when he opened it, thankful it was unlocked.

"Looking." He studied the box, knowing these desks often held secret compartments. Removing an inkwell from its compartments did exactly what he wished—a small lock was released and applying pressure to the wood at the bottom of the desk, the compartment lifted, and three hidden drawers came into view. He silently thanked his mama for having a similar desk that he'd played with often as a boy, and now all he could do was pray this was where the letter was. Surely, if Riddledale was hiding his correspondence anywhere, it would be here.

Pulling open the first drawer, Elizabeth's hand shot out and clasped the missive. "It's here. This is the letter." He smiled, putting the writing desk as it was before and closing the lid quickly. The relief on his future bride's visage was all the thanks he required.

"I'll lock up the other desk, and we'll go. We need to leave."

"Yes, you do, but not before giving back the letter you've just stolen."

Elizabeth gasped, clutching the missive against her chest.

Henry laughed; he doubted his lass would be giving up the missive any time soon. "Ye mean the letter you stole, Riddledale. How amusing ye are." He clasped Elizabeth's arm and pulled her toward the door. "Good night to ye."

"I can still cause a scandal for you, Lady Newland, do not mistake. It would be best if you gave me the missive and do as I bid. You will marry me, my dear. Make no illusion."

"I will never marry you."

Henry turned at the abhorrence of her tone, and he could not blame her. To be saddled with Riddledale would be torture. "She'll not be marrying ye no matter what rumors ye spread to try and tarnish her or her family. Elizabeth will be my wife, and there's the end to it. She will never be yours."

Riddledale snarled, idly walking toward the door and leaning against its dark wood. "Have you not read the missive, Lord Muir? You're accommodating for a man whom I would've thought reading the letter would've caused great hurt to you."

Henry frowned, unsure of what he meant by that. "I know what's disclosed in the letter."

"Really?" Riddledale scoffed, his tone mocking. "Elizabeth, have you been honest finally? I doubt you know the whole truth, Lord Muir."

Henry looked to Elizabeth and noted her quietness and wont of color on her face. He took her hand, shaking it a little. "Elizabeth, pass me the missive."

Her eyes widened and she stilled. "Henry...I—"

"Give it to me, lass." With reluctance, she released her grip on the note and gave it to him. He walked over to the desk, held the note beside the candlelight, and read it.

The words jumped out at him, words like ruin, child, pregnancy, honor, marriage, father... He slumped against the desk and fought not to cast up his accounts.

He was a father? Samuel was his?

He strode to Elizabeth, fisting his hands at his side. The despair written on her face was clear, but he ignored it. Damn the woman. All the weeks he'd been back in town, the promises of no more lies, of them being friends, lovers, and she'd not thought to once be honest with him. He'd given her plenty of opportunities to tell him of their child had she wished to, but she had not. For a moment he wondered if she ever intended to tell him.

He swore, clasping her arm and pulling her toward the terrace doors, needing to be away from Riddledale, this house, the ton—everyone. Henry strove to control his temper, which he was just keeping leached. It wouldn't bode well for either of them should he lose it. And, unfortunately, this was just such a situation as he was likely to.

He was a father... The notion rumbled bout in his head like a drum.

"You're leaving so soon?" Riddledale asked, laughing. "Come now, stay, perhaps I can offer some advice on your predicament."

Henry ignored the cur and pulled Elizabeth out the door before turning about and facing Riddledale. "You may spread any tales ye wish, we don't care. We have the letter, so it's hearsay from this night on, but be aware that should ye push me with your relentlessness on having Lady Newland as your wife, I will be forced to push back, and it'll not be to your liking. Do ye understand?"

Riddledale scoffed, pouring himself a brandy. "I don't take well to being told what to do or how to act, but in return, Lord Muir, I will tell you this. I always get what I want. Always."

Henry didn't bother with a reply, but left, walking Elizabeth toward the mews and where the carriages were stationed. He spied his driver and motioned him to ready the carriage. Helping Elizabeth up into the squabs, he joined her, slamming the door shut.

She watched him, her eyes wide and, for the first time in the entire duration he'd known her, she was quiet. Good. Best she didn't speak until he'd tempered his anger to a controlled level.

It was only a few minutes before they were on their way, the houses of Mayfair beacons of light and wealth along a darkened road. He saw none of it.

"Say something, Henry. Please."

His eyes narrowed and he shook his head, beyond furious. "You lied."

---

*E*lizabeth nodded. She had, and the guilt of such an untruth had eaten at her from the moment she'd decided Henry should never know of Samuel. "I did, but you must see why I did such a thing. It was not purposefully done."

"No? And pray tell me how ye come to that conclusion? Because to me, it most certainly is purposeful." Henry sat back against the leather seats, crossing his arms, his face a mask of hurt and fury.

"You must see that we tried. We wrote to you, begging your return. It was not my fault that Riddledale took the missive and made use of it for his own agenda." She swallowed the panic clawing at her throat and strove to calm. Surely if Henry could see the truth behind all the mess she'd made of the situation, they could make something work. Have some kind of future happiness.

"My son has the name of another gentleman. Instead of the Scottish earl he should be, he's taken the roll of a mere English viscount. How dare you."

Tears smarted, and she bit her lip. "I didn't have any choice. When we received the letter back from you, even though I know now it was a fake missive, my parents did what they thought best. I was dragged to Wiltshire and married before I could draw a calming breath."

"And ye fooled another gentleman. Allowed the fellow to die always believing he'd fathered a son, an heir for his lands and estate, when he had not. How can ye live with such a falsehood?" Henry shook his head, distaste clouding his every word.

Elizabeth fought to right the wrong, a wrong she'd really had no say in. Had Riddledale not stolen from them, none of this would be occurring right now. The life she longed for, the life she wanted, started to pull further from her reach. She clasped the chair for support, needing something to keep her upright.

"Newland came across me in the garden at his estate, being sick on his perennials. He guessed the urgency for our visit and due to his riding accident, which left him unsuitable for most of his social obligations, he asked me to marry him." And she'd loved him in a small way from that moment on for saving her, even though he didn't have to. He could've thrown her to the wolves and watched her be ripped apart.

"He knew?"

She flinched at the whipping accusation. "Yes, he knew, and he adored Samuel, cared for him like he was his own child, and I'll never let anyone, not even you, mar that memory for me. He saved me, Henry, and had you been able to, had you known the truth, I know you would've done the same, but I didn't have that option. I did what was necessary to secure my son's future."

"My son's future, which will forever be a lie."

She looked out the carriage window, hating that his words were cold, cutting and the truth. "Samuel will be known as Lord Newland one day, yes. I will not allow you to try to change that. My family supports my actions, and should you try, Henry, I will fight you on it."

"How so, madam?" His lip turned in disdain. "I hardly know ye."

The carriage rocked to a halt, and Elizabeth was surprised to see he'd brought her back to her family's London home. "You cannot prove anything, Henry, and that you're threatening me when I'm as innocent as you in this muddled past is beyond forgiving. I did not tell Riddledale to steal our letter. I did not tell him to write on your behalf and shout lies and insults in my face. What did you expect me to do? Have a child out of wedlock? I could not, I would not do that to my family."

"Ye should have."

"And that, Lord Muir, is where we will forever differ. If I had my time again, I would do no different. Lord Newland was a loving and caring husband, and I'm forever grateful for him. I'm sorry your son now bears another man's name, but it is what it is, and you should make peace with it, for it'll not ever change, no matter how much you wish it to."

Henry opened the door, gesturing at the space. "Get out. This conversation is over."

Elizabeth started, but did as he bid, climbing down without assistance and not looking for any even if he had offered it. "I think all that needs to be said between us has been said. I wish you well, Lord Muir."

"And what about my son? Do ye dare keep him from me?"

"You may visit Samuel whenever you wish, I'll not stop you, but heed my warning, Henry, do not overstep your bounds. I will not have it."

He slammed the door in her face, glaring at her. "We will see about that, Lady Newland." The rap on the carriage ceiling was loud in the quiet street, and Elizabeth turned away, her eyes smarting and making the steps that were nothing but a blur.

She made it up to her room in a haze, unsure how she got there, but thankful when her maid undressed her and helped her into bed. Elizabeth pulled the blanket over her head. Her life was over, no future in Scotland with Henry beckoned, as there was no chance he'd ever forgive her for her dishonesty.

Elizabeth allowed the heaving sobs to burst free, and she muffled them as much as she could against her pillows. He hated her, and the loathing on his face when she'd stood outside his carriage left her with little hope of reconciliation.

This time they were done. It was over, and nothing she could say or do could change that awful truth.

CHAPTER 18

A month passed, the time endless and seemingly longer than the years Henry spent abroad. Elizabeth had stayed in town for some days after Lord Riddledale's ball in the hopes that Henry would seek her out, beg to have her back, to say sorry for what they'd both said, ask for forgiveness and a chance to start again.

But she'd been wrong, had fooled herself into a false hope that eventuated to nothing. Henry's silence spoke louder than any words could, and so Elizabeth had made the decision to return to Dunsleigh before the season ended. Her family, still in half mourning, wished to accompany her, and so the London home was closed up, and they left.

Women's voices sounded from her mother's sitting room upstairs, and not in the mood for company, Elizabeth walked into the family's private drawing room at the rear of the house—a sunny, well-lit space during the morning— and sat before the terrace doors, watching as the gardeners weeded the flower beds outside.

"A letter has arrived for you, my lady."

The footman handed Elizabeth the missive and she

thanked him. She scrutinized the note's messy writing for a moment before breaking the seal.

Courtship is a fool's errand.
And love makes fools of us all.
Do not dally forever more.
Or all you fools will fall.

Elizabeth scrunched up the note, hating the fact her hands shook with the action. Lord Riddledale had more hair than wit and she should've known the man had not the smarts to give over. At least he could not harm her or Samuel any longer. The letter had been duly burned and, should he pronounce her indiscretion, it was her word against his, and no one would dare slander the Worthinghams without proof. Riddledale had lost.

Determined to shake off her melancholy and enjoy the beautiful day, Elizabeth stood and headed to the stables. Her flighty Argo poked his nose over the stall door in welcome and she refused her groom's offer to saddle her mount, instead opting to do it herself.

Once saddled, she led him out to the mounting block, took her seat, and cantered from the manicured grounds, jumping the outlying fences before urging Argo into a blistering speed toward the grassy fields beyond. The wind made her eyes water, hairpins dislodged, and soon her light locks cascaded about her shoulders. Still, she pushed Argo, blaming her tears on the impressive speed her mount could accomplish and not the loss of a certain Scottish earl.

Time ticked by, and eventually Argo's steps slowed. She led him under a copse of trees and dismounted, seeking out a fallen limb to sit on. Elizabeth looked up at the branches of the grand oak, the leaves swaying in the pleasant breeze.

Memories of Henry haunted her every thought. Of their

racing these very lands, of picnics and endless summer days before coming-out balls and necessary trips to America were a concern.

How life had been so much simpler then.

She shut her eyes as her body heated recalling their last day together here at Dunsleigh where their beautiful son was conceived. How together they'd transformed from youths to adults before the slow flowing waters that Henry had taught her to swim in.

What a mess she'd made of things. And worse, she didn't really know if a future together was possible, or if Henry had walked away from her for good. Her heart stopped beating at the thought. It couldn't be over. She'd not allow it to be. She would have to speak to him again. Perhaps he'd returned to Scotland, and she would write him a letter, detailing everything that had happened and her reasoning behind her actions.

Maybe it would work.

A crack of a branch sounded from behind, and she looked over her shoulder, but it was too late to react. A filthy cloth came up hard against her mouth and covered her nose. The assailant pulled her up against his body, and Elizabeth kicked at him as best she could. The man was large, a bandana covering half his face. His strength was immovable, and he took what punches she could deliver, but nothing budged his tight hold.

Her eyes grew heavy and it was a fight to keep them open. Her knees gave out just as blackness swamped her senses, but not before her last conscious thought was that Lord Riddledale had made his final move.

*E*lizabeth woke with the notion she was not alone in the equipage. The carriage rocked, gravel crunching loud under the fast-paced wheels. Still her senses screamed for caution. Without moving a muscle, she peeked at her surroundings, spying a pair of spotless, high-gloss boots. It wasn't hard to guess to whom they belonged. His lordship had always been a pompous ass even in kidnapping it would seem.

"Ah, I see you are awake. Welcome, Lady Newland. I hope you had a pleasant sleep."

Elizabeth struggled to sit up and gasped as Lord Riddledale bent down and pulled her to sit across from him. His hands slid down her arms and checked the knot holding her wrists together behind her back. Elizabeth struggled to breathe with the vile-smelling bandana across her mouth.

She tried to tell the fiend he was a curse upon society. His lordship's reaction to her feeble attempt was a hefty laugh. The man's fragile mind had finally snapped, she was sure of it. His fingers slid over her cheek, then down to outline her top lip before he wrenched the bandana from her mouth, his nails cutting into her cheek.

Elizabeth took a breath of fresh air and fought down nausea rising in her throat. "My brother will ensure you hang for this. How dare you kidnap me?"

His calculating smile chilled her to her core. "He will not kill the Marquis of Riddledale, his new brother-in-law."

Elizabeth sat as far back against the squabs as she could and watched with distaste as Lord Riddledale's eyes lingered, his mouth almost salivating over her form. She looked away and tried to block out the thought that he may hurt her, take liberties that were not freely given.

"You should have accepted my proposal when I first

asked. Had you done so, none of this would've been necessary, my lady."

"Again, my lord, you fail to understand the English language. I said no." She tried to calm herself, but it was a battle she was losing. "Perhaps you should listen more attentively the next time you ask a question."

He chuckled as if the whole situation was amusing. A lark to be settled by marriage. Damn him.

"All women play coy and hard to please. You are no different."

Elizabeth looked out the windows and tried to gauge where they were, in what direction they traveled. The carriage was not new or fashionable, the upholstery was torn and dirty, much like herself, she mused. The rattling door was held shut by a frayed piece of rope. And here sat Lord Riddledale in his best attire, fresh and well-kept just like a Mayfair dandy.

"I thought such a vehicle would be less conspicuous. I can't have mine being seen; all of them sport the family emblem on the doors, you see." He smiled, and she glared. "We're not being followed, and we'll make our destination by morning."

Elizabeth swallowed, not wanting to know where the lout was taking her but knowing he would tell her in any case. Threats such as these seemed a trait of his nature,

something he craved as much as having her for a wife. "Would you like to know our destination, my dear?" Her eyes narrowed at the endearment, but she refused to be drawn into his game. Dreadful prig.

He laughed, sat forward, and tweaked her nose. "Never mind, I shall tell you. You'll be happy to know the town in which you'll become my wife in the truest sense, and I'm not just speaking of our vows, is Gretna Green. You may now announce your excitement."

Elizabeth tested her restraints, having never hated a man as much as she hated the one across from her. "How dare you."

He shrugged. "I've been daring for years; you just didn't know it."

She met his gaze and hoped he read the hate in her eyes. "You'll pay for this treachery."

"And so will you should you not do as I say. I know all the scandals your pretty head almost crashed down upon the Duke of Penworth's lofty head. I know everything, Elizabeth."

Elizabeth lifted her chin. "You have no proof of them, and the letter you did steal has since been burned. My brother has kept the correspondence you sent on behalf of Lord Muir, which he's passed along to Bow Street for investigation. It will not be long before you'll be outed as a thief, scorned by your betters. Ruined."

He smirked, and she wanted to scratch the smug smile off his face.

"Did I fail to tell you, my lord, that when we were looking for my father's letter, we came across notification of your debt? A lot of it, mind. My brother has since bought up all your IOUs, and now you owe his grace a hefty sum. If my brother has need to call in those debts, well, it shall not end well for you, I believe." Elizabeth raised her brows. "Are you sure you wish to continue with this ploy, your lordship?"

"I have no debt to your brother," Riddledale said, his voice no longer so sure, his face turning paler than usual.

"I do not lie. My brother did buy up most of what you owe, and now your fortune could be lost. So unless you wish to be poor, I would turn us about now."

His alarmed face cleared when his hand settled on her knee, his fingers clenching her skin. Elizabeth fought not to vomit. "He'll not ruin his brother-in-law, and that's exactly who I'll be in a matter of hours."

He leaned away, folding his hands in his lap, seemingly a man without a care. "I've always watched you, Elizabeth, and you were lucky the day you laid like a whore, spread your legs like a Covent Garden hussy for Lord Muir, that I didn't have my flintlock with me. If I had my time again your esteemed Henry would be long dead."

She shut her eyes, hating the thought of a vile creature such as Lord Riddledale intruding during an act that was brought on by affection and, above all, love.

"After Muir left it was easy to have incoming and outgoing mail diverted to me to ensure no letters from America made the salver nor any of your missives made his. I'm so glad we're neighbors," he said. "It makes one's life so much easier, don't you think?"

"You bastard. A family friend who deceived us all. You ruined my life." Tears welled, and she pushed them away, not wanting him to see how he could affect her so. She would never give him such power if she could help it.

"You ruined your own life. My intention was only ever to marry you. I love you."

Elizabeth kicked his shins, happily landing a good blow before his hand was about her neck, the accompanying squeeze ensuring she stopped her assault.

"You thought to marry your bastard Scot and have his baby, no heed to your duty as a duke's daughter or what's expected of you." He squeezed tighter, and she fought for breath. "It would be a slight upon England for a Worthingham to marry such highland scum." He paused, snarling. "Well, you will not marry him, Elizabeth. I would not allow it then, and I shall never allow it now. You will be the future Marchioness of Riddledale, or you'll be nothing at all should you refuse to do as you're told. With your distress at losing your dearest Henry, it is all probable that a woman of your mental insecurities could befall an accident. All of London has watched you fawn over the gentleman since his return, and I've whispered into enough ears to ensure an accident would not be a surprise. Such a sad ending for a woman so unlucky in love." He laughed, his eyes gleaming in triumph. "How the ton will enjoy such a sad tale of woe for years."

"The hell I will," Elizabeth said, loathing lacing her tone. "And you will not have to push me from the cliff, for if it's a future with you or death, I pick death. I would rather die than let you win."

Riddledale raised his brows. "Well, we will see, shall we not?" he said, tying the bandana across her mouth once more and watching her with a silence that left her ice cold.

CHAPTER 19

*H*enry cantered down Dunsleigh's drive, going over every word he would say to Elizabeth when he saw her in only a matter of minutes. He beat back the doubt that continued to gnaw at his gut that Elizabeth had walked away from their love, had believed their final night in London together was the last they'd ever have.

It would not be. Could not be.

"Stupid fool," he cursed aloud, pulling his mount up to a walk the last mile. How he could've said such things to her, been so cruel, so callous, without a moment's thought to what she was actually saying, what she was trying to explain. All of which within a matter of weeks he'd come to see the sense of, even if it was a knife to the gut that his son would not inherit his estate. But that was hardly Elizabeth's fault. Riddledale had been the one he wanted strung up and dealt with, but the bastard had fled town, and something told him he'd followed Elizabeth back to her ancestral home.

Soon the grand sandstone building came into view, and he kicked on with his plan, a plan he was determined would not fail. Elizabeth would be his. He loved her, loved Samuel more than anything else in the world, and deep down he knew she loved him. Enough time had been wasted. It was their due to have a home and family, to be together as husband and wife and father and mother to their boy.

Henry pulled his mount to a stop, noting with some amusement a young stable lad, flustered and red-faced racing about from the side of the building to take his mount. Dismounting, he pulled off his gloves just as the ducal carriage barreled around the corner and stopped in a cloud of dust before him.

The sense that something was wrong flared alarm within him. Footmen raced from the house with luggage, the servants seemingly in some sort of uproar. Henry quickly went inside, the front door wide open, and strode toward the library where he could hear the duke barking out orders to his staff.

"What's going on?"

His grace sank into his chair, his gaze weary. "Lord Riddledale has taken Elizabeth."

"What!" Henry felt the blood drain from his face. He stood, stunned for a moment before his mind caught up with his rapid heartbeat. "What happened?" He tried to calm his growing apprehension, but the thought of Elizabeth in that fiend's clutches made his blood run cold.

Oh dear God, what had he done. He'd left her. Alone. Again.

"Victoria was out riding this morning. She saw Elizabeth on Argo from a distance. She also saw a great oaf of a man put something over Elizabeth's face and then carry her away. From the description she gave, it's the same man Elizabeth mentioned seeing in London, the one the runner assumed to be working for Riddledale. I've no doubt she is with him now."

Henry slumped into a nearby chair, his mind frantic over

where he may have taken her. He knew Lord Riddledale had an estate not far from here, but unless the man was as thick as he was foolish he doubted he'd take her there. So where?

Henry met the duke's gaze. "What's ye plan?"

"Victoria, the smart girl that she is, followed them for some distance and watched Elizabeth be placed into a carriage just out of Penworth. They then headed north on the road to London."

Henry nodded, making a mental note to thank Victoria for her forthright thinking. "London then Gretna?" he suggested.

The duke cursed. "Yes, it seems most likely. He could certainly force her to marry him there if enough money changed hands, but I really do not know. It's a guess only." He stood pacing. "I'm going to ride up to Gretna. It'll be a lot faster than a carriage. But I will be sending Alice up in the family vehicle. No doubt Lord Riddledale has set lookouts along the road, and if he thinks I'm chasing them by carriage, he'll not quicken his pace to Scotland or panic and do something foolish he'll live to regret."

"And we therefore make Scotland around the same time on horseback." Henry clenched his fist. He welcomed the meeting with his lordship and bestowing some well-deserved Scottish punishment on the English prig.

His grace nodded. "I assume by your arrival you were looking to reconcile with Elizabeth."

Henry nodded. "That's right."

"You love her." It wasn't a question.

The thought of Elizabeth warmed his soul, and he smiled at the duke, finally seeing resignation and acceptance in his soon-to-be brother-in-law's gaze. "I always have."

His grace chuckled wryly and went to the decanter, lifted the crystal, and poured two glasses of brandy. He handed one to Henry. "I suppose since you're here, you've come to see

that our family had little choice in keeping Elizabeth's reputation intact and giving Samuel a father. It was not done out
of spite to you, Lord Muir, and although I've yet to forgive
your actions beside the lake that day, my sister does love you,
and therefore I must concede defeat."

"Does this mean I have ye blessing to marry her, your
grace?"

The duke finished his drink. "Well, that you're here
proves to me that my assumptions of you are correct. You
love her as we do, so yes, you have our blessing. Father
always suspected you were innocent of the crimes we laid at
your door, had stated something didn't add up quite right."

Henry smiled, relief pouring through him like the amber
liquid in his hand. "The late duke will forever be remembered fondly. He was a good man." Henry smiled at the
memory of Elizabeth's father, who'd always given affection
and advice to his children and never faltered being there
when they needed him.

The duke sighed, running a hand over his jaw. "Riddledale has been playing with this family for a long time, and
it's past time he received his comeuppance for all the
heartache he's caused." The duke paused. "I had to dismiss
two maids who work under Elizabeth's lady's maid. I found
they were the ones who betrayed our family and were
working for the blackguard along with the one who ran
away in London."

Henry felt ill at the knowledge. "His actions have been
truly disgraceful and I'm sorry for it. And I must thank ye for
the blessing. I'm glad to have it, but ye know," he continued,
catching the duke's eye, "I would've married Elizabeth
without it, just so ye know."

"I know you would have. Don't the Scots always take
what they want, English or no?"

"Aye, they do." Henry chuckled. "I think it's time we left.

We've given Lord Riddledale enough of a lead. It's time we chased him down."

The duke's eyes lit with retribution that was soon to be theirs. "I couldn't agree more. Let's be off."

Minutes later, Henry stood next to his mount and checked the girth. He rolled his shoulders, ready for the forthcoming ride. At the sound of female voices, Henry turned and watched as Alice ran from the house, followed by a maid carrying two small bags, Victoria following close behind.

"Victoria, go and change. You're not traveling with Alice looking like that," the duke said, his voice hard.

Henry tried to hide his smile over Victoria's attire, consisting of men's breeches, shirt, and jacket. He would let his future brother-in-law deal with his hellion sister.

"That's because I'm not traveling with Alice, brother." Victoria turned to the stableman. "Is my horse ready, Tony?"

"I demand you go and change this instant. You look—"

"Oh, do be quiet, Josh. You know I'm not going to listen to you in any case. With my cap, no one will recognize me as a woman. Now stop this and let us be on our way. I believe there's a wedding we have to object to."

Henry watched in amusement as the duke realized he wouldn't win the battle. The man cursed then mounted his horse and turned toward the gate. "Let's go."

They took off at a punishing speed, making London in less than half a day. They called into Smithfield and queried the publican at the coaching inn with no luck. Lord Riddledale had possibly traveled straight through the capital without pause.

At Stamford, they missed them by only a few hours. Pushing on to Retford, they changed horses for the third time and partook in refreshments.

With the persuasion of gold, the patrons at the coaching

inn's tavern described in detail a man with a woman passenger heading north. One lodger mentioned it seemed strange: the whole time the young miss fought with the gentleman and looked rightfully annoyed. How very insightful, Henry mused as burning revenge and punishment cooked away inside him. Lord Riddledale would not enjoy their arrival in Gretna.

After watering the horses they continued north at a blistering speed. Their time was precious, and every second counted. Elizabeth's well-being was at risk, for what type of man kidnapped a woman, no doubt threatening her with God knows what to make her do as he bid.

It was imperative they reached Gretna at the same time as Riddledale, if not before. After everything Elizabeth had been through, she didn't deserve to be forced to marry. Henry would kill the bastard, a long and painful death, if he harmed one hair on her body.

They pushed their mounts hard, changing horses regularly. He could almost taste his revenge, taste Lord Riddledale's comeuppance.

They stopped a mail coach whose driver told them of a carriage up ahead that had nearly run them off the road with its reckless speed.

"Should we pull them over and demand her release, or would ye prefer to sit back and follow them into Gretna?" Henry asked the duke. "Make Lord Riddledale believe he's made it safely and without incident?"

His grace thanked the mail coach driver and looked at Victoria. Henry noted the satisfied glow in the duke's eyes, knowing his quarry was not far away.

"We'll wait and follow them into the town to ensure others are about. Not that I wish to gain witnesses, but it should calm Riddledale to not try anything stupid. And if I know the man at all, he will not waste time securing a room at an inn, but try to marry Elizabeth without haste."

Victoria shifted in the saddle. "Shall we go then, gentlemen?"

They kept their distance, but soon they were close enough to see the moving carriage through the trees some distance ahead. Revenge tempted his palate, and it was sweeter than elderberry wine on his tongue.

---

*E*lizabeth looked out the window, refusing to talk no matter how aggravating Lord Riddledale's questions were. She would rather die than speak to the man again. By the excited gleam in his lordship's eyes, Elizabeth knew Gretna could not be far away. After a full day and night in a carriage, with few stops, she would be thankful for that, at least. The fresh air would be a welcome respite.

The fields soon gave way to outlying farming cottages, and those cottages eventually gave way to the busy streets of the bustling town.

"Come, my dear, do not let us go on in such a manner. We are about to be married. Don't make me use force when the time comes to speak your marriage vows."

Elizabeth gritted her teeth. She wanted to scream that she would never marry him, duress or not. He would have to use force if he wished to hear her voice again. And even then it would be only to say "I don't" and not "I do."

Her hands, still tied behind her back, made it a struggle to keep her seat when the carriage turned a corner. Blacksmiths and inns passed by the window. Couples, many of whom looked quite pleased with themselves, walked the main thoroughfares.

Elizabeth wondered if the couples were newly married. If

they had thrown aside all strictures society placed on their lives and married the one person they loved anyway. The word "love" reverberated about in her mind, and regret threatened her sanity. Henry.

How she adored him and had hurt him beyond redemption. She wondered where he was and what he was doing right at this moment. Wondered if he still resided in London or had traveled north. The distance that separated them tore at her soul, and tears pooled in her eyes. None of it mattered now, for it was too late.

"If you are wondering if you will be rescued, my dear, I'm sorry to disappoint. My men have informed me your brother is a day away, traveling by coach. He will not make it in time to save your precious...well..." His lascivious grin made her skin crawl. "There is nothing to save, is there, my dear, for you've already given away your prize, but I shall enjoy taking my fill of you."

Her eyes narrowed, and she fought against her restraints. "I'll never be yours, and I'll die before I'd allow you to touch my person, you bastard." She cursed herself for breaking her own promise not to speak to the bastard again, but the look of fury on his face made her lapse in concentration worth it.

The rope cut into her skin as she tried to work the knot free. Why would Josh take a carriage? Surely if he knew where she was, he would come on horseback. She refused to speak and again looked out to the cobbled streets beyond. Were they coming? Anyone?

Please don't let this be my fate.

The carriage rocked to a halt.

"Here we are, my dear. Let me untie those ropes. No need for further restraints. I'm sure you will not try to escape with John not far away."

Elizabeth looked out the now-open carriage door and recognized the brute who had taken her from her home.

She sighed in relief when the rope unwrapped and fell away. Elizabeth brought her hands around in front of her and rubbed the red, swollen welts about her wrists. Then, with all her might, all the anger and frustration she could muster, she punched Lord Riddledale in the nose.

His lordship, not suspecting the attack, reeled back onto the squabs, holding his face and screaming over the blood that spurted onto his fingers.

John, Riddledale's henchman, stilled beside the carriage, his eyes wide with shock, and Elizabeth made use of his surprise and leaped for the opposite door. She jumped from the carriage and gasped as Lord Riddledale seized her skirt, the material pulling tight against her legs, making her lose balance. Elizabeth fell hard against the carriage step, her chin hitting the graveled road.

Sitting up, she touched the stinging cut on her jaw as people gathered and watched the goings-on in the carriage. She turned and looked into the vehicle just as Lord Riddledale yelled for John to catch her. The demand acted like a bucket of cold water. She scrambled to her feet and took off as fast as she could go. Heavy footfalls sounded behind her, and Elizabeth glanced over her shoulder, noted the pursuing John only steps behind.

Looking forward again she didn't see the gentleman step in front of her in time and, with an almighty oomph, she hit a wall of muscle. The familiar comforting tones whispered against her ear made relief swamp her, and her knees threatened to crumble.

She wrapped her arms tight about his waist and sobbed.

Henry.

The click of a pistol at her side stopped the brutish John in his tracks and, for the first time in two days, Elizabeth's heart raced a steady beat of reprieve. She tightened her hold on Henry and welcomed his supportive hand that wrapped about her back and held her tight.

"Move in any direction and I promise ye it will be ye last action ever made upon this earth," Henry said, his tone laced with deadly intent.

Elizabeth shuffled behind to allow him to concentrate on the burly John and Lord Riddledale, who, leaning out of the carriage door, still held his bleeding nose with a handkerchief.

The sound of another gun preparing to shoot clicked near them, and she looked to her left, her jaw falling open at the sight of her sister, Victoria, clad in men's clothing and looking all the more comfortable for it holding a steady pistol at Lord Riddledale's head.

John didn't dare move, but his eyes narrowed in contemplation, no doubt wondering if he could chance it and make a run for freedom.

"That warning goes for you as well, Lord Riddledale," Josh said, coming up from the opposite direction.

"I haven't committed any crime. Your sister came with me willingly to marry me in private."

"Well," her brother drawled, "I'm sure the magistrate will think differently. Victoria saw your brute kidnap Elizabeth on my property. You, my lord, are henceforth penniless, as I call in all your debts, which I know you're unable to pay. You are ruined, in every way possible. I hope you enjoy debtor's prison or even Newgate; either would pacify me."

At that moment, the town magistrate, a large rotund man, ran into the mêlée, guards following close on his heels. He profusely apologized for the misdemeanor that had befallen the Duke of Penworth's family and had the disgraced Lord Riddledale and his brute John taken away without further ado.

Elizabeth watched with loathing as the man who'd caused

so many troubles for her was led away, his shouts of denial and undying love echoing off the walls of Gretna's shops.

Turning away, she looked up at Henry and was rewarded with an explicit oath. She stepped back instinctively before he tore off his cravat and placed it against her chin.

"Let me have a look," Victoria said, pulling the bandage away a little.

"Is it bad?" Elizabeth asked, ignoring the sting their prodding caused.

"It's a nasty cut, but I don't think it needs stitching. Come, we will check into an inn, clean it up, and have a better look."

Elizabeth met Henry's eyes, deep pools of concern that twisted her heart. "You go ahead with Josh. I wish to speak to Lord Muir for a moment."

Josh nodded, taking Victoria's arm. A smile quirked her brother's lips, and Elizabeth wondered what had happened between the two men to bring them about to be so accepting, friendly even, when they were usually at odds.

"Are ye well, lass? He didn't harm ye in—"

"No," she said, shaking her head. "He didn't touch me at all. How is it that you're here?"

Henry relayed how he'd traveled to Dunsleigh to call on her and was confronted with the house in uproar over her kidnapping. Elizabeth stifled a giggle at the image of everyone planning a counterattack against Lord Riddledale. "Thank you for coming to save me." She looked at him, fixing his shirt where his cravat had been. "For what were you coming to Dunsleigh?"

Henry ran a finger down her cheek, careful not to hurt her wound. His warm breath mingled with hers and for one wicked moment, Elizabeth thought he might kiss her on the street. Instead, he leaned down and kissed her cheek, the gesture as soft as silk, but his eyes remained guarded, giving her no hint to his thoughts. He stepped back, and Elizabeth felt the loss of his contact deep inside her soul.

"I traveled to Dunsleigh to beg forgiveness, to ask ye to forget all that I said, and marry me. I'm sorry, lass, for everything. I was shocked and upset, and I should've come sooner, but I've been a stubborn fool."

Elizabeth clasped his hands. "We need to talk, Henry, but not here. Later..." She swallowed her nerves. "Will you meet me later? Alone?"

Elizabeth caught the flicker of heat in his gaze that only she'd ever been privy to, and her nerves disappeared. Thoughts of what they'd done together when alone bombarded her mind, and for a moment her attention snapped to his lips. How she wished to kiss him, to feel him against her, to seduce him.

"Where?" Henry asked, his husky voice sending her pulse to race.

"I'll come to your room tonight. I'll wait until Victoria's asleep."

"I'm not sure that is wise, Elizabeth."

Elizabeth pushed away the hurt his reply brought forth. "I think it is. I'll not be put off." At his nod, Elizabeth walked into the inn, ready more than ever to declare herself to the man she loved and anyone else who wished to know.

---

*I*t seemed to take Victoria an eternity to fall asleep. Elizabeth thought it would have been much quicker since they partook in a lovely roast beef dinner followed by warm baths and fresh clothes. And yet since Victoria was in haste to explain everything that had transpired during her kidnapping they hadn't sought their beds till well past midnight.

Elizabeth lay in the dark room, watching the flickering light from the fire cast moving shadows across the walls. Victoria's breathing eventually slowed with sleep and, with the gentlest care, Elizabeth inched from the covers, pulled on some socks she'd left beside the bed, and headed for the door.

She looked once more at her sister, a smile quirking her lips when she realized half the battle to see Henry was accomplished. Now she had to make it to his room without anyone catching her.

Opening the door a bit, Elizabeth peeked into the hall. A lone sconce burned near the start of the stairs, but no one materialized anywhere; only the muffled voices from the taproom below stairs sounded, and the smell of stew, which hung in the air.

Elizabeth thanked the noise for masking her footsteps as she ran across the hall. Without knocking, she entered Henry's room and shut the door with the least amount of noise possible. The sight of him—shirt open, bedraggled locks, the faintest shadowing of hair on his chest—made it impossible to move.

He was glorious.

Heat and longing pooled at her core, and she wanted nothing but to be with him again. She bit the inside of her lip to stop from throwing herself at his head.

"No one saw ye?" His voice held concern and yet a gentleman to the last, no matter his rakish looks.

"No. Victoria is asleep, and there was no one about." Henry paused beside the fire before walking to the small round table and pulling out a chair for her to sit. She did as he bade, watching his every move as he sat across from her, his nearness, their seclusion, tangible in the small room.

He cleared his throat. "Before we discuss anything, there is something you must read. It is from Miss Andrews."

Elizabeth pushed the letter away. "I do not need to read her letter."

"Please, I want ye to read it."

She shook her head, taking his hand instead of the letter. "When I was in the carriage with Lord Riddledale, I thought he'd finally won. The thought of never seeing you again was more than I could bear, and I knew I had to try, at least once more, to be free of his lordship." She paused. "I'm sorry for what happened between us, Henry. I'm sorry I did not tell you of your boy. I never meant to hurt you; you're everything to me. You were always everything to me."

Henry's thumb stroked the top of her hand, and shivers raced up her arm. "Are ye saying ye love me still, and wish to marry me?"

Elizabeth's heart stopped at the raw emotion she heard behind the question. "If your offer of marriage still stands, Henry Andrews, Earl of Muir, I will marry you, because I love you. I have always loved you and will never love another."

*enry reached across the small space that separated them and pulled Elizabeth onto his lap. Her body fit his like the kid leather gloves she often wore, and he reveled in the feel of her in his arms.

"I'm glad to hear it, lass." He skimmed his lips over hers before taking all that she offered. She held nothing back, and his body hardened at her ardent response. Her sensuous touch teased and beckoned, her hands greedy at his ripped-away clothing, pooling at their feet. But the chair was no place to make love to his future countess and standing, Henry swept her into his arms and carried her to the bed. He dropped her onto the coarse but clean white linen and chuckled when she bounced.

She watched him appreciatively as he stripped off his breeches before crawling up the length of her body, holding himself above her as he took in the beauty that was his Elizabeth.

The smell of jasmine rose from her milky white skin. The scent had always been a reminder of what he'd left behind. It had often tested his resolve when living in America, had made him homesick in an instant. He lay beside her, gently tracing the outline of her profile, her sweet perfect nose, lovely chin, now sporting a cut, thanks to the bastard Riddledale.

"Henry, is anything other than your finger going to touch me tonight?"

He growled at her brazen question and took her lips in an equally shameless kiss. Her body undulated beneath him, her breasts teasing his chest, her mons pushing against his hardened length and pulling forth a growl of need.

"Tonight I shall explore every inch of your beautiful soul."

She sighed, running her hands across his shoulders. He lifted from her, kissing his way down her stomach, clutching her breasts, licking the inside of her thigh before running his tongue between her wet folds, enjoying the feel of her at his mercy.

"Henry! You can't!"

His cock hardened at the breathless need, the words opposite to her clutching hands that pulled at his hair telling him to continue, to stay where he was and bring her to orgasm against his mouth. "I can, and I will. Lie back, lass, and relax."

She did as he asked, and he stole a look at her. Straight white teeth clutched her lower lip firmly between their grasp, her eyes closed, a slight blush on her cheeks.

He suckled her again, running his tongue between her sex, flicking her hardened nubbin with even strokes.

"Oh, Henry. What are you doing to me?"

Loving her... It wasn't long before she was close; her labored breathing, her hands more adamant against his head, her legs moving on the linen sheets told him so. He wanted her to find release against his mouth, had dreamed of being with her in this way for an age. He would not stop now.

Moving his hand, he slid a finger into her wet heat and groaned at the tightness he found there. She undulated against his face, riding him as he would soon ride her, pushing her with each glide of his tongue, with each stroke of his finger, to orgasm.

She called out his name when she shattered beneath him. Henry savored every delicious shudder that ran through her, wanting to hear his name on her lips for the rest of his life.

He pulled away, coming over her and settling his heat between her legs. "I have to have ye." His words sounded strained even to his own ears.

She looked at him, her eyes a stormy ocean of wonder and need. "Yes, please."

Her brazenness snapped the last of his control and, hitching her leg high on his waist, he pushed deep and made her his. He moaned, having never felt anything so right as being this close with her. Elizabeth pulled him down and kissed him hard, her tongue no longer tentative or meek, but demanding, controlling. His body roared for release with each glide within her tight core. It was a struggle not to lose himself, to take what she offered and come.

"I didn't think sex could enthrall me as much as your tongue, but I was wrong."

He growled at her words, increasing his pace, needing her to orgasm with him buried deep within her core. She moaned, pulling at the hair at his nape, the sex frantic and fast, their bodies becoming one and the same.

"Elizabeth…I love ye," he gasped. "Love ye so very much."

Their gazes locked as he continued to push her, stroke her, tempt her to ecstasy and then, her mouth opened on a sigh, her green orbs looking up at him in awe as she climaxed tight and long, bringing him to completion with her.

"Lass…" It was all he could manage, anything else he was going to say died on his lips.

Her body went limp, a well-satisfied grin lifting the corner of her mouth. He lay beside her, pulling her into the crook of his arm. She kissed his chest, the lightest strokes that made goose bumps rise on his skin.

"I'm absolutely, incandescently happy, and it's all thanks to you. Thank you for being you, Henry."

He kissed her hair, contentment making him drowsy. "I love ye as well. And come tomorrow I'm going to marry my bonny English lass."

She cuddled into him, and he could feel her smile against his chest. "Yes, you will."

CHAPTER 20

Over breakfast the following morning, Elizabeth sat with a contented smile upon her face as she nibbled the delicious toast before her. Even the tea in this establishment was delicious. Not to mention…well, not to mention one Scottish man who occupied the seat across from her. He was delicious, too.

Her attention stayed fixed on Henry as he ate the hearty meal of ham, eggs, and strong coffee. Victoria and Josh had already eaten and were waiting in the inn's yard to rendezvous with Alice, who was due at any moment. Elizabeth sipped the sweet tea and devoured Henry in his morning attire. He looked like the young man she once knew, the one she fell in love with all those years ago. Carefree and happy just as they would be again.

Elizabeth hid her smile as she sipped her tea, watching as he read the paper and ate. She tried not to think over what they had done the night before and why he was so ravenous this morning, but it was hard to concentrate on something other than his lips…

"Anything interesting in the paper?" Elizabeth asked.

A servant came in and placed a fresh pot of tea on the table, curtsied, then left. Elizabeth waited for the door to shut before leaning over and kissing Henry, welcoming the spark of desire she lit within his eyes.

"Nothin', lass. Although I could get used to such breakfast delights as the one ye just bestowed."

Elizabeth chuckled and, sitting back down, nibbled on a piece of toast. "I believe Alice will be arriving any moment. I think Josh wishes to depart later today. Will you be traveling with us back to London?"

Henry remained silent, his expression guarded. "Henry, will you be traveling with us?"

He shut his paper and regarded her for a moment. "It occurs to me that perhaps we could marry much sooner."

"I don't understand," Elizabeth said.

He took her hand, clasping it with both of his. "I know we spoke of marriage last night, but why travel back to London to have the nuptials. Let's marry here, in Gretna."

Elizabeth's eyes widened at the possibility, hope blossoming in her chest. "I think that's the most wonderful idea I have heard in a long time."

"Do you think his grace will deny us? Ye family are not present, and your mama may prefer a London wedding."

Elizabeth pushed back her chair and wiggled onto Henry's lap. "I think Josh has come to terms that my choice is made, and you seem to be on much friendlier terms than you were a few months ago, which is promising. You will see, Josh will walk me down the aisle as he should. And by nightfall I'll be legally yours."

Henry kissed her again, this time much longer and more satisfyingly than she ever remembered. It was as intoxicating as the finest whisky in Scotland.

"Ye were always mine," he stated, grinning. "I just had to remind ye of the fact."

*T*he marriage was a quick affair. Alice was overjoyed to have arrived in time, and after a little private discussion with her brother, Elizabeth secured his agreement to walk her down the aisle in a blacksmith's shop in Gretna Green. Not the most appropriate location for a duke's daughter to marry, but what was that when two people who loved each other wished to make their union official.

The blacksmith, who was also the priest, stood before a wooden table lined with a white tablecloth and smiled in welcome as a duke walked his sister toward a smiling earl. Henry waited, hands folded before him, his features filled with love and adoration for her.

The service was short and sweet, as they wished, and it couldn't have been a more perfect wedding had all of London been present in St. James. Later they ate a celebrative lunch with her family at the inn's private sitting room. Josh notified them of his intention to travel back to London within the hour.

"Will you be traveling back to the capital, Lord Muir, or have you other plans, now that you are a married man?" Lady Alice asked, grinning.

Henry laughed at the question and sipped his whisky.

"I sent a note this mornin', notifying my staff to have little Samuel meet us here in a day or two, with his nanny, of course, and then I'll be taking me lass home to the highlands. I want her to see Muirdeen Castle."

Elizabeth looked over to Henry and noted he seemed a little uncertain of his plans. She read the question in his eyes, that she may not wish to leave England and travel to the wild highlands. He couldn't have been more wrong. It was everything she had ever dreamed.

"I would love to see my new home, Henry." She reached for his hand and turned to her brother. "Will you have Newland Estate closed up for me, brother, and all of my possessions and Samuel's sent to Henry's estate? Of course, I will write to Mama and explain my wondrous news. Will you do that for me?"

Josh nodded. "Of course," he said, catching Henry's eye. "Lord Muir, although I never thought to be uttering these next words, may I welcome you, wholeheartedly, to our family. I wish you and Elizabeth all the happiness in the world."

Elizabeth blinked back tears, smiling from her brother to Henry. "I think we'll be the happiest people on earth. Thank you for marrying me, Henry," she whispered so only he would hear.

"My pleasure," he replied, kissing her before all her family. Soundly.

EPILOGUE

Six months later

*E*lizabeth strolled out into the outer bailey of her highland home and looked through the gates toward the highland mountains that now glistened with white, crisp snow atop them. With Samuel down for his afternoon nap, she took the opportunity to read her mail that came monthly beside the castle walls. Elizabeth looked over their lands, taking in the loch beyond that changed from the deepest blue to silver depending on where the sun was in the sky.

From the moment they had arrived here, she'd loved it, just as much as she loved Henry, who, as promised, adored her and Samuel unconditionally and made her laugh more than she'd ever thought possible. She broke the ducal seal of the letter from her mama, the perfect, flowing script easy to decipher.

My dearest Elizabeth,

I hope this letter finds you well. We're all ensconced at Dunsleigh for the winter, but the girls are looking forward to spring and returning to town for the season, or so they declare, although I'm yet to believe their admonitions.

I'm glad you love your highland home, and I hope to travel there in the not too distant future. I miss Samuel dreadfully, and I can only surmise how much his lordship has grown. I'm ecstatic to hear your happy news that Samuel will soon have a sibling. You're a wonderful mother, and I don't believe I've said how very proud of you I am. Your father, also, I know would be smiling down on his beautiful, loving daughter.

If you happen to visit your sister Isolde at Avonmore, please try to persuade her to come to town next season. It is time she came home and found happiness of her own. The last letter I received from her was very low of spirits, I believe, and I worry for her wellbeing. If you can, please persuade her to come back to England; she deserves happiness such as yours.

I hope your winter is not too harsh and you're all safe and well. I will write again next month as I hope you will, too. We miss you, dear girl, do remember to come and visit whenever the time suits. You and Henry are forever welcome.

I embrace you.

Your loving mama

Dear Reader,

I hope you enjoyed, *Only an Earl Will Do*, book one in my To Marry a Rogue series!

I'm so thrilled you chose my book to read, and if you're able, I would appreciate an honest review of *Only an Earl Will Do*. As they say, feed an author, leave a review!

If you'd like to learn about book two in my To Marry a Rogue series, *Only a Duke Will Do*, please read on. I have included chapter one for your reading pleasure.

Alternatively, you can keep in contact with me by visiting my website or following me online. You can contact me at www.tamaragill.com or email me at tamaragillauthor@gmail.com.

Tamara Gill

ONLY A DUKE WILL DO

TO MARRY A ROGUE, BOOK 2

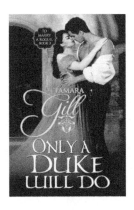

Without a Season, Lady Isolde Worthingham captured the Duke of Moore's heart at a country dance. But on the eve of her wedding, a scandal that rocked the ton and sent her fleeing to Scotland alone and unwed, leaves her perfectly planned future in a tangle of disgrace and heartbreak.

. . .

*Merrick Mountshaw, the Duke of Moore loathes the pitiful exis-
tence he hides from the ton. With a scandalous wife he never
wanted, who flaunts her many indiscretions, life is a never-ending
parade of hell. When the one woman he loved and lost returns to
London, he knows he can no longer live without her.*

*But vows and past hurts are not easily forgotten. Love may not win
against the ton when a too proper Lord and Lady play by the rules.*

CHAPTER 1

Mountshaw Estate, Wiltshire 1805

Isolde Worthingham, the second eldest daughter of the Duke of Penworth, spooned syllabub into her mouth and grinned at her betrothed, a man she had known for only one year, yet it felt like she'd known him her entire life. Merrick Mountshaw, the fourth Duke of Moore, was a gentle soul, much like herself, and suited her more than she'd ever dreamed. So much so it was almost like they'd been made for each other.

He smiled back, his eyes sparkling with humor. How was it that in only a few hours they would be married, finally promised to each other before God and all those they cared for most in the world.

Excitement thrummed through Isolde's veins. She'd waited for what seemed forever for this day to arrive. How lucky she was to be marrying for love, something that she and her sisters had promised to uphold after witnessing such a union from their parents' own match.

And she had found it with Merrick. The last dinner

together as an unmarried couple carried on around them, and was enjoyable and hearty. The conversation was of nothing but the forthcoming nuptials and the joining of two great families of southern England. The event of the Season some said.

It did not surprise her that the wedding was titled as such, with half of London having traveled to Mountshaw, Merrick's ancestral home, to attend. Everyone who was anyone would see them state their vows, their promises to each other, tomorrow. She couldn't wait.

Merrick took her hand, pulling her from her thoughts, placing a lingering kiss on the inside of her wrist. Warmth spread across her cheeks, and she bit her lip.

"I cannot concentrate on this dessert when there is something all the more delectable at table," he whispered, leaning close.

She laughed, looking about and hoping no one heard his words. "You tease, Your Grace."

"With you, I tell only the absolute truth." He smiled and answered a question from her brother Josh across from her. It was always pleasant sitting next to Merrick. In fact, she preferred it to the other end of the table, where she would hardly be able to see him between all the fruit and flower arrangements lining the great expanse. And if she sat away from him from tomorrow onward, she wouldn't have the delightful feeling of his boot rubbing up against her silk slipper.

There is no hope for the man. I've ruined him.

She inwardly chuckled at the thought. Once one of Town's most-loved rogues, Merrick had been quite a sought-after gentleman, not that Isolde had known anything about him until last year, when they'd met. She watched as he spoke with her brother about having some celebratory drinks after the women retired. Merrick was animated in conversation; his strong jaw teased her to stroke it, to drag him down for a kiss by lips that still distracted her when she looked at him. He was, in her estimation, perfect.

And she loved him so very much. He enjoyed life and all it offered, always imagined the best of any bad situation. The duke cared for his friends as much as his tenant farmers and staff. He was unlike anyone she'd ever known. The best of men.

Isolde sipped her champagne, the bubbles tickling her tongue, and the day's tension slipped away as the dinner progressed. Everything was ready for the wedding. The flowers were set, the trestle tables were on the lawn, waiting for the servants to set them for the wedding breakfast tomorrow morning. Her trunks sat packed in the entrance foyer for their trip to the Continent, and her wedding gown hung against her armoire. All Isolde had to do was try not to blubber uncontrollably as she promised her heart and soul to the man beside her, something she would absolutely fail at.

Isolde leaned over toward him, gaining his attention. "Must you, Merrick? I can hardly concentrate on this meal as it is, never mind having your foot dancing along my leg."

"It is only fair, as I've not been able to concentrate for months." He winked, picking up his glass of wine and taking a sip. She watched him, entranced when he licked a droplet of the drink off his lips. He caught her watching him, and understanding dawned in his gaze, hot and full of promises.

He picked up her hand and kissed her fingers, paying homage to the square diamond he'd given her in celebration of their betrothal. The ring had been his grandmother's, and now it was hers, and God willing, their son's wife, one day.

Heat pooled in her belly with the tantalizing stroke of his mouth against her body. The thought of the wedding night left her breathless, and she took a fortifying sip of champagne.

"I love you," he said, loud enough for all to hear the endearment.

"And I you." Her response was automatic, natural, and she blessed the day her best friend, Miss Hart, had introduced them at a country dance one year earlier. From that day forward, Merrick had been attentive and unrelenting in his pursuit of her, and she reveled in the fact she'd brought to heel one of London's devilish rogues.

Her father, the Duke of Penworth, cleared his throat, watching them with mirth. Her dearest papa all but glowed with pride. "I would like to propose a toast to the Duke and the future Duchess of Moore. May your life be full of love, good health, and happiness."

Her father smiled, and she noted the sheen of unshed tears in his eyes. He'd always been an emotional man, and they loved him all the more for it. "Moore has proven himself this past year to be a determined and honorable young man, and was I not assured he'll do nothing but strive to make my beautiful daughter happy, I would not have allowed the union to go on. But tonight my heart is full and joyful. Isolde has chosen well. It fills me with contented pleasure knowing you will forever be safe and blissful. So please raise your glass to the future Duke and Duchess of Moore."

The chorus of cheers burst from the table, and Isolde smiled at Merrick when he kissed her hand a second time. She looked around the long, marvelously decorated table, smiling her thanks to all her family and the few close friends who were present.

Her gaze halted on her best friend, Miss Leonora Hart—Letty to her. A frown marred her usually perfect forehead, and her lips were thin with displeasure. Letty looked distracted, worried even, and Isolde paused, promising to find out what ill her friend was feeling before the night came to an end.

Perhaps it was because Isolde was about to be married and Letty wasn't going to have a Season in Town due to finances at home. Her father, the local vicar back in Surrey, was not fluid in funds, and had refused the Duke of Penworth's offer to give his daughter a Season. Isolde had thought his decision very unkind, and unfair for Letty, and not being able to help had made the situation even more frustrating. And Letty's father's decision was final. He was not a vicar swayed by persuasion.

She would speak to her father again about the situation before she left for her wedding trip to Paris and Switzerland. Letty was practically her sister, after all, having known each other since they'd been in braids. There was nothing Isolde didn't want more for her friend than to have the happiness she herself had right at this moment with Merrick.

Finally, the dinner came to an end and the men stayed behind for their port and cheroots. Isolde made her way to the withdrawing room, ready for the night to be over so the next day could finally begin. Her wedding day... How amazing that sounded.

Want to read more? Get Only a Duke Will Do today!

LORDS OF LONDON SERIES
AVAILABLE NOW!

Dive into these charming historical romances! In this six-book series, Darcy seduces a virginal duke, Cecilia's world collides with a roguish marquess, Katherine strikes a deal with an unlucky earl and Lizzy sets out to conquer a very wicked Viscount. These stories plus more adventures in the Lords of London series! Available now through Amazon or read free with KindleUnlimited.

Lords of London

KISS THE WALLFLOWER SERIES
AVAILABLE NOW!

If the roguish Lords of London are not for you and wall-flowers are more your cup of tea, this is the series for you. My Kiss the Wallflower series, are linked through friendship and family in this four-book series. You can grab a copy on Amazon or read free through KindleUnlimited.

LEAGUE OF UNWEDDABLE GENTLEMEN SERIES AVAILABLE NOW!

Fall into my latest series, where the heroines have to fight for what they want, both regarding their life and love. And where the heroes may be unweddable to begin with, that is until they meet the women who'll change their fate. The League of Unweddable Gentlemen series is available now!

LEAGUE OF UNWEDDABLE GENTLEMEN

To Marry a Rogue Series
ONLY AN EARL WILL DO
ONLY A DUKE WILL DO
ONLY A VISCOUNT WILL DO

A Time Traveler's Highland Love Series
TO CONQUER A SCOT
TO SAVE A SAVAGE SCOT
TO WIN A HIGHLAND SCOT

Time Travel Romance
DEFIANT SURRENDER
A STOLEN SEASON

Scandalous London Series
A GENTLEMAN'S PROMISE
A CAPTAIN'S ORDER
A MARRIAGE MADE IN MAYFAIR
SCANDALOUS LONDON - BOOKS 1-3 BUNDLE

High Seas & High Stakes Series
HIS LADY SMUGGLER
HER GENTLEMAN PIRATE
HIGH SEAS & HIGH STAKES - BOOKS 1-2 BUNDLE

Daughters Of The Gods Series
BANISHED-GUARDIAN-FALLEN
DAUGHTERS OF THE GODS - BOOKS 1-3 BUNDLE

Stand Alone Books
TO SIN WITH SCANDAL

OUTLAWS

ABOUT THE AUTHOR

Tamara is an Australian author who grew up in an old mining town in country South Australia, where her love of history was founded. So much so, she made her darling husband travel to the UK for their honeymoon, where she dragged him from one historical monument and castle to another.

A mother of three, her two little gentlemen in the making, a future lady (she hopes) and a part-time job keep her busy in the real world, but whenever she gets a moment's peace she loves to write romance novels in an array of genres, including regency, medieval and time travel.

www.tamaragill.com
tamaragillauthor@gmail.com